Visions

by

Lisa Compton

The Olivia Osborne Crime Series,
Book 3

Visions

Cover Art by *Lisa Dawn MacDonald*

The Wild Rose Press, Inc.
PO Box 708
Adams Basin, NY 14410-0708
Visit us at www.thewildrosepress.com

Publishing History
First Edition, 2024
Trade Paperback ISBN 978-1-5092-5362-3
Digital ISBN 978-1-5092-5363-0

The Olivia Osborne Crime Series, Book 3
Published in the United States of America

Dedication

To Shevawn Barron. My own personal cheerleader and the only person to have bravely read everything I've ever written.

Praise

Mickey - 5.0 out of 5 stars A thriller from the start! This series is fantastic, and I can't wait to read another Lisa Compton book.

****

Cynthia G. - 5.0 out of 5 stars Must read!

Lisa had me hooked in the first couple of sentences! She really made it hard to put the book down. I was very disappointed when I finished because I was so caught up in characters and story. Can't wait for her next one! She combined my love of mysteries and paranormal and did it in a realistic way.

****

Sheila - 5.0 out of 5 stars Awesome book!

Lisa Compton is my new favorite author! She drew me in quickly to get lost in this book. Her metaphors and colorful descriptions keep me enthralled.

Prologue

"Forgive me Father for I have sinned."

The archbishop gave his guidance without pause.

"God the Father of mercies, through the death and resurrection of his Son has reconciled the world to himself and sent the Holy Spirit among us for the forgiveness of sins; through the ministry of the Church may God grant you pardon and peace. I absolve you from your sins in the name of the Father, and the Son, and the Holy Spirit. Amen."

Olivia raised her head and looked him in the eye. "Even after what I confessed; you'll still grant me absolution? Did you even hear what I said?"

"I heard you. More than that, so did God."

Nicefero Saldaña Mendoza knew this day would come. Her past was written before her birth. The only thing missing was her ending. It was near.

"You showed remorse. Without it, you wouldn't have come. Seeking forgiveness is what separates you from the darkness."

The archbishop was wrong. She made a deal with a demon. There was no coming back from that. Her confession was an admission, but he was missing the point. Absolution had many meanings.

Olivia was seeking freedom. Not forgiveness.

Chapter One

A thousand tiny legs inched across her scalp, marching in tandem. The energy surrounding her buzzed just below her periphery like white noise. Olivia struggled to keep up with the two men ahead of her, the protest from her feet reminding her why she never wore heels. She was supposed to be sitting in a board room reviewing the security needs of her new client, not traipsing around dungeons.

The San Antonio State Hospital, SASH for short, was an inpatient psychiatric facility. As with any other hospital, the goal was to treat the patient's immediate needs and discharge them back into the community. However, behind these walls also resided those no one liked to talk about, individuals who had committed crimes so heinous a court of law had found them too dangerous to set free. If a tour had been on the agenda for today, Olivia would have expected it to be to the locked forensic unit where they kept the real-life Hannibal Lectors. They were the individuals Dr. Olivia Osborne was famous for hunting.

Instead, Olivia found herself traversing the bowels of the facility, wading deeper into levels of latent energy. What started as a low hum had morphed into a screaming locomotive by the time she reached the bottom of the narrow staircase. Hospitals were storehouses of discarded emotions, and this one had more than a century's worth of storage space. Gripping the skinny iron railing, Olivia fought through the fog of the past to return to the present. She opened her eyes to see her journey end in a cramped hallway. The low ceiling added the extra ambiance of claustrophobia.

Olivia released the stair railing and flexed her fingers. The waves of nausea she battled during her descent subsided, and she focused on her physical surroundings. Closed doors lined the hallway. This had once been part of the original hospital, back when it was known as the Southwestern Insane Asylum. The small window positioned at eye level told Olivia these were once patient rooms. She resisted the urge to look inside. Physically they were empty, but remnants of long-ago events still lingered here, their energy trapped forever.

The men were waiting for her outside the room at the end of the hall. It was the only one with an open door. Her companions parted as Olivia crossed the narrow threshold alone. The muggy dampness of the confined space was oppressing. This room was larger than the others, telling Olivia this was where procedures, now considered barbaric, were once performed. Echoes of long-ago events remained, like the sobbing coming from the corner. Olivia avoided looking in that direction lest she found herself pulled into a past she couldn't change. Anchoring herself to the present, Olivia focused her attention on the voice of the groundskeeper. The name on his badge identified him as Armando. He was pointing to the dingy materials bunched up in the corner. In a pinch, they could serve as a blanket and pillow. Not far away, trash was collecting.

"You're worried someone is staying here," Olivia voiced. It wasn't much of a leap.

Recent unfortunate events across town at another medical facility prompted local news reporter Jessica Tate to turn her investigative sights on the state-funded hospital recanting its own long history of also misplacing patients. Fearing inquiry from the state and local officials who allocated their funds, the hospital board members turned to an expert who could understand not only their clients but the need for safety. Dr. Osborne was a nurse before earning her Ph.D. in forensic psychology and consulting for the FBI's elite Behavioral Analysis Unit. Her resume was what landed her on their grounds and inside their dungeons.

The maintenance man looked to his boss, receiving a nod of confirmation. "Yes, ma'am," Armando replied.

Geoff Vines, the hospital administrator, was the one who suggested the tour Olivia mistakenly thought would take her anywhere but here. Now she knew why, but she put those concerns aside for now.

Slipping into investigative mode, she took stock of her surroundings. "Access in and out?" Olivia asked. In addition to the blanket and pillow, paper bags littered the floor. The smell of deep-fried grease still clung to them. Only a select group of residents were kept under constant lock and key. Most of the population had reasonable freedom within the walls, but this was something else. This was a hideaway for someone who had access to the outside.

"Both have been eliminated," the administrator assured her.

Olivia studied him. Vines was concerned about his job.

"When did you cut off access to this room?" she asked Armando. The groundskeeper knew more about the day-to-day activities than the man in the suit.

"Six, eight months ago, not long after that other fella escaped from across town."

Armando was talking about the infamous Good Samaritan Killer. Jamie Lynne Smythe escaped custody while under lockdown at University Hospital. Ironically, here was where Olivia secretly hoped Jamie would end up one day. He could easily qualify for the locked forensic unit. She would have been more than happy to scream her recommendation to anyone who would listen.

"You're sure your previous elopers are all accounted for?" she continued.

"Part of our new protocol was to relocate those particular clients to other parts of the facility making it more difficult for them to escape," Vines explained.

Clients. The description sounded better than patient or inmate.

"I can assure you they are all accounted for. We started keeping logs to prove it. This isn't one of ours." A good administrator knew how to cover their ass. Olivia had worked in enough hospitals to know.

"This section of the facility is part of the original structure and only used for storage. The doors aren't accessible by an employee key card. These doors require an actual key," Vines explained.

"If this room is supposed to be off limits, then how did you find this?" Olivia wanted to know.

"Water leak," Armando answered. "Since then, I've been keeping an eye out." He picked up one of the paper bags. The red and white logo was a familiar one.

"We keep finding these. It's how we know it's still happening."

Olivia knew the place well. The food was fast, cheap, and one of the few places that still employed carhops. She felt a sudden craving for a soda with a shot of vanilla.

"I need you to pull the schematics for this area of the hospital. Make sure there is a detailed assessment of the entries and exits to this room," Olivia said, turning her attention back to Vines.

Over her head, Vines nodded to Armando to go.

"If we could keep this to ourselves," Vines suggested once they were alone.

"You sat in the boardroom today and assured your superiors this kind of thing had stopped," Olivia reminded him. "It's one thing to lie to them, it's another to lie to me."

Her tone caught Vines off guard. The man with all the answers didn't have one.

****

Silas Branch felt at home in the neighborhood. Older homes surrounded by stately lawns reminded him of his beloved Virginia. Silas never believed anything could persuade him to leave the place he grew up, but after marrying Olivia, he realized home wasn't a place but a person. He left Virginia and the BAU for the local FBI station chief position, and Olivia traded killers for hospitals. They were committed to building a new life together.

Rounding the block toward home, Silas spied his next-door neighbor, Ross Forester in his driveway with Martin Mendoza. The two were locked in what looked like a tense discussion. Ross and Lily moved into the neighborhood with the intent to renovate. They were looking for someone they could trust, and Olivia was happy to introduce them to Martin. He had worked wonders renovating Olivia's childhood home. The project was the beginning of a friendship, and the couples spent many nights drinking on the porch and commiserating about the pitfalls of home renovation.

Seeing the two men gave Silas the excuse he needed to slow down. A run through the neighborhood was part of his daily routine, but his knee had stiffened a block back. It was happening more and more lately. The past had a way of recurring. Two knee injuries on the college football field cost him an NFL career. The last surgeon warned him he was looking at a knee replacement before he hit fifty. Silas felt six years was a generous estimate.

Martin saw him first. "Agent Branch, how is Dr. Olivia?" It was the first thing the contractor always asked.

"She's very well, Martin." Silas smiled. His wife collected followers. He wished more of them were like the contractor. "I'll tell her you asked."

"Glad you stopped by, big guy," Ross interrupted. "I have something I want to give you," Ross said before turning his attention back to Martin. "So, next Tuesday at the latest? You promise?"

"Yes, sir," Martin assured him with a ready smile.

The tightness around the corners of the contractor's mouth told Silas Martin was glad for the interruption.

"The kitchen is useable, but still a mess. Half of the tile for the backsplash was cracked so now we're left waiting on another order," Ross grumbled as soon as the van pulled away. "It's always something, right?"

"I don't envy you." Silas wasn't around for the transformation of Olivia's house. He could only imagine what the disarray had done to his wife's sense of order.

Silas followed Ross through the side door leading to his home office. Ross reached inside the small fridge and came out with a bottle of water. "Looks like you could use it. Maybe one day, I'll join you, if you promise to go easy on this old man," Ross grinned.

Silas knew Ross had recently traded his golf games for going to the gym. Silas admired the change. He couldn't help but wonder if Ross' attempt to get in shape was a mid-life crisis or part of the empty nest syndrome. Ross and Lily claimed the move and house renovation was their fresh start since both kids were out of the house and off to college.

Ross pulled an envelope from inside his desk and handed it over. "Something the landscape guys found when they were laying pipe for the sprinkler system. I thought Olivia might be interested."

The weight inside piqued Silas' curiosity, but he would wait and let Olivia open it. Her family originally owned all the plots on the small offshoot of their street, but time and events eroded their hold on the land, a regret Olivia still held. She was disappointed when they returned from Virginia last summer to learn her great-grandparent's house came on the market and sold before they even knew it was available.

"Did Olivia ever live here, in this house?" Ross asked.

"The plot was sold before she was born," Silas told him. The question sounded like there was more to come, but the buzz coming from Silas' pocket ruined the moment. He didn't usually take his phone with him on a run, but Livie had texted, saying she was running late. He had wanted to keep in touch. Squinting at the screen, Silas saw it was Patrick Monahan, his former boss and the only other person Silas would stop whatever he was doing to answer.

"Gotta take this, sorry," Silas said and headed out the door, bracing for whatever awaited him on the other end. The Director of the BAU didn't call with good news.

****

"They found a body in Eden."

Silas' gut seized as he sank down on the front steps of his porch. Eden was a bump in the road of a little back woods town in rural Florida. For Silas, it was home to the case. The one that never felt right or finished. Five girls, three still missing, and two dead.

Silas recalled the image of their killer sitting calmly in his duct-taped, vinyl recliner confessing to the murder of two twelve-year-old little girls. Larry Wayne Pittman never blinked, just stared glassy eyed at something no one else could see.

"I want in," Silas responded. It wasn't a question.

"Why do you think I'm calling?" Patrick was Silas' friend before he was his boss. The transfer agreement to San Antonio stipulated the BAU had the discretion to call on their former special agent when needed. Like when an old case he had handled reopened. "We're still waiting on an ID but, based on the location, my gut tells me it's one of yours. I think Olivia should take another run at Pittman."

"No one wanted Livie there the first time," Silas was quick to remind him.

Not even the man who was now asking and certainly not the FBI. Pittman didn't fit her typical criminal profile. They saved the nastiest for her. As for the locals, they had a confessed killer and that was good enough for them. They wanted the nightmare to end and the FBI to go away. The case was closed, and the missing became forgotten. But not for Silas.

Patrick ignored the outburst. "If anyone can get to the truth, it's Olivia."

"She did that last time."

"Pittman has had some time to think about it. Maybe after passing on an insanity plea, he's looking for a way out. Besides, you know how they are with her."

Maybe that was the problem. Silas did know how they were. The killers they hunted were Livie's biggest fans. It was unnerving how predators looked at her—not like prey, but something higher on the food chain. Olivia knew evil, and evil knew her.

"Unless you're telling me there is some reason she can't," Patrick said when Silas didn't answer.

Not only was Olivia some kind of miracle worker with the crazies, but she had also somehow tamed Silas's wandering eye. He debated his next words, only because Patrick was a friend first. Livie was trying to put the FBI behind her. Not only were they building a future together, but she was exploring her past by helping someone that reminded her of herself. Bringing more missing girls into their life would disrupt those plans. Olivia had saved Kimmy Burleson from Andre Roche, but Silas didn't want his wife to feel like she had to save them all. Silas wanted her to save herself. Something had happened that night in the barn with

Roche that she still hadn't put behind her.

Silas opted for an abbreviated version. "She just took on a new client."

"Believe me, the FBI is aware." No matter how contentious their relationship was, the Bureau was still interested in how Dr. Osborne spent her time when she wasn't working for them.

Knowing his friend was stonewalling, Patrick moved on. "How are the classes going?" Silas always was a good front man for the Bureau. If the Bureau had a recruiting poster, Silas Branch's picture would be on it. Currently, the station chief was putting his talents to use by hosting educational sessions for local law enforcement. Not only was it community outreach, but also a recruitment tactic.

"Good. Well attended. They seem engaged."

"The important part—anyone showing an interest in coming over to our side?"

"One or two guys out of the last class. This class, Sergeant Will Ibarra for sure."

"Have I heard that name before?" Patrick asked.

"He's SAPD. The Atascosa County case was his first."

Literally a barn burner. Patrick let out a slow whistle. "What a way to get started. How old is this guy?"

"Older than you think. Early thirties, master's degree in education, spent most of his career teaching at SAPD academy. He transferred out just before the Good Samaritan case. It was his rotation algorithm that located the car Smythe stole from the third victim. After that, Bartholomew took him under his wing and Sergeant Ibarra slid over to major crimes and took

Mark Austin's slot."

"Lieutenant Barry Bartholomew." Patrick savored the name. "I do remember him." The lieutenant was a hard man to forget. He was the stoic figure who delivered a heartfelt eulogy for his former partner, Mark Austin. He had also been with Olivia in the barn. According to Bartholomew's statement, she saved his life.

"Ibarra was also the one to uncover the route Smythe took when he dumped the knife," Silas said.

The find had been invaluable to the FBI. The sergeant's discovery proved Olivia's hypothesis regarding the location of the missing weapon used to kill Mark Austin. It also reminded everyone Dr. Osborne was as good at tracking evidence as she was monsters. The knife would be the nail in Smythe's coffin in the state's case against him. If they could ever find him. "Will would definitely be an asset."

"Sounds like he's good with analytics," Patrick agreed. "And I can tell he has your endorsement." It was the use of the first name that gave it away. "And Bartholomew?" Patrick was curious. Like a dog with a bone, the lieutenant was the kind no bad guy wanted on his case. He had also successfully dodged any FBI follow-up on the Atascosa County case. Not a simple feat. Bartholomew was definitely one to watch.

The pause from Silas gave both men's thoughts time to wander. Things between Bartholomew and Silas were strained before Sergeant Austin's death. Since Olivia was the one who requested help from the Bureau for the Smythe murders, Patrick could only surmise she was the reason.

"How's the lieutenant going to take it if we lure his

boy away?" Patrick wanted to know.

"Personally. Bartholomew has difficulty letting go of things he thinks should be his."

Chapter Two

Barry tried not to look at her as he approached but couldn't help himself. Her attire was a cut above the Bureau's standards. The skirt ended just above her knees, and the navy heels she wore accentuated her toned calves. Her hair was blonder and longer than he remembered. It looked good on her.

They had seen little of each other over the last year since the slow deconstruction of the task force searching for the Good Samaritan Killer dwindled. The two of them had never discussed what happened in Atascosa County, and so far, he'd dodged a formal inquiry from the FBI. Maybe the powers that be wanted the mess put to bed as quickly as possible. Sometimes it was better not to know the truth. Barry wished for the same kind of ignorance. It would make sleeping easier.

After the events of last summer, he went back to the daily grind at SAPD. Olivia was still consulting, but no FBI fieldwork, not after what happened that night in the barn. Barry wondered if the career decision was her choice or someone else's. Maybe it had to do with the whole marriage thing. It all happened so fast. His eyes drifted to her hand. The ring was hard to miss.

Olivia raised her soda can to him as he approached. She was missing the vanilla she wanted earlier, but the sugar and caffeine were enough to satiate the hunger that came out of nowhere. "I never expected them to send me a lieutenant," Olivia said with a smile.

Barry wondered if that was code for, I didn't ask for you. Still, she looked happy to see him. For that, he was grateful. With Sergeant Will Ibarra unavailable, Barry took it upon himself to fulfill her request. Something his faithful secretary Norma knew he would do when she passed him the message.

"Will is currently indisposed," Barry explained. He wondered if she knew her husband was the one responsible for Will's absence. Silas was teaching a class at SAPD Academy; education and recruitment all rolled into one. From what Barry had heard, the new San Antonio station chief was good at captivating an audience. If SAPD wasn't careful, they were going to lose Sergeant Ibarra to the Bureau.

"I didn't know who else to call," Olivia admitted. "I'm hoping to keep this on the down-low in case it's nothing." Even with his sunglasses on, Olivia sensed broodiness lurking behind them. Barry had his walls up. They were each waiting on the other, seeking a space between them they could both safely navigate. The last time they'd seen each other, the emotions had flowed freely. Near-death experiences would do that.

Barry watched Olivia center herself. She had waited outside for a reason. Even he felt the heaviness of the building looming behind her. Inside those walls would be a host of shadowy specters, all competing for her attention. She had fled the ghosts, but she had yet to find her grounding. He knew because she was chattier than usual. She was seeking a solid point against the turning world. According to T.S. Elliott, it was the place where the past and future gathered. Was it this place, or was she still as stuck as he was in the empty space between them? Barry shook his head, scattering the thoughts. Such mental wanderings were what he got from a philosopher father and a literature-loving mother.

"So, what am I looking for?" Barry asked.

"An interloper."

Barry took note of her interesting word choice. It implied an intruder or even an imposter.

"The administrator, Mr. Vines, says they have cut off access to the outside."

"You don't believe him?"

"It's not about that, exactly. He's under a lot of pressure. They all are," Olivia explained.

"Thus, your presence."

Olivia gave him a *what are you gonna do* shrug. "Truth is, I don't know him well enough to trust him. He's young, and inexperienced. Deep down he's afraid he's going to lose his job."

Barry returned her shrug. "Plight of trying to administrate a hellhole like this place."

"I went up to some of the units and interviewed the charge nurses. They insist they're not missing patients. After reviewing their protocols, I believe them." Working in Alzheimer's units, Olivia was familiar with housing mentally fragile patients with a tendency to wander. Vines had told her their process was secure. After seeing it for herself, she agreed. "Still, I'd like an independent assessment."

"You picked up on something," Barry said what she wouldn't. "You used the word interloper. That tells me you think they have an intruder. Someone is breaking in—not out." Barry stepped closer, stripping off his sunglasses with a swipe of his hand. He needed her to hear him, and she couldn't do that if he hid behind the shades.

The gesture reminded Olivia of the first time they met. He was conflicted. Looking into his serene grey eyes brought a flood of memories rushing in to fill the void between them. They hadn't talked since the night she saved his life, and he rescued her from a place she should never have gone.

"Is *It* back?" Barry couldn't bring himself to say the word demon.

Trading one life for another may have released Jamie Smythe, but not her. *Alleracsap* wasn't gone. The demon had just moved inside her head. Free flow communication was the price she paid for making a deal with a demon.

"After what we went through, do you really think there's anything you can't say to me? I owe you my life." Barry's confession was brutally honest, full of raw emotion. It leaked through no matter how many walls stood between them.

Images of Andre Roche holding a knife over Barry, threatening to end his life rolled around inside her head. The only way to save Barry was to give herself over to a monster. *Alleracsap* handed her the keys to unlock the gifts inside her. Once taken, she couldn't put them back. Once unlocked, Olivia no longer had to wonder who the monster was.

"There's a lot of energy here. But no monsters." It's why she took a consulting job with a hospital and not the FBI. "All I found was an echo I can't place." Despite no physical connection to this place, the feelings Olivia experienced were personal. "Armando, the groundskeeper, will take you to the little room. I can't go back in there. Not again. Not today," Olivia said, sharing some honesty of her own.

Being inside the room set off a whirlwind of old and new connections to the other side. Her psyche had been all over the place for weeks now. Today was just another example.

"Walk the perimeter, just the two of you. Away from the others, Armando may give up the story he has to tell." Olivia would have done it, but the groundskeeper was cagey around her. Maybe because she had been inside his head. Having been there also told her he was more comfortable talking to a man.

"The room feels like a way station."

Another noteworthy description. "If not a patient, then who?" Barry asked.

"Maybe a former one who can't let go. Doors swing both ways, don't they?"

Barry let out a sigh. Olivia once said no one called her for normal. "You know, it takes a special kind of crazy to break into a mental institution, don't you?"

His comment produced a smile that reached all the way to her green eyes. Barry had never seen eyes so vivid. Paired with her pale skin and blonde hair, she was an uncommon beauty. He loosened his tie and gave himself a moment to pull his shit together. He told himself it was the heat but knew that was a lie. All the time away from her had changed nothing. She stirred emotions in him that he never knew existed.

"I am familiar with crazy," she conceded. "If this is a break-in, then that makes this SAPD's jurisdiction. I heard the neighborhood around here is pretty organized. I'm sure they wouldn't hesitate to report a rise in opportunistic crimes or file a complaint."

"You sound like a detective or maybe a federal agent. Looks like the hospital got a good deal when they hired you."

"I'm not real FBI, remember?" Olivia repeated the confession she made when they first met.

She was still smiling when they parted ways. He had work to do, and she had a husband waiting at home. Seeing Olivia left Barry wondering how many more nights with Amanda Greene it would take to purge her from his memory.

Chapter Three

Olivia followed the smells to the kitchen, where she found her husband barefoot, stirring something that smelled almost as good as he looked. Silas Branch had ditched his FBI suit in favor of shorts and a t-shirt. Olivia took a moment to appreciate her new life. Before marrying him, domestic was not a word she would have used to describe the man who had been her work partner for eight years. With his good looks and charm, Silas had quite a history with the ladies, but he had traded all those habits to be with her. Olivia had never felt so safe, secure, or loved.

Silas felt the weight of her stare from across the room. He turned to find her leaning against the doorway to the kitchen, her shoes dangling from her hand. Late, and now shoeless, something told him the first day with her new client hadn't gone well. Good thing he had a glass of wine waiting for her.

"Bad day?"

The glow in her emerald eyes shifted, signaling something else.

Silas turned down the burner. "This should probably simmer."

"Good," Olivia said and dropped her shoes where she stood. "I could use an appetizer."

Silas caught her in his arms.

They never made it upstairs.

****

"So, you liked it?" Silas asked, watching her dip her finger in the remaining rosemary sauce and swirl it around her plate.

Olivia stopped herself. She had eaten all of the bread. She sucked the remaining flavor from her finger and pushed her plate away. "You are fabulous in the kitchen as well," she told him with a bat of her lashes. She reached for her glass, only to discover it was empty.

"Let me," Silas told her, retreating to the kitchen. Couch night was his favorite. It reminded him of their first time.

He noticed her wine sitting untouched on the counter. "You want wine instead?"

"No, thank you. Just not feeling it." The thought of alcohol made her stomach roll.

Silas was mildly surprised. After the day she had, a glass of wine would have been in order. He returned with a bottle of her favorite sparkling water instead. The way she was going through it, maybe they should consider buying in bulk.

"Want to tell me about your day?"

"Not really," Olivia told him. Discussing hospital bureaucrats just wasn't the same as the killers they once hunted.

"The Forester's sent this over," Silas said, sliding her the glass of water and the envelope he had left with her wine. "The landscapers found whatever that is buried in the yard. It could belong to your family."

Eager to see the mystery inside, Olivia ripped through the paper. One look at the inscription, and she knew. A tingle raced up her arm as she let the coins slip through her fingers and onto the table. She typically wasn't good at reading inanimate objects, but as soon as the first coin touched her hand, she felt the blessing in them despite their age.

VRS. "Vade retro Satana," she whispered.

Having been partners long before they were married, Silas sensed something was wrong even before she started speaking Latin. "Do I want to know what that means?" he asked.

"Step back Satan."

"I caught the Satan part," Silas assured her.

"It doesn't mean Satan was the intended one," Olivia clarified. "The coins were blessed by a priest and buried on the property as a sign of protection. We have them here." She shook her head at the thought these coins no longer served their purpose. The defense they once offered was broken.

"I also know *why* we have them," Silas reminded her, not wanting to bring up the matter of the demon in the living room. He never saw it, but it had left its mark on the floor where Father Dominic pierced it with his cross. Silas' eyes were drawn to it every time he crossed the threshold of their home. Like a greeting.

"All Saint Benedict medals carry the inscription. It doesn't mean it's demonic."

From the look on her face, Silas wasn't sure if Olivia was reassuring herself or him.

"There are other reasons for the coins, less threatening ones," Olivia said, digesting the information. She was limited in her family history, having only the books Gran left behind as a reference. The house where Lily and Ross lived was older than hers. Surely somewhere within the stored reams of paper, her ancestors documented the reason for the coins.

"If the coins were buried for protection, then there must have been a reason," Silas said what she was thinking. "Do you think it was to keep something out?" It's what they had done here.

"Or in," Olivia suggested, doing nothing to ease his anxiety. At one time, her family owned the whole block. The house she and Silas shared was the only one that still bore the Osborne name. It was built to keep her great-grandmother with the family. Her ancestors held on to things.

"Could removing them have let something loose?" Silas asked.

"What do you mean? Loose?"

"Maybe now's the time I tell you I saw a dead girl in the bathroom."

"You saw a dead girl?"

"You sound surprised," Silas scoffed. "You don't think I've picked up a thing or two from you?" Olivia had many talents. The fact the dead liked to commune with her was only one. "I can even notice when Alice is around," Silas told her with pride.

Olivia reached over for his hand, lacing her fingers through his. "Of course, you can, Silas. Alice likes to turn the lights on and off." The friendly poltergeist had been with Olivia her whole life, shifting from imaginary childhood playmate to protector when Jamie Smythe showed up in her living room. Alice's light trick induced a seizure and gave Olivia time to retreat. She and Silas both put a bullet in him that day. The demon may have escaped but they caught a serial killer. Jamie Smythe would always be a part of their lives and never be classified as an unknown subject again. He would forever be known as the *Good Samaritan Killer.*

"Alice also plays with the water, which she hasn't done, lately," Silas told her.

When Alice was alive, she and Gran were friends, but that was eight decades ago. Gran believed Alice lingered here because she was killed in an accident in front of the house. Olivia remembered the first time she saw her. Interestingly, Gran had never mentioned Alice until she did. It was the same day her mother abandoned her. Alice stood watch over her as she slept her first night back at Gran's house. Because of that, Gran believed Alice could be her guardian angel.

Olivia rubbed the coins back and forth between her fingers, ignoring the static that came with them. "How long do you think Alice has been absent?" she wondered aloud.

"Hard to say, since we don't hear from her every day. The last few days though seem different somehow." Silas reached over and laid his other hand over Olivia's. Touch would bring her back from wherever she had gone. "What are you thinking?"

Olivia was reminded how lucky they were to be together. How many other couples could have great sex, fantastic food, and discuss the dead all in one evening? Life with Silas was definitely never boring. "A haunting could have sent Alice into hiding."

"So, the girl in the bathroom is a haunting?" Olivia might be the expert, but Silas had picked up the lingo. "Is it like the thing I heard in the shower at the hotel?" he asked, referring to their one and only stay at the Emily Morgan Hotel. The historic landmark was located just across the street from the famous Alamo.

"Yes, like that. The place is full of ghosts," Olivia agreed. Not only was the hotel located near the scene of a bloody battlefield, but the building had once been a former hospital. Now it was a hot spot for ghost hunting.

"Did the girl in our bathroom say anything?"

Silas shook his head. "Nothing. Maybe she was waiting for you to get home."

Olivia smiled at the remark. Silas liked to joke. The quips helped alleviate the horrors they saw working for the BAU. "Was today the first time you saw her?"

"Uh, no. I've been catching glimpses of something darting around for the last couple of days. But today I got a good look at her. I'm inclined to think it's been her all along."

"What were you doing when you saw her?"

"Washing my hands. I had just come inside from feeding the dogs."

Mention of the dogs set Olivia in motion. "We should walk and talk at the same time," she suggested, noting the shadows falling outside. Strolling the neighborhood with their fur babies was all part of the cherished routines they had adopted as part of their new life together. One where they made time for each other and the future.

As was their custom, Silas took Daisy. Olivia may have rescued the greyhound from the racetrack, but Daisy defected with Silas's arrival in their life, leaving Olivia with Alvin. The tiny gray and white schnauzer was also a rescue, but from one of Jamie Smythe's victims. Initially, Alvin wasn't a fan of the leash, but he learned to accept it as part of their nightly strolls and visits to the Alzheimer's Units. The visitations were one of Olivia's community volunteer projects with Father Dominic.

"Were you feeding them people food again?" Olivia asked once they were on their way.

Anyone else might have forgotten his earlier slip of the tongue, but not his wife. She was relentless. Silas liked that about her. "What gave you that idea?"

Her look said it all.

"There might have been a few chicken trimmings I didn't want to go to waste," Silas admitted. He couldn't keep anything from her. Not only did she have otherworldly skills, but she was also a trained FBI profiler. "They eat the same thing every day. Don't you think they get bored?" Silas suggested with a smile. He was resigned to the role of the fun parent if they ever managed to have kids.

Olivia smiled. She couldn't stay mad at him. "Why don't you tell me more about the dead girl?"

"After feeding the dogs, I stopped in the downstairs bathroom to wash my hands. When I looked up, I saw her in the mirror. Hanging out in the shower."

"What did she look like?" Olivia asked using her interview voice.

"About your height. Well below my shoulder." Standing six feet three, Silas dwarfed her. Olivia could stand behind him unnoticed if she wanted, but that wasn't her way. She didn't hide from anything. His petite, demure wife was a bad ass who faced down demons.

"Any distinguishing features you remember?

"Her face was covered by a tangled mess of hair that hung down to the top of the gown she was wearing."

"What kind of gown? Sleeping? Wedding?"

Silas paused to nod at the couple they passed on the opposite side of the street. With his outgoing personality, it didn't take Silas long to get to know the neighbors. Silas had been part of a team his entire life. Olivia, on the other hand, had always been a loner. She walked quietly beside him, content to let him lead. Clad in her non-descript yoga pants and a t-shirt with her golden hair threaded through the back of the Notre Dame baseball cap, she looked nothing like her FBI press photo.

Silas considered the options. "Neither. It was something old fashioned, with a scooped neck and ruffles. There was something around her neck. Maybe a necklace."

Olivia nodded. She was in full agent mode now, building a timeline in her head based on his description. "Age?"

Silas tried to reconstruct the skittish specter. "Not a child, but not old. Hard to say without the face. Maybe late teens, early twenties based on body build. Dark hair."

"You're doing great," Olivia coaxed him.

"Thank you, Agent Osborne." Silas caught the hint of a smile from her at the term. She wasn't an agent anymore, but he knew she preferred the title over Doctor any day. Personally, Olivia went by Branch. Professionally, she stuck with Osborne. There was a lot of paperwork involved with changing her professional license. Besides, they still worked together. In her opinion, it was better for Silas, professionally, if they stuck to separate names. He was a star with the FBI, while she was the stepchild no one wanted to talk about. After less than a year together, the Bureau kicked her out only to come crawling back when they realized there were things out there only she could understand.

"Anything else you recall?" Olivia asked.

"She was wet. She was gray, and she was dead. That about sums it up."

****

Silas was rummaging through their bathroom medicine cabinet looking for something to ease the ache in his knee, when he ran across a familiar pink and blue package. He hadn't seen one in months. After more than a year of trying, Silas knew Olivia believed it should have happened by now. Since she wasn't talking about it, he would.

Silas slipped into bed, and Olivia inched her way into the protective circle of his arms. Before Silas came along, she barricaded herself behind a wall of pillows to mask feelings of loneliness.

"You know, if it's just the two of us, going to bed like this for the rest of our lives, I'll be just as happy," he whispered as he stroked her hair. It was the only silky thing on her at the moment.

Olivia turned to face him. "You mean that?"

Silas reached out and tucked a stray strand behind her ear, his gaze never wavering until her eyes locked with his. "You know I do."

"And I love you for it."

Olivia buried her face in his chest, and he held her tight, waiting for tears that never came. Maybe she had cried them all away.

Chapter Four

Once the sun dipped below the horizon, Barry moved to the front balcony of his condo. His perch from the thirteenth floor offered an unobstructed view of the north-south interchange that stretched through San Antonio. Rush hour was long over, but it was summer and the height of tourist season. The steady stream of oncoming traffic led downtown to the famous San Antonio River Walk. The taillights dotting the causeway in the opposite direction belonged to residents heading home to their families. A few miles to his right, nestled beneath the canopy of trees, was Olivia. She should have made it home in time for dinner.

Barry quickly stopped the flow of memories. Seeing her today had already prompted a stop by the wet bar. So far, there was only a splash of Crown in his diet soda, but too much emotional wandering, and he would be pouring more. Since the incident in the barn, Barry had learned the more alcohol he consumed, the worse his dreams. Barry redirected his thoughts to the present and what he found at the hospital.

A walk with Armando along the fence found it breached in more than one place. From there, they followed a well-worn trail leading to one of the old doors Vines told Olivia about. One that required more than an employee key card. Whoever entered this one definitely didn't have a key. Someone had jimmied it. Considering its age and exposure to the elements, a child could have done it. Once inside, the door led to a forgotten trail of stairs and straight to the abandoned room. Olivia was correct, the hospital had an uninvited guest.

Barry recognized the logo on the fast-food bags. According to Armando, there was a location within walking distance. Barry decided to bag the contents to make himself feel better and aid with a timeline. The receipts were still there, but unfortunately, all purchases had been made in cash. If there was any forensic residue left behind, it would be easy enough to trace to staff or patients. All employees would be in the system due to the conditions of their employment. The evidence bag was sitting in his office while he waited to hear back from Geoff Vines. By the time Barry had finished his inspection, it was after five, and the administrator was nowhere to be found. Perhaps Vines didn't want to stick around for more bad news.

A review of his findings left Barry's thoughts as jumbled as Olivia's senses. Knowing her, she had probably already constructed a profile of what kind of individual would voluntarily sneak into a mental institution. Maybe it was a former client who wasn't ready to return to the pressures of society or one that had nowhere else to go. Those were rational, mainstream explanations, ones fed to hospital administrators. Realistically Barry knew the suspect list was full of damaged, potentially dangerous individuals.

His first assessment of the scene was as a cop, looking for physical clues. The second time was different, thanks to Ana Lutz. The witchy brew she force-fed him the night in the barn flipped a switch inside of him, awakening a heightened set of senses he didn't know he had. Entering the forgotten door fanned a flame that had been on a slow burn ever since. The jumble of someone else's thoughts filled his head. For the first time, Barry wondered if this was what it was like living inside Olivia's world. He should probably talk to someone. Maybe someone in robes. Father Dominic would be a good start. The priest knew his feelings for their shared cause.

For now, Barry filed an official police report along with a request to step-up nightly patrols around the hospital. He also decided to run a check for any recent activity reports from the same area. Like a hunted animal, the visitor was desperate. They might have tried other nearby accommodations before seeing this place as their last resort. Maybe, he could find a physical lead to go with his emotional one. Barry constructed a set of parameters and sent an email requesting information on burglary and trespassing calls in the neighborhood surrounding the hospital.

Since they hadn't met in person, Barry also sent an email to the hospital administrator and copied Olivia, outlining his recommendations for security cameras but downplaying his concerns regarding the room. Scaring Vines into compliance was Olivia's job, not his. Still, she needed to know his findings and his thoughts. None of those were suitable for an email or a phone call. It meant seeing her.

Thoughts of her sent him brooding again. Barry pushed aside his empty glass, vowing not to drink another one. He was wondering how long the promise to himself was going to hold when his phone came to life. Considering the hour, his first thought was it was the watch commander requesting clarification on his patrol request. He hadn't specified if they needed to begin tonight. He was happy for the distraction—until he wasn't.

Barry stared at the screen making no move to answer. The call eventually slid to voicemail. If she left a message, he would delete it without listening.

Most men he knew would be happy to have a woman like Dr. Amanda Greene calling at this time of night. She was a beautiful woman with a successful career as a psychiatrist specializing in damaged cops. Barry probably needed therapy more than anyone he knew. She could have been just what he needed, but it wasn't like that. For either of them. Their relationship was anything but professional. He shot her down as his therapist the day she showed up at his condo to conduct a wellness check after the death of his partner. She settled for his bed instead.

He wasn't looking for anything permanent. He had done the marriage thing before. Twice. Both ex-wives described him as emotionally absent. Barry knew himself well enough to know they were right. Amanda was just someone to help him forget the losses he had chalked up before meeting her. So far, there had been only one woman who filled him with a tidal wave of emotion. So much so, he hid behind it in a selfish act of self-preservation. It was a costly mistake he was still paying for. Today was a reminder. He was still mourning his past while Amanda was planning for her future. That's what buying the fancy new house with a yard was all about. Amanda was just a placeholder he used to help him forget Olivia. It wasn't Amanda's fault she couldn't help him. No one could.

****

"Yea. Sure, I'll be right there."

It was three in the morning, but Silas didn't sound like he had been asleep for almost four hours. He sat up and rubbed his hands over his face.

"Who was that?" Olivia mumbled, clearly not awake. She had been sleeping soundly lately. Silas suspected it was because she wasn't working a case.

"Ross. Something tripped the house alarm. He sounds kind of freaked out. I told him I would come take a look."

Since the call didn't involve anything dead, Olivia snuggled back down in the covers.

Silas bent down and kissed her cheek. "You go back to sleep. You're probably exhausted. I should know."

****

Silas spied the half-empty snifter of bourbon on Ross' desk. "You're sure the alarm went off?"

Silas had already asked the question but repeated himself, hoping for some elaboration. It was too bad they were never able to finish their earlier conversation. It might have provided some context. From the looks of him, Silas figured Olivia was probably better suited for this particular situation. Too bad for Ross. He was stuck with him. For now.

Ross stared at the gun shoved in the waistband of Silas' shorts. Ross knew what his neighbor did for a living. He had just never seen him in full FBI mode before. He was used to seeing Silas with a drink, not a gun.

Noting the look on his neighbor's face, Silas slid

into the chair across from Ross, putting them on equal footing, and more importantly concealing the weapon.

"Yea. The alarm went off. I'm sure of it," Ross told him.

Silas believed the part about the alarm. "You should have the security company come out tomorrow and do a system's check," Silas suggested. "Maybe the renovations caused some kind of electrical problem. I found nothing suspicious outside. Nothing inside either."

Silas continued to study Ross. He was still sipping. His knuckles were white from gripping the glass. "You want to tell me what's really going on?"

For the first time, Ross looked relieved. "I think maybe I should be talking to your wife."

****

Olivia stirred as Silas slipped back into bed. "What was it?"

"He's still a little fuzzy on the details, but something tripped the alarm. He's pretty sure he saw something. He's not sure what came first." Silas settled down next to his wife, hoping sleep would come. He had an early start in the morning. "He's still processing, but he and I agreed he should talk to you." Silas turned toward her, burying his nose in her hair. The smell of vanilla and honey filled him with a sense of home.

"Me?"

Silas couldn't tell if she was annoyed or sleepy.

"He's your friend."

"It's really your area. You know, the usual, spooky shit," Silas said, closing his eyes. "He's picking Lily up from the airport in the morning. Then they'll be by for a chat. I told him to bring your favorite almond croissants from that little bistro place you like."

****

Silas checked the medicine cabinet the next morning. He wasn't snooping, just curious. The test was still there. For a while, Olivia had been obsessed with their lack of results. Maybe the fact she wasn't talking about it meant she was working through it in her own way. Their own self-imposed timeline was looming. No matter what the outcome, they would be united in their decision.

At forty, they both knew time was not on her side. It's why they had planned ahead. Before they started, they made a pact. Natural was best. If they couldn't conceive on their own, there would be no fertility testing for either of them. Theirs was an equal partnership. Silas remained supportive, never wavering in his feelings. He wanted a baby too, but he stood by what he said last night. He was content to live the rest of his life with just her by his side.

****

Olivia told Silas goodbye from bed, waiting until he left the house to creep to the bathroom and stare at the box. It was her last one. They had been trying for a year with not so much as a false alarm. A temperature chart confirmed she was ovulating, but she knew that before they started. The rhythm method was the only birth control she had ever used. She was in tune with her body enough to know when she was fertile. Getting pregnant wasn't something she had to worry about. Before Silas, the intimate part of her life was sporadic at best. She was too busy hunting monsters. That and being sensitive to the emotions of others made for a complicated personal life. Silas started out the same way, but after years of working together, he ended up being the most surprising man Olivia had ever met. Maybe that's why it worked with them.

Chapter Five

Ross and Lily arrived armed with croissants as instructed. An air of uncertainty hung over their arrival. Olivia blamed herself. She had her own cult following due to her extrasensory abilities, but that was her professional persona. Her relationship with the Foresters was personal. They were the first married friends she and Silas had. If it were up to her, Olivia would keep what she did for a living to herself. The Good Samaritan case made that impossible. After murdering Mark Austin, Jamie Smythe came for her. Shooting a serial killer in her living room was a hard thing to keep from the neighbors. The fact Jamie Smythe still roamed free made it unforgettable.

Olivia suggested they move to the backyard, hoping a more tranquil setting might help. Silas' suggestion of food was a good one. They often either drank or ate with their neighbors, but after Ross' brief update on their home renovations, there was more awkward silence. This time Olivia didn't blame herself. Away from a couple's setting, Olivia sensed a deep river of secrets between them. The longer she spent with them in silence, the more Olivia was sure Ross shared little with his wife. And not just about last night.

Beneath her silence, Ross began to fidget. "Can't wait until I have one of those," he said, his eyes avoiding Olivia to land on the stainless-steel grill behind her.

The patio hadn't been part of Olivia's original renovation plan. She added the space later as a wedding gift to Silas. Her husband loved outdoor living, and the warm sultry weather of South Texas offered more than they could ever find in Virginia. Olivia spent more than a decade there in graduate school and then working for the FBI. She fully expected Silas' career climb to take them back one day. With her robust consulting portfolio and writing career, Olivia could work anywhere. As much as she loved her home, she had made peace with the potential relocation. Marriage was about compromise, not secrets.

Lily was finally the one to break the stalemate. "We came here to learn about the coins, not drool over Silas's toys," Lily said it with a smile, but Olivia heard a barb in there. And it wasn't because she returned to an unfinished kitchen. It went deeper than that.

"I was going to look the coins up online but never got around to it. Are they valuable?" Lily asked with a mischievous smile.

"That depends on what you're using them for," Olivia said. "I don't think we've discussed it before, but are either of you religious?"

Ross avoided eye contact while Lily shook her head. "We were raised conservative Southern Baptists. We got married in a church."

"We really didn't have a choice," Ross muttered.

Lily shot him a glare.

Olivia paused, making sure they were done. "They're Saint Benedict medals. Typically, they are blessed by a priest and buried on the corners of a property as protection. We have them buried around our house as well. They were a wedding gift from the archbishop."

The Triple Blessing was one of the Church's oldest rituals. Blessing the property and each room she shared with her husband conveyed hopes for a fruitful and prosperous union. By Church standards, that meant offspring.

Olivia hoped by sharing with them that she and Silas had the same medals would alleviate their concerns. Given the amount of tension rolling off of them, Lily and Ross appeared to have bigger problems.

"Is it a Catholic thing?" Lily asked. "I noticed the little silver cross you always wear."

Instinctively, Olivia reached for the necklace. It was her most precious gift. Gran gave it to her for her fifth birthday, the day she legally became Gran's. "For some, yes, but you don't have to be Catholic to have your house blessed."

"Kind of like hanging crucifixes above the doors?" Lily suggested.

"I'm guessing blessings and burying medals is a little more involved than hanging crosses," Ross interjected, his tone dismissive. "They must mean something in particular."

"The Saint Benedict medal is one of the most honored medals used by Christians. Its purpose is to provide protection," Olivia said smoothly.

"Protection from what?" Ross wanted to know.

Olivia took a breath. There was no easy way to say it. "The medal has been used to ward off evil since the fifteenth century."

"Are we talking about the devil? Is there something evil in our house?" Ross asked before Lily could. Her mouth was stuck in a perfectly round 'o'.

Olivia rushed to derail him. "Evil doesn't necessarily mean the devil. Evil can come in many forms."

"Like that boy you shot," Lily said, finally finding her voice.

Olivia had shot that boy, but it had more to do with the thing inside the boy than the fact he was trying to kill her, but now wasn't the time for a lesson in demonic possession. Before she could find an answer, Olivia was distracted by a glimpse of the distorted vision of something white flowing near the garden. It was a small, old woman. Her long white hair billowed in the wind. Except there was no wind and no woman. Not a real one anyway.

"If it's not the devil, then what is it?" Ross snapped her back to attention.

Olivia blinked her eyes. "Any number of things. The medal can protect against hauntings or temptation. Poison, disease." She could go on, but she was searching for the woman.

"Your family lived there. You must know something," Ross probed.

"Medals are also placed to protect someone who is tormented by dark spirits. Or tempted by witchcraft."

"It's your family, isn't it?"

"Ross," Lily snapped. She looked embarrassed by the accusation. "What kind of question is that?" When her husband had no answer, Lily composed herself and turned back to Olivia. "What would your family have to do with coins in our yard?"

"Tell her," Ross said, looking at Olivia. He already knew the answer.

The vision of the old woman was gone, all that was left was the truth. "My family, I believe, had many beliefs," Olivia said, the admission coming with ease for once. "My ancestor, Sarah Osborne stood trial in Salem." It was one of the few stories Gran did share.

"So, there are witches in your family?" Lily asked.

Olivia hesitated, conflicting thoughts filling her head. Most of her ancestors thrived deep in the shadows. *Alleracsap* taught her that. Did the archbishop believe the same? Was that his reason for the Triple Blessing? Or did he just want her to be fruitful and multiply?

As Olivia struggled to find an explanation, the woman reappeared, hovering on the edge of the garden. Her land was blessed. The Saint Benedict medals protected against haunting influences. The woman wasn't a ghost. She was a vision.

"You believed your ancestor," Ross answered for her.

Olivia cleared her throat, grounding herself in the present. "Sarah Osborne denied being a witch. She claimed evil spirits were harming others while assuming her appearance. Under the influence of another, she was unaware of her actions and therefore could not be held accountable. Given this explanation, the court was forced to find her innocent."

Olivia was familiar with the defense. It was still used today. An insanity plea was a last resort, but the odds were in their favor with Dr. Osborne on the stand. After the Bureau revoked her status as an agent, Olivia gained a stellar track record as an expert witness defending those who found themselves victims of a similar fate. Olivia believed her success rate was what prompted the Bureau to ask her back. If she was hunting killers, she couldn't defend them.

"Sarah Osborne died in prison before she could be released. As an innocent. Not as a witch." Keeping the details of history was important. Maybe not to the Foresters but to Olivia.

"You based your dissertation on her story, didn't you? *The Seven Second Theory.*" Ross caught the look from his wife. "I found it online," he explained. "I thought you were one of those 'head' doctors," he told Olivia.

She took that to mean a psychiatrist.

Lily looked at her husband like she didn't know who he was.

"I was curious, so I looked her up." Ross' tone was more accusatory than apologetic. "I looked up Silas too. He played tight end for Notre Dame. Could have gone pro."

"Ross." Lily didn't even have to raise her voice, and magically Ross stopped talking. Olivia wondered if it was some unique skill acquired with marriage or motherhood.

"What can happen in seven seconds?" Lily asked.

It was a question Olivia had answered many times throughout her career.

"The notion of free will and its implications is one of the longest-running debates between philosophy and religion. Through modern technology, we can now see the brain at work. It has been demonstrated there is a lag time between the initiation of thought and the physical act of movement. It can last as long as seven seconds. The debate remains about what happens during that delay? Some believe it leaves the host vulnerable. During that time, can they lose themselves and transcend into another world?

"To me, that sounds like what Sarah Osborne described when she claimed something took control and stole her free will. In science, this experience is known as the *Seven Second Theory*. In religion, it is known as possession. Basically, it gives credence to the old saying, the devil made me do it."

Lily looked horrified. "That's terrifying."

"You're right. It is. Because it's real," Olivia assured her.

Lily paled. "You got all that from your ancestor?"

"It was a start. But any good hypothesis requires proof. Before I earned my Ph.D., I was a nurse. I worked with Alzheimer's patients. Some of the things I saw got me thinking. I was looking for answers. When science or medicine can't provide them, I'm willing to look elsewhere..." Olivia let her voice trail off. Lily's face said she had heard enough.

"My Gran left behind some family albums. I'll do some research on your house and see what I can find." Olivia shifted her attention to Ross. The door was open. If he wasn't going to walk through it, then she would see that he did. "Until then, the best chance of me helping you is for you to tell me exactly what you heard and saw last night."

Olivia watched Lily turn on her husband. "You didn't tell me you saw something." There was concern in her voice with a hint of something else.

Maybe it was an accusation, but Olivia wasn't sure. She got a flash of something red but shut it down. She didn't want to know. It wasn't her business.

"I didn't want to worry you over the phone," Ross

said, patting his wife's hand without looking. It was a patronizing gesture. One Olivia was sure he used often.

"Did this thing show up because the medals are gone?" Ross asked.

"Possibly. That's why I need you to tell me what happened and describe this thing you saw."

"I heard sounds coming from the shower. Have you ever been in a house where the ventilation system comes through the floor?"

Olivia nodded, encouraging him. Her apartment in graduate school was on the second floor of an old, converted home in Richmond. Sometimes she could hear the newlywed couple downstairs. Most times, she wished she couldn't.

"That's what I thought it was, some kind of weird acoustic trick. I heard moaning coming from the drain. I thought it might be an animal outside somewhere." San Antonio was one of the most inhabited cities in the US, yet wildlife still roamed free. The dense trees in their older neighborhood provided ample cover, especially for raccoons and opossums.

"What came first? The moaning or the house alarm?" Olivia wanted to know.

"The moaning. The alarm didn't come until the end. Almost gave me a heart attack." Ross shifted in his chair. Beads of sweat dotted his upper lip. "We have a pretty bright night light in the bathroom, so I got up to check it out. When I walked in, I thought I saw something moving in the shower. It was blurry, shadowy at first."

"The shower is glass, Ross. Are you sure it wasn't your reflection?" Lily asked, seeking a tangible solution. Just like Ross, her mind reached for the familiar. Reality was a safe place.

"It wasn't me," Ross snapped. "It was a dead girl. She was wet. I thought she was standing at first, lurking in the corner. Then I noticed her feet."

"What about her feet?" Olivia asked.

"They didn't touch the ground. There was a rope around her neck. She was hanging."

Chapter Six

After Ross and Lily left, Olivia trekked outside to the shed in the corner of her backyard. After the house renovations, she didn't really need it, but she kept it for sentimental reasons. She couldn't bear to tear down what her grandfather had built. When she was young and just discovering her gifts, she often sat in that space gliding her hands across wood slats she knew he had touched, willing him to come, but he never did. At least not there.

Her grandfather went off to fight the Germans shortly after he married her grandmother. The man who returned was a shell of the one who left. This small shed was his retreat, his safe place. Once he was really gone, Gran used it for storage and practical purposes. Olivia grew up lugging dirty clothes all the way across the yard to do laundry. When the time came for renovations, an inside laundry room was as important to her as a new master bed and bath. Since then, the little building had turned into a retreat for Alvin and Daisy, complete with a large doggy door. Inside it doubled as a storehouse for an assortment of family history.

Gran might not have been big on sharing family stories, but the volumes of old leatherbound books told Olivia someone was. They were the first place she went after the demon *Alleracsap* showed up in her living room. The claim that she owed him a debt forced her to explore her family's past. Olivia began with a mother she never knew, but her journey was short-lived. After learning Sarah Larsin's troubled teen years led her down a path that intersected with Ana Lutz and Andre Roche, Olivia never finished the story.

What she didn't know, she couldn't share with the FBI or the human trafficking task force hunting her mother. Olivia wasn't sorry when she heard the lead investigator, Mason Deveroux, dropped off the radar and out of their lives. As for *Alleracsap*, she found a way to atone for promises made centuries before. Andre Roche and Ana Lutz paid her family debt with their lives.

Olivia pulled out the step stool to reach the cabinets where she kept the books. She might not want to read them, but like the little building, they were a connection to a past she couldn't release. She stored them in plastic bins that still smelled like Gran's favorite soap, a mingling of past and present.

Sorting through them, Olivia was overcome by the combination of summer heat and the smell of lavender. Clutching books older than Gran, she felt unsteady. As she sank to the floor, a welcome blast of cold air filled the room. Olivia leaned her head against the cabinet behind her until the spinning stopped. She opened her eyes to find mounting shades of grey. The morning sun was gone, replaced by silent rivets of rain sliding down a milky pane of glass.

Olivia stood and slowly made her way to the window, only to find her neighborhood gone, replaced with open land. She watched as plowed fields turned to mud. A clap of thunder sliced the air, and she felt another wave of vertigo. Olivia closed her eyes, willing the scene to end. The buzzing in her pocket brought her back. She clutched her phone like a lifeline as the world outside righted itself.

"Olivia, is that you? You don't sound like yourself."

Silas had told her about Patrick Monahan's call, and that he had taken the liberty of refusing his offer for her.

"My answer is still the same," Olivia replied, exiting the building and taking the books with her.

Patrick acted like he didn't hear. "Pittman is fighting his lawyer on continued appeals. The state of Florida will kill him sooner rather than later. You have to get to him before that happens."

Larry Wayne Pittman had passed his psych eval. With it, an insanity plea was off the table. That's why he would spend the rest of his days in prison and not in a mental hospital. Death was the price of his freedom.

"It sounds to me that Mr. Pittman has accepted his fate."

"Maybe he's seeking absolution," Patrick suggested.

It was the same word the archbishop had used.

"Pittman wasn't asking for forgiveness. He knows what he did. He told me so," Olivia reminded him.

They needed kill'n.

"He asked for you."

"He did that last time." And she gave him what he wanted. Her presence. "Pittman didn't kill the other girls," Olivia countered. "They wouldn't be missing if he did."

"I believe you."

Olivia and Patrick had worked together before.

After one fateful night, ending in the death of a veteran agent, the Bureau cut her loose, and Patrick was shuffled to the BAU. Two years later, he was faced with a case he knew only Olivia could solve. Her return was contingent on working exclusively for him.

"Pittman's request to see you was months ago, before the body was found," Patrick revealed.

The news settled over Olivia as she deciphered what it meant. This had nothing to do with Patrick or the BAU. "Why am I just now hearing about this?"

"I just heard myself."

With Silas behind a desk in the San Antonio field office, the BAU lost both of them. Patrick had hoped the request for her services was an attempt to get her back. It was only after Patrick told his bosses Dr. Osborne wasn't interested that he learned the truth. As usual, the Bureau's interests were self-serving.

"It's the Justice Department. They're the ones dealing with Pittman. They told him the only way they would let him talk to you was if he gave up the location of the other girls."

DOJ, FBI, BAU. The acronyms no longer mattered. They were all the same. Olivia was tired of being the prize they dangled. It was time she freed herself from her handlers. She vowed this would be the last time. Even Jamie Smythe couldn't bring her back. She could hunt him down on her own. Besides, Olivia wasn't so sure she wanted the FBI to find him. Smythe had proven he wasn't easy to manage, and she had found alternative solutions to dealing with the likes of him.

"Do you have an ID on the body?" Olivia asked.

"Not yet, but the decomp time is a match. Given

Pittman's request, the FBI is moving in. There's a plane leaving in a few hours. Silas has agreed to be on it. I need you to go with him."

Olivia let her silence speak for itself. Moments later, she felt the vibration in her hand.

"Those are your boarding passes." Patrick had already booked her a flight. He knew she wouldn't say no, not to him. At least not this time.

So did the FBI.

****

Airports like churches and hospitals were cesspools of energy. Travelers rushed through this waystation on their way to somewhere else, carrying their heightened emotions with them like baggage. The pressure of so many open, unbridled minds swirling around her forced Olivia to retreat. Behind the walls she built to shield herself, she envisioned a garden, like the one in her backyard. Minus the old woman. Sometimes it was the only place she could hear her own thoughts. Events of the morning churned just below the surface, waiting for her. Not the mundane ones, but the ones that mingled between both her worlds. The past was haunting her. The vision she experienced in her grandfather's shed was a glimpse in a time when her ancestors inhabited her land. Their tales awaited her in the books she retrieved.

Thoughts of Sarah Osborne bubbled to the surface. The story Olivia had shared with her neighbors was a recital of a hypothesis she had created fifteen years ago. The notion of one being under the influence of evil was solid. The *Seven Second Theory* was based on science, with her ancestor as the blueprint. What troubled her now was the motivation she assigned it. Now, older and wiser, Olivia forced herself to consider that decision with an entirely new perspective.

The younger and considerably more naive version of herself clung to the notion her family was good and that the shadows lurking in her mind were merely her imagination. Olivia had learned much since then. Demons were real. So were the shadows. With them came gifts and acceptance. Sarah Osborne made a deal with a demon and cast her bloodline into the shadows.

More than three hundred years later, history repeated itself. What were those consequences? What future course had she set for her offspring?

A soft touch on Olivia's shoulder brought her back. It was Silas sliding into the chair next to her. Her lack of reaction didn't mean she was ignoring him. Like the old rule never to wake a sleepwalker, he knew she was somewhere else. He knew she would return on her own.

"So glad you decided to join me," he said, and Olivia smiled, as his lips brushed hers. She had only tipped her toe in the water of her thoughts, but already she was glad for the reprieve.

"Thanks for taking care of everything." Silas rushed through his morning lecture. In his wake, he left behind his reluctant second in command, Jon Sharpe. "Everything good to go?"

"Pretty much."

Her first concern had been leaving her client so abruptly, but after scrolling through Barry's emails regarding his findings at the hospital, Olivia felt confident Barry could fill her unexpected absence with his suggestions for updated security. That would keep the hospital administrator Vines busy for a few days. After that, she could focus on more personal matters, like what to do with the dogs. Ironically, Barry helped with that as well.

Her preferred doggy motel was closed for renovations. Getting them in somewhere else would require paperwork and time she didn't have. Briefly, Olivia considered asking Lily to watch them but didn't want to impose. Between the house renovations and whatever had just happened, she didn't think Lily was up to it. With no other alternative, Olivia sucked it up and reached out to the woman trying really hard to be her friend.

Amanda Greene had been the woman in Barry Bartholomew's life since the incident in the barn. Olivia might have saved Barry's life, but Amanda was the one who nursed him back to health. When Dr. Greene wasn't mending cops, she volunteered her services to rape victims. She offered her services pro-bono to Kimmy Burleson, the girl Olivia rescued after spending eight months as Andre Roche's captive. Over the last year, both Amanda and Olivia had helped the young girl piece her life back together, each in their own way. Kimmy's gifts, like Olivia's, made her a target. Roche, with his interest in black magic, exploited them. Olivia was the only one who could understand. It was one aspect of Kimmy's recovery Amanda couldn't help.

Amanda's attempt at friendship felt artificial. Olivia wondered if it was because Amanda knew the girl was keeping secrets, or something else, like Barry. Either way, because of their vested interest in Kimmy's recovery, Olivia went along to get along. Acquiescence was a familiar fallback. All Olivia ever wanted as a child was to be like everyone else. That meant having friends.

"I called Amanda and asked her to take the dogs," Olivia confessed.

Silas was mildly surprised. "How did that go?" He wanted Olivia to have a friend, but he wasn't sure Amanda Greene was the best choice. Silas saw Amanda's efforts for what they were. It was Amanda's romantic relationship with Barry Bartholomew that pushed her to get close to Olivia. Dr. Greene was smart enough to know, just as he did, how Barry felt about Olivia. No matter how she dressed it up, insecurity was Amanda's motivation.

"Of course, she said yes." Amanda didn't strike Olivia as the warm fuzzy type, but she had taken to the dogs the night she was at the house for Kimmy's graduation party. Amanda mentioned once she bought a house, she wanted a furry companion to go along with it. Olivia never had a pet until after Gran died. Daisy became her substitute for human interaction. It was nice to know someone was waiting for her when she got home. What void was Amanda seeking to fill?

"Did she also remind you of her housewarming thing on Saturday?" Silas asked. He wondered if Bartholomew was feeling pressured yet.

"Of course, she did. I suppose I'll have to go now." Gran was big on manners. It was the polite thing to do.

Silas reached over and patted her knee. "I'll make it my mission to see you're back in time," he said with a devilish grin. He knew how much his wife hated social gatherings. He was also trying to lighten the mood. Silas couldn't build the same walls as his wife. The tension of the trip they were about to take was building. Silas hadn't forgotten what was left behind.

****

The flight from San Antonio to Tampa was shorter than a hop to DC. Silas waited until they were at cruising altitude before asking what he really wanted to know. "Anything else you want to talk about?"

"All I want right now is a nap." Maybe it was the events of the morning, or what she knew was waiting for them in Florida, but suddenly Olivia felt exhausted.

Olivia leaned her head back and closed her eyes. It was easier to deliver the news that way. "I didn't take it," she told him. Silas was out the door before she got out of bed. The package insert said a morning urine sample was the best. It contained the most HCG, the hormone found in pregnancy. Olivia really needed to pee, but she let the sample go to waste. She left the box sitting on the shelf, waiting for her to return.

"Do you want to talk about it?"

"No."

Silas reached over and squeezed her hand.

"I just wasn't ready."

Silas nodded silently, settling into his seat. At his feet was the briefcase containing his notes from the Pittman case. Silas preferred his own handwritten notes to the sanitized electronic version. He wondered what Patrick said that made Olivia change her mind.

"There are still three missing girls, and we have no idea what happened to them," Olivia answered Silas' unanswered question. Behind her closed eyes, the past still stalked her.

"What was the first thing Larry Pittman said to you?" she wanted to know.

"They needed killin." Silas had never forgotten it. "What did he say to you?"

"I see them too."

Just like her.

"It was more of an admission than a confession. I thought maybe I missed something." Olivia confessed.

Maybe they both did.

She told Patrick Pittman wasn't seeking absolution.

Neither was she.

Chapter Seven

Silas was silent all the way to the car. Seeing the Eden case file stuck in the outside pocket of his briefcase told Olivia how he spent his flight time and the reason for his mood. With a two-hour drive ahead, they both could use a distraction. There would be plenty of time to discuss the real reason they were there later. Until then, they could catch up on their day.

"Ross and Lily didn't take the news well," Olivia said once they headed north down I-75.

"Maybe calling it a haunting had something to do with it. You didn't lead with that, did you?" Silas asked. The smile that spread his lips was slow, a sign that maybe he had missed her. She had slept the whole time.

"I didn't use those words," Olivia assured him.

"What kind of words did you use?"

"We started with the medals. They're not Catholic and didn't know the meaning of them. The simple explanation was enough to spook them, so I had to tread lightly."

"You didn't speak Latin, did you?"

Olivia smiled this time. "No. I also chose not to share the literal translation."

"Good call. I heard discussing Satan before lunch is bad manners. So, what's your diagnosis, Dr. Osborne? Do they have more visits in their future?"

"I'm sure of it. Last night's event wasn't the first."

"You sure? Ross was pretty spooked."

"Ross isn't the only one who lives there," Olivia reminded him. "And they have a night light in the bathroom. I'm assuming there's a reason behind that."

"Good catch. So, what did you tell them?"

"Without using Latin, I took the path of the dark arts. If you read up on the medal *to destroy witchcraft* comes before *to give protection against evil spirits*. Considering my family history, I went with witchcraft."

Silas was glad to see she was back in agent mode. The nap must have helped.

"Now that I talked to Ross, do you want to go over with me again what you saw?"

Silas recounted his description.

"What about her feet?" Olivia asked when he was done.

"I couldn't see her feet." The downstairs bathroom still had the original claw foot bathtub. A showerhead had been added decades later.

"So, you saw the dead girl in the mirror and not in the actual bathtub?"

"Absolutely. Just her reflection. When I turned around, she wasn't there."

Olivia nodded, digesting the information, wondering if there was any correlation between Silas' visions and hers, but kept the thought to herself. Her experiences seemed more like shifts in time.

"You mentioned something about a necklace. Was there anything hanging from it? A locket maybe?"

Olivia was obviously looking for something in particular. Silas replayed the incident. His brow wrinkled at the revelation. "It wasn't a necklace. It connected somewhere outside the view of the mirror, from above." He took a moment to process. "It was a rope. She was hanging." A glance over at Olivia told him he was right. "Did Ross see the same woman?"

"Sounds like he did."

"Is she related to you?"

"I'd bet on it," Olivia told him.

"Why does it matter if I saw her in the mirror?"

"The medals were removed from the Forester's house, releasing the protective binding. That's how she could appear in their shower. Our house has been blessed. While that doesn't mean things can't get in, it just makes it harder for *certain* things. My theory is correct. This is a good ole fashioned haunting."

Silas nodded and reached for her hand. "I acquiesce to your expertise in these matters. I think you're onto something about your family."

Her family was a vast untapped well. One she was just starting to explore.

"Knowing what you do know, would your ancestors have buried medals and blessed the house if this was *just* about witchcraft? Not to beleaguer the point, but didn't a bishop bless our house and yet things still seem to find their way inside?"

Silas had a point. His assessment gave more validity to new thoughts about her ancestor. Communing with demons might not be such an uncommon occurrence in her family. Archbishop Mendoza had commented how her ancestor Sarah Osborne, an uneducated woman, delivered a defense clever enough to escape execution. She had no legal representation. Was it some unholy alliance instead?

Alleracsap's words haunted her. *You owe me a*

debt. Demons didn't measure time the same way as humans. If Sarah Osborne's life was the debt she owed, then Olivia paid it that night in the barn.

"You asked for one. I gave you two. That should settle my debt and the boy's."

"And now he is free. Are you?"

It was never about Jamie.

"Why the mirror?" Silas asked, snapping her back to the present.

"Mirrors provide a passageway between the living and the dead. It's why people of Jewish faith cover the mirrors during shiva, the time of mourning, to keep evil spirits from attaching themselves to the living. Some people cover their mirrors at night. That's when the dark comes. I didn't have one in my room growing up. I don't know if you've noticed, but we don't have unnecessary mirrors in our house."

Silas hadn't noticed their lack of mirrors. Conducting a quick mental inventory, he discovered she was right. They had no decorative mirrors, only practical ones in the bathrooms and closets.

"Old mirrors can be problematic. Over time they see and capture many things. As you can imagine, not all of them good. I was sentimental when redoing the house, in particular the downstairs bathroom. I only replaced the frame because it was cracked, but I left the original glass. For all I know, it could have come from the Forester's house. That is where my great-great grandmother lived. Our house was originally built as a wedding gift for Gran's mother. I should scrub the glass with salt water when we get home."

Silas cocked an eyebrow her way. "A condiment will get rid of the scary girl?"

"Salt was once considered a precious commodity. It's a pure substance, made of the earth and sea. Cleansing with salt water restores innocence. If there's something maleficent lurking in our mirror, the process should set it free."

"Sounds like lore," Silas commented.

"It's reality with a dash of magic." Most of Gran's teaching moments happened in the kitchen. It was there Olivia learned her family did things differently. Her beliefs were considered superstition to most people she knew. That's how she learned to stop sharing things about her family. Gran would have called the cleansing ritual a family tradition. Gran was a witch whether she wanted to admit it or not. The traditions and beliefs were hardwired in her DNA. Just like salt's connection with the earth and the sea, Olivia couldn't escape the roots of her family no matter how many prayers Gran said. She knew that now, too.

****

Dr. Greene had only been to the house once—for Kimmy's graduation party. Kimmy looked to Olivia like a sister or a mentor. Olivia's part in the girl's recovery was still a mystery. Just like so many other things about the good Dr. Osborne. Maybe there was some kind of bond between the rescuer and the victim. Hours of analysis still hadn't uncovered the real reason.

Amanda put the thoughts aside and concentrated on her surroundings. Standing in the living room like a voyeur, she told herself there was nothing wrong with wanting what Olivia Osborne had. The new house was one step. Barry Bartholomew, whether he knew it or not, was the next.

Amanda heard the crunch of gravel in the

driveway, signaling he was there. His parking spot was a sign of familiarity. She wondered how many times he had made that turn. Barry didn't come to Kimmy's party. Something about working a case. It was his go-to excuse, but Amanda knew that wasn't it. She had given him a pass, but no more. It was time he moved on. Olivia obviously had.

****

At least Barry now knew why Olivia hadn't returned his call or his email. Amanda was the one who told him she left town. What he didn't expect was to meet Amanda here—of all places. Any other time, Barry would have balked, but she needed him for practical purposes. Her sporty little car wouldn't hold both dogs, specifically the lanky greyhound. At least he wouldn't run into Silas.

Approaching the house, a swirl of memories began, beginning with the morning he said goodbye and the apology he made to go with it. Stepping onto the porch, Barry remembered the kiss he and Olivia shared on the steps. Looking ahead, Barry spied the camera over the door, wondering if Olivia ever changed her passcode and whose birthday she commemorated with it.

Inside, the familiar smell of vanilla and honey filled the air, tugging him back to the night he spent here. The way she felt. The way she made him feel. He had been standing on the edge of a cliff, willing and ready to fall.

It was quiet. No dogs. No Amanda. Barry's eyes searched the room. Daisy's bed sat tucked in the corner, surrounded by her toys. The greyhound was still guarding her territory. The feeling of familiarity faded as the differences rushed in. The TV had grown. The couch was upgraded to leather, surrounded by matching chairs. All classic signs of a male presence.

The patter of feet racing across the wooden floor snatched Barry free of the past, his memories tumbling right through his fingers, just like Olivia.

The little schnauzer made it to him first, prancing around in excitement until Barry bent down and stroked the back of his neck. The nub of a tail told him the pooch hadn't forgotten him.

"Look at you. You have a fan already."

So caught up in the reunion, Barry didn't hear Amanda come in. Maybe because she shouldn't be here.

"Alvin and I go way back. I was there the night Olivia rescued him." Barry recalled the bloody pawprints leading him to the first horrific scene he found in Wendy Florren's house. The other one he kept locked inside a box inside his head.

Amanda knew what everyone else knew about the Smythe case but, since Barry didn't talk about it, she wasn't privy to the nuances, like this tiny little detail. She wondered what other ones kept him tethered to Olivia Osborne.

Chapter Eight

Ocala, Florida, was a sleepy little town of fifty-five thousand. From November to March, the population swelled with flocks of northerners who fled there to escape East Coast winters in some reverse tourist season. By June, the crowds were gone, and the sidewalks rolled up at sunset. The only things left were horse shows and an occasional sighting of John Travolta.

Once they arrived, Olivia dropped Silas off at police headquarters while she checked them into their hotel. She felt very domestic, but the role didn't bother her. This had always been Silas's case. She didn't arrive until after Pittman's confession. Silas had called her late one night, admitting something just didn't *feel* right.

She caught the first plane out then, too. Agent Branch wasn't one to question his actions. He swam with confidence, yet something about this case caused him to pause and tread water. Something neither one of them could explain. Olivia returned to the thought that Silas had been onto something.

****

"Seven months. Five girls. Three missing, and then these two." Silas populated the board while he talked, adding school photos of the girls whose murders ended the case. "Ava and Dorcas McCleary, age twelve and thirteen. Their bodies were found on the side of a small dirt road not far from where they lived." Silas used a black marker to divide the board with a mark down the middle and added more pictures. At least these didn't have faces.

"Less than forty-eight hours ago, a couple of college boys from Oklahoma took their drone up for a spin. It crashed on top of this shallow grave." Silas pointed to the photos supplied by the forensics team. Olivia focused on the curious mound of debris. The configuration tickled the back of her brain with an odd familiarity.

"Looks pretty remote." The observation came from Agent Sean Tunney. He had been dispatched from the Tampa field office, replacing Harry Dunn, the local agent who worked the case with the BAU. Dunn retired shortly after and dropped dead of a heart attack a month later.

"If not for the drone, it could have gone unnoticed," Silas agreed. "The condition of the body suggests it had been there at least a year, which matches our time frame. A preliminary forensics review determined the bones to be female. The size and other precursory anatomical findings suggest an age range compatible with the missing girls. While the location is remote, it is easy walking distance to where the two girls were murdered and near where all the girls lived."

"Eden—instead of a garden, it looks like a wide space in the road to me." It was Tunney again.

"The population is listed at six hundred and eleven. It boasts a main street, a town square, a local convenience store and a couple of stop signs. The average resident is seventy-five. Given the stats, you can see why missing adolescents caught the attention of the BAU."

The FBI always thought it took the locals too long to get them involved. They chalked it up to reluctance to involve the government. The small community was a close-knit bunch. Silas still wondered who or what they were hiding.

"Our prime suspect, Larry Wayne Pittman currently resides in the Florida state prison outside of Gainesville. He confessed to shooting the McCleary girls. Their bodies were the only ones recovered."

"No more dead girls since you put this guy away?" Tunney asked.

Pittman put himself away. But Silas didn't stop to correct him. "No."

"So, did he do the other three?" Tunney gazed at the photos as Silas added a third column. It was the faces of girls still missing. Silas didn't want them forgotten. The gathering tonight was just the FBI show, mainly to bring Tunney up to speed.

Olivia stared at the smiles frozen in time, wondering which one it was.

"At this point, I would like to keep speculation to a minimum. I expect a new investigation. The parents of those still missing deserve as much. The first officer onsite was a state trooper who had the good sense to keep the news quiet. The fact the drone owners aren't local is a plus. The town endured enough scrutiny last time around," Silas explained. "Before the murders, a reporter out of Orlando wrote an expose` just in time for Halloween entitled *The Monster of Eden*. My hope is to avoid such macabrely again. I've asked local law enforcement to keep quiet the FBI's back in town."

Tunney nodded and snuck a glance across at the woman who hadn't said a word since the big guy introduced her as Dr. Osborne.

"Dr. Banigo, the medical examiner who worked the case last time, and Dr. Sheppard, a forensic anthropologist sent in from Miami, are currently examining the remains. They will brief me in the morning. Hopefully, we'll have an ID by end of tomorrow. Agent Tunney, I would like you and Agent Osborne to go to the dump site." Silas let Tunney believe Olivia was also an agent. No matter what had happened, she had earned her place in the Bureau, besides, a consultant title didn't inspire the kind of loyalty Silas needed from this man he didn't know. "The trooper who worked the gravesite will meet you. We'll circle back after lunch and compare notes."

Seeing they were finished the local police chief stuck his head inside and requested Silas to join him down the hall. Olivia remained where she was absorbed in a file that had been waiting for her, courtesy of the DOJ. It contained information on Larry Wayne Pittman she didn't have the last time. Mainly his juvenile record. It was expunged and sealed when he turned eighteen. Pittman was a fighter in his youth. Each time he was the aggressor, but maybe not without reason.

Pittman's trouble started in middle school just about the time puberty hit. It began on the playground with a schoolyard bully, followed by an alleged neighborhood peeping Tom, escalating to a shop owner from Panama City. The owner and Pittman got into a physical altercation when Pittman accused him of trying to lure a little girl into the back of his store. No one came forward to dispute Pittman's story, but no one stood up for him either. Pittman could have gone away for the assault, but the shop owner dropped the charges and pressed for property damages instead.

A yellow post-it with a handwritten note by someone with the initials of *MS* revealed the shop owner was murdered a year to the day later. The case remained open and unsolved. Given the additional information on the shop owner as well as his reluctance to pursue charges he was sure to win, Pittman could have been right. Olivia wondered if Pittman saw himself as an avenger of sorts? The boys at Justice would never see it that way.

"Since you're a doctor/agent, does that mean we're looking for more bodies tomorrow?" Agent Tunney asked all smiles. While Olivia had been busy absorbing Pittman's past, the agent had saddled up next to her. Leaning against the table beside her, Tunney focused on the clingy blouse she wore. She must not have been in the office when she got the call to hit the road. He would enjoy the view now before she got conservative in the field tomorrow. She was definitely a nice distraction from the FBI poster boy in charge. Tunney considered he might have been mistaken on the dullness associated with a middle-of-nowhere cold case assignment.

Olivia barely looked up. She was in the zone. "Not that kind of doctor," she muttered.

Agent Tunney slid into the chair next to her, determined to get Olivia's attention. His hand crossed over into her personal space to get a look at the folder she was holding. He saw the DOJ stamp and Pittman's name.

"Oh, I see that now." She must be a shrink sent by

the BAU like the big guy. It meant she was smart and took no crap. Nice. Tunney never would have guessed by looking at her. "Why not confess to all of them?"

"Maybe because he didn't do all of them," Olivia suggested, readjusting herself. She distanced herself from him and the wave of stale cigarette smoke that followed.

The agent gave a small laugh. "If he did two, why not the rest? What's three more? The state can only kill him once, right?"

"That's my point. He confessed to two. If he did the other three, why not just say so?" Olivia parroted back. From what she recalled Pittman was honest. Not entirely forthcoming, but she hadn't gotten the impression he was lying either. He also made no attempt to hide what he had done. He left the two girls where they fell, right out in the open. He didn't even pick up the shell casings from the floorboard of his car.

Tunney nodded. "So, no speculation."

Olivia finally looked up long enough to give him a brief once-over. Tunney was younger than her and looked like he liked to have fun. He probably didn't have to look far to find it, not with his easy smile and soft baby blues. The smoking was recreational to go with a drink in his hand. He was definitely on the prowl, and not just for drinks. "Those were Agent Branch's instructions. We are here to assess and verify," Olivia reminded him.

Spoken like a by-the-book agent. "I see," Tunney mused.

Olivia doubted his statement. He had been too busy ogling her to see much of anything. She remembered when she put the blouse on that morning how big her boobs looked in it.

"Since you've been here before, I thought you might know where to grab a drink, maybe some dinner," Tunney suggested. It was a leading statement.

"Stay on County Road 200. It's the main thoroughfare through town, the only one actually. If you can't find what you're looking for along the way, then they don't have it," Olivia told him.

"Do you drink?" Tunney inquired.

Olivia took her eyes off the paper and closed the file for good. "Not currently."

"Hmmm. What do you do? I hear this place doesn't have much to in the way of entertainment."

"The sidewalks do roll up pretty early," Olivia agreed. "Even in the busy season the average tourist is pushing seventy."

"Exciting," Agent Tunney said, gazing down at her bare legs with a slow crawl back to his original destination. He wasn't opposed to some indoor recreation.

Olivia smiled politely. No one had hit on her since she got married. She sensed Silas' return even before he got close enough to rest his hands on her shoulders. Tunney didn't hear him come in. It was his mistake.

"We like *Mimsy's*. For nightcaps or breakfast. Either one."

The Tampa agent lifted his eyes to the agent in charge, carefully bypassing another once-over of Olivia. Tunney nodded. "Thanks for the tip."

"Do you need another one?" Silas asked.

"No, I don't believe I do."

"Good. I hate repeating myself," Silas told him. "Please meet Dr. Osborne in the lobby of our hotel at nine in the morning."

"Yes, sir." The agent nodded at Silas and gave a quick one Olivia's way without making eye contact.

Silas didn't take the seat next to her until the agent cleared the room. "So, did the big boys send over anything interesting?" he asked with a nod toward the file she had discarded.

"I saw nothing in there that would give Pittman a reason to want to talk to me privately." That was all she was concerned about, not what the boys at Justice thought. She needed to stew on what she had learned, but not now.

Olivia snaked her hand over and rested it on Silas' thigh. It brought his tension level down a notch. "You were subtle," she said. "Why don't you just grab me by the hair and drag me back to your cave next time?"

Silas's eyes darted back to the door the agent had exited.

"You don't think I could handle him?" Olivia asked.

"I just thought he should get the lay of the land sooner rather than later. Didn't want any misdirection."

"It's not the first time I've been hit on, Silas."

"It's the first time since you became my wife," Silas reminded her.

Olivia nodded and gave his leg another squeeze. "I like it that you're protective."

Silas's eyes finally found their way to hers. "I didn't like the way he was looking at you. It infuriated me." Silas invaded her space this time.

Olivia took a moment to look at him and remind herself of how her husband appeared to other men. Physically, Silas was formidable. Personally, he was principled and passionate. Crossing him would be a mistake. She hoped for Tunney's sake he was a fast learner.

"How about we go to the little family place I saw on that billboard on the way into town? They were advertising a chocolate brownie with vanilla ice cream and a strip of bacon on the side."

Silas smiled at the suggestion of food. "Since when do you eat dessert?"

"I had a late breakfast, no lunch and then you drug me to this exotic place. After you feed me, you can take me back to the cave," Olivia suggested with a mischievous grin.

****

Barry was on edge after leaving Olivia's. He was quieter and more broody than usual. Dinner and a tumbler of whiskey helped soothe him. He had noticed he drank more when he was with Amanda. What she noticed was they ended up at her soon-to-be-vacant apartment rather than his comfortable condo.

Uncharacteristic of recent events, Barry made the first move, the sex fueled more by alcohol than desire. He waited for the rhythmical sound of Amanda's breathing before slipping out. By now, his pre-dawn escapes were the norm. Sneaking out prevented him from coming up with another excuse when what he should be doing was telling the truth. It wasn't her. It was who she wasn't.

Tonight, it was something else. There was an image Barry couldn't get out of his head.

He found himself back in front of Olivia's empty house. The street was dark under the canopy of trees, perfect for lurking or surveilling. No unmarked car anywhere in sight. That was good for him. Just the same, Barry bet the neighborhood patrols were back in place since Smythe's escape. He couldn't be the only one who thought the kid would one day make his way back for her.

Barry took a slow crawl past the house, circled the half street, and swung into the driveway. He cut the headlights and surveyed his surroundings. The soft glow of light inside the house mimicked the ambiance of someone home. The was a light on over the sink in the kitchen and one upstairs in the master bedroom. Barry had come in at the end of the renovations and knew there were two more rooms waiting. He wondered if Olivia had plans to fill them, but just as quickly decided he didn't want to know. It was too late for more alcohol, but the pull down memory lane was strong.

Barry drifted back to the time he brought her favorite bottle of wine. They started out talking about an UNSUB and ended up talking about feelings, mainly the ones Mark had for her. Olivia believed it was because she was the last connection he had to his dead brother Jason. Barry could have told her they went much deeper than that, and she could have told him about her feelings for Jason, but neither of them did. They were too wrapped up in each other.

The first tentative steps they took that night were heading somewhere important. Instead, they were shattered by life and death. All Barry had to show for it was a key to a door he couldn't open. He shut down the thoughts, shifting his focus to the memory that brought his return. Barry recreated his last night here—the one when Daisy almost died.

He was sitting in the driveway, just like now, questioning his motives for being there when lights flashed in his rearview mirror. Looking up, Barry had caught sight of a car making a U-turn in front of the house. The high-end sports model looked like it belonged, but it didn't. Cop instinct told him it was a drive-by. Surveillance but not the official kind.

Fast forward to a few hours ago. After getting Daisy settled in his car before exiting the driveway, Barry caught sounds of an argument next door. The man exited the house, overnight bag in hand, and headed for the car in the drive. He never even slowed his pace, despite the pleas coming from the woman on the porch.

Barry watched the man get in the car and never look back. Barry knew he should do the same. That's when tonight's memory returned. The lights of Amanda's sporty little Lexus had lit up his rearview mirror. Watching her make the U-turn in front of Olivia's house was a replay of the year-old memory he carried inside his head. A look back to a mystery he had never solved. *Until now.*

Chapter Nine

Agent Tunney was relieved to see her exit the elevator alone. He headed her way when he got cut off. The guy in the suit looked Bureau, but he wasn't packing underneath the jacket. The man stopped the doctor in her tracks.

"Dr. Osborne, Marc Singer with Justice." He offered a card, but Olivia didn't take it. "Did you get the file I sent?" He took her non-answer as a sign to keep going. "I need to speak with you."

"Not now." By then, her eyes had found Tunney.

"It's about Larry Wayne Pittman."

"I'm aware."

"Then you're aware we need to talk," Singer pressed.

He stepped into Olivia's personal space, electrifying her senses and signaling her he was growing impatient. His emotional rise was fuel for her fire.

"What I'm aware of is I should have had access to this information before, yet I did not," Olivia countered.

"There was nothing of relevance." Singer was dismissive, a familiar maneuver. He stared down at her but couldn't maintain her gaze. There were a lot of rumors about her at the Bureau. She was supposedly different. No further description was given. The ones who had worked with her, like Patrick Monahan, refused to talk about it. The Bureau had been known to dabble in recruiting those with unique abilities. In the 1970s they recruited people who claimed to have ESP abilities to spy on the Russians and anyone else the government deemed a threat. Apparently, the Bureau had moved on to bigger and better things—like Dr. Osborne. Except she was a wild card. They didn't make her. She was an original.

Before he knew it, Singer found himself explaining to her. "It took some time to find Pittman's juvie records. They were under another name. Suffice to say we learned there were no murder or weapons charges. Happy?"

"No. There are still three missing girls," Olivia reminded him.

"According to you, Pittman didn't do them."

"He didn't but somebody did." Olivia was bored with the conversation. Tunney was loitering in the corner waiting to see if she needed assistance. The agent edged closer, but she headed to him.

"Where are you going?" Singer protested. He reached out as if to stop her, but a look from her stopped his hand in mid-air. "I need to know about those other girls, Doctor." Singer called after her.

"Yes, you do. Which is why you need to let me do my job."

"This isn't over. In case you forgot the Bureau answers to us," Singer reminded her, but his threat lacked confidence.

"In case you forgot, I'm not a federal agent. Not anymore."

Tunney followed on Olivia's heels. He snuck a look back to see if they were being followed.

Fortunately, the Justice guy was still standing by the elevators looking lost. He was smarter than he looked.

****

"We have time for coffee, The state trooper sent me a text saying he was going to be a little late," Tunney told her.

Olivia held up a mini bottle of sparkling water. There was more stashed in her purse. "Help yourself," she told him.

"I'm sorry about last night. I had no idea," Tunney said, as they sat in the drive-thru for coffee. He had gone back to his hotel room last night without the drink he wanted and did some research.

Olivia looked at him, giving him full opportunity to explain himself.

"It was rude and disrespectful of me. I know now that you and Agent Branch have worked together for a while."

"We did. Now we're married. I'm here because I worked the original case."

Tunney nodded. It was worse than he expected. More than partners. *Great.* The big guy alluded to that last night. "You should wear a ring or something," Tunney suggested, trying to diffuse the situation. He flashed her a grin different than the one last night.

"We don't when we're working a case. Knowledge of a personal relationship is a liability. You never know when you're going to be put in a situation where someone is going to use anything they can against you." Olivia thought of Andre Roche as she said it. She was Barry's weakness when he went looking for her and found Ana Lutz instead. Roche had used Barry to try and control her. It had been a miscalculation on his part.

Roche only thought he knew who he was dealing with and what she would be willing to do to save those she cared about.

Tunney got his coffee, and they were on their way. "Before we get to the scene, can you describe what it is you do, besides talk to the crazy ones?" It was also probably why Singer from Justice wanted to talk to her about Pittman. "It's why you're in the field with me, isn't it?" From what Tunney read, what she knew didn't come from BAU training. It was some kind of a gift.

"It's called *claircognizance*—the gift of knowing. My training as a profiler, aside, it means I can sense what happened at the time of death, like reading a story." If there was enough energy left behind, she could manipulate it. It was a new skill she learned in the barn.

Gran told her she was gifted, but she had shared very little about what that meant exactly. Olivia didn't know if it was because Gran didn't know, or she didn't want Olivia to know. According to the archbishop, Gran's greatest fear was her granddaughter would follow the same dark path as their ancestors. The emergence of the new ability proved both sides of Gran's theory.

"Every living creature gives off electric energy. It's how readers, like me, can see the crossover from one plane of existence to another."

"So, reading energy, is a real thing? Not magic."

"Who says reality and magic don't go hand in hand, Agent Tunney? It happens in nature with animals. Sharks for instance."

Tunney put his coffee away, knowing he wouldn't touch it again.

"Whitetip sharks hunt on the ocean floor in the dead of night. Beneath the waves, under the dark sky magnetic particles are released each time a fish's heart beats or their tail swishes. The energy created by this movement leads the predator to its prey. Death extinguishes the energy, like blowing out a candle. What's left is a vision of what once was."

The way she said it sounded beautiful—if she hadn't been talking about death.

****

Barry was in the office early despite his late night. He began by rummaging through DMV records. If he remembered correctly, Amanda bought her Lexus about the same time they met, the same time as the drive-by. After losing Mark and ruining things with Olivia, the details during that time of his life were a little fuzzy. Barry was looking for a way to eliminate what his gut said was true, but the query only confirmed what he already knew. At the time of the drive-by, Amanda's new car was sporting temporary tags. Just like the one he saw at Olivia's a year ago.

The incident occurred before Kimmy's rescue. At the time, Amanda didn't even know Olivia. But she did know him. They had just met, yet Barry already knew Amanda's interest in him wasn't professional. Had she been stalking him?

The ping of an incoming email pulled Barry away. It was the reply to his request for police reports from the neighborhoods surrounding the state hospital. Someone, probably a summer intern, had taken the time to compile the findings on a spreadsheet in chronological order with names, addresses, and missing items. Barry appreciated the effort—definitely someone with time on their hands or hopes of a job.

His request was for the previous six months. Surprisingly, he found more incidents than expected. The stolen goods were the typical easy-access items, push mowers, weed-whackers, fishing poles, and hand tools. According to the notes, some of the homeowners admitted to leaving their garage doors open during the day. They were long-term residents not used to being vigilant. More than one complained the neighborhood wasn't what it used to be. Due to the opportunistic nature of the crimes, Barry's initial theory was the thief was one of their own, maybe a bored adolescent. Until the last incident changed the profile.

Up until then, the items were low in value, and easy to unload at the nearest pawnshop, but not this one. Taking this one was different. The local pawnshop wouldn't do. Too many questions. Barry wondered what prompted the change in pattern. Before he could skip to the description column for details, more emails arrived. Both from the hospital administrator, Geoff Vines.

The fence repairs Barry identified during his walk-through with the groundskeeper were underway. Vines had also been granted financial clearance to install the cameras Barry recommended.

Barry wondered why two emails when he noticed the second one only included him and Olivia. It was a follow-up to another of her questions. Had anyone talked to any of the roamer residents about any unusual encounters? Probably not something Vines wanted to share with his bosses.

With the possibility of a breach Vines, made some inquiries, discretely Barry was sure. According to staff, two residents known to frequent the forbidden zones claimed to have encountered someone they didn't know. The descriptions were similar enough to convince Barry they were describing a real person, not an imaginary one. It wasn't much to go on from questionable witnesses, but the results fit. Someone from the outside was responsible for the breaks in the fence line.

Barry glanced to the corner where he stashed the paper bag containing the blanket and pillow. He should take it to forensics. Like running Amanda's plates, the contents might not give him the answer he was looking for, but it would eliminate one. He still wanted to know who would be crazy enough to sneak into a mental hospital. The description didn't fit his bored teenager theory.

Olivia had mentioned a neighborhood watch group. Barry looked across the room at his own special project. He was compiling data and plotting a case. His hope had been if he stared at the cluster of pins long enough, he might eventually see what he couldn't find.

One rabbit hole at a time.

He should stick to tracking missing property. Not ghosts. Barry sent a return email, thanking the sender for the spreadsheet and asking for more. He worked better with a visual anyway. Barry pushed away from the computer screen. He had spent enough time on administrative duties for one day. He wanted to roam, not shuffle paper and study spreadsheets. It was the main reason he was resisting his captain's push toward promotion. A fancy title brought more paper. He headed toward the bullpen, looking for action, when a text pushed him out the door, whether he was looking for a rescue or not.

Chapter Ten

The roads narrowed as they left the highway. Some were barely wide enough for two vehicles. Luckily, they were the only ones on this particular road. For Tunney, the landscape was familiar. It must have been why the agent in charge asked him to drive.

The place was a maze. Olivia was sure she could never have found her way through the unmarked territory. The palm trees disappeared, choked out by weepy trees with tendrils of grey moss hanging from their branches. Her view from the front seat looked identical to the crime scene photos from a year ago. Time might march on but not here.

Tunney detected the change in surface. There had been a lot of recent vehicle traffic. Most likely from the forensics team. Tunney confirmed they were in the right spot when he saw the sleek, black highway patrol cruiser. Trooper Bauman was an impressive sight in his hat and uniform. He was eight years into his tenure, polite and all business.

Tunney and Olivia tried to be less conspicuous, trading their typical Bureau attire for jeans. As Tunney predicted, Dr. Osborne went conservative. She tucked her blonde hair in a slick-backed ponytail and holstered her sidearm below the cover of her untucked button-down. The shirt was open far enough to show a navy tank top underneath. Tunney told himself not to look when she shed the outer layer later due to the heat.

"This seems pretty out of the way for you." By Tunney's calculations, they were several miles off of I-75.

"You'd be surprised what goes on back in here," Officer Bauman told him, his eyes scanning the terrain. Despite the fact, they were only a few feet off the dirt road, the veil of trees drastically reduced their visibility. "All municipalities have to work together to stay one step ahead of the riff-raff."

"Drugs or poaching?" Tunney suggested.

"Both. Marijuana is easy to grow here. The location is remote enough for cooking meth and then there are the gator nests. I suspect that's what the college boys were looking for with the drone despite what they said. There is no other reason to be out here."

"It's the right habitat and the June rains are coming," Tunney agreed.

Olivia did a slow turn, gathering her bearings. The place was calling to her. Whispers hung in the trees much like the grey moss if she would only stop and listen. Or if she knew the language. There were some very old things here. Ancient mystics, Gran would have said. As religious as she was, Gran taught her their beliefs weren't the only ones. Beliefs, like people, had a way of coming together.

Across the dirt road from the dumpsite, the trees parted to a small clearing. Olivia spied the boulder-sized rock. She remembered it from her last visit. It was too big to ignore. It would have been a gathering place for the local kids.

"How close is this to where the McCleary girls were found?" Olivia asked.

Trooper Bauman pointed to the path to his right. "If we were in the city, probably not more than two blocks that way."

"If you keep going you end up at a pond, right?"

"It's where this road dead ends." Bauman confirmed. "Are you from around here?"

"No. I visited the murder scene last year." Olivia turned and looked back over her shoulder, toward the way they came in. "If you walk that way, and take a right, you eventually end up at the girls' house, correct? The McClearys." Melanie and Terry were Ava's parents, Dorcas' aunt, and uncle. The murdered girls had been cousins.

"Yes, ma'am."

"Did they drag the pond for the girls that went missing?" Tunney asked.

"No. By the time the locals opened up about what was happening, it was too late," Bauman explained.

"Gators?" Tunney asked. Parts of this stretch of I-75 were known as Gator Alley.

"They're here alright, but actually in that particular watering hole, the problem is crocs."

Tunney let out a whistle. "Crocodiles, this far north?"

"They're migrating. Anywhere they can find a bit of saltwater," Bauman explained. "A result of human encroachment according to the wildlife guys. But to hear the locals tell it, that particular pond has been around since the beginning of time and the crocs with it. A photographer was out here last year. Her dog got eaten right in front of her. She said the croc came right up out of the pond like someone rang the dinner bell."

Olivia felt a lurch in her stomach at thoughts of

Daisy and Alvin meeting such an end. She turned and faced the opposite side of the road. The dumpsite was across the way through the trees. She couldn't see it from here, but Olivia knew it wasn't far off the road. Pittman shot them without ever getting out of his vehicle. The location itself was far enough not to attract attention. She agreed with Silas. If not for the drone, they might never have found the remains. The terrain was definitely on the side of nature. Another summer in the elements, coupled with seasonal rains, and they might never have found the bones.

"Show us what you found," Olivia suggested and headed toward the site. Bauman and Tunney followed without question. She stopped at the stakes and small flags planted by the forensics team. They had removed the bones and anything else they thought might be helpful to the investigation. Olivia recalled the piles of brush in the photos. She wanted to see them in person.

Bauman reviewed the story as they marched through the undergrowth. "Lucky for our aviators the GPS tracker wasn't damaged in the crash. Otherwise, it would have gone missing just like these little girls."

"Unless they really were looking to poach," Tunney suggested.

Olivia didn't care what the boys were doing. Poaching was the least of their worries. "How much of the scene do you think they disturbed?" she asked instead.

"From what I saw the grave was pretty shallow. It didn't take long to find the remains. Whoever did this, didn't try very hard to hide them."

"Or they were coming back later," Tunney theorized.

Bauman hesitated at the seed the agent just planted. "The boys moved the covering around. It would have looked like a gator nest. The drone was off to the side."

"Based on the photos we saw last night it makes sense," Tunney said with a nod toward Olivia. "Female alligators build their nests from soil, vegetation, and debris. Kind of like this," he explained.

Olivia knew then he wasn't here just for his driving skills. Tunney was a native with another career before the FBI.

"The boys obviously dug through the debris enough to find the bones but didn't get too far because one of them ended up losing his lunch over there by the tree," Bauman said.

Olivia hadn't seen the body, but given the conditions, there would have been remnants of skin and muscle still clinging to the bones and maybe even hair. Enough to look ghoulish.

"Did you notice anything unusual about the covering? I couldn't tell from the photos, but something about it piqued my interest."

Bauman shook his head. "Sorry, ma'am. Didn't notice. They moved the ground cover off to the side. I tried to make sure nothing else was disturbed before forensics got here."

Sensory wise Olivia was picking up little. Maybe there was too much going on in the trees. There were no sounds except their voices, only the weird muffled whispering from the trees only she could hear. Maybe death hadn't come here. She couldn't help but wonder, if someone went to the trouble to move the body, why didn't they do more to conceal it? The actions certainly didn't fit with what Pittman did with the two girls he murdered.

"You know the area. Tell me, how did this shallow grave go unnoticed for over a year?" Olivia asked Bauman.

"It's isolated. This is an ideal place as any to bury a body, deep or not."

With nothing else to add, Bauman left them. He had patrols to make. Agent Branch had requested his presence at Ocala police headquarters that afternoon for a joint meeting.

Tunney suggested a stroll down to see the crocodile pond.

"With three girls missing, who lets their kids wander around down here?" Tunney asked.

He had a point. It was the same one Silas made the last time they were here. Olivia grabbed a bottle of sparkling water from their vehicle and followed him. Her phone buzzed as soon as they headed on their way. Silas. Olivia motioned for Tunney to keep walking.

"I pushed our afternoon meeting to four. We might have just caught a break. Local kids under the age of seventeen, who are Medicaid eligible, which happens to be most of them, are serviced by a state funded dental program. The dentist just happens to be in the area this week making his rounds. We're hoping his records can help us with an ID." With the dentist onsite, it cut down on the red tape and greased the wheels of bureaucracy.

"How's it going with Tunney?" It was the first thing Silas had wanted to ask. He had called the Tampa field office to check him out. From all accounts, Sean Tunney was a solid agent. He had been with Florida Parks and Wildlife before the Bureau, so he knew his way around the area. He had just been hoping for something more glamorous than Tampa.

Olivia kept her eyes on the road. The agent was still close. She didn't want him to know they were talking about him. "By the book."

"Did he apologize?"

"Yes. I'm sure you'll be briefed later."

Silas was relieved. "At least he can follow direction. Anything on your end?"

Now would be a good time to tell Silas about her encounter with Marc Singer, but they had more important things to discuss. The Department of Justice could wait. "It's early yet, but the dumpsite is not the kill spot. I'm almost sure of it."

"Any more thoughts on Pittman?"

"My initial reaction was he only did the McCleary girls. Just like he said. Being back here has done nothing to change my mind. In fact, the longer I'm out here the more convinced I am."

Olivia caught the subtle change in Silas' breathing. He knew something, but he wouldn't say. Not yet. Considering Silas had spent his morning at the morgue, he probably already knew the cause of death for their nameless victim. When it came time, he would have her tell her tale before the coroner. It was how he converted the nonbelievers of the audience.

"Do we have more pics of what was used to cover the grave?" Olivia asked, quickly steering them away from what would come later.

"No, just the ones from the drone. The boys moved it to get to the grave. What was left was in shambles. We've got some techs reconstructing it based on the photos."

"Good. There's something about it," Olivia mused.

"Are the college boys around the area? I'd like to talk to them."

"They're located this side of Gainesville. Shouldn't be more than an hour drive."

"Since we have time, I think Tunney and I should drive over and have a word."

Olivia caught up with Tunney by the pond. "That was Agent Branch. Our meeting got pushed until later. Silas is sending you the contact info for the drone owners."

Tunney's phone buzzed, but his attention didn't leave the body of water in front of them. Olivia's gaze followed Tunney's. She spotted the ancient reptile sunning itself on the opposite bank. It appeared sedate, but she wondered how quickly that could change. The ragged line of teeth framing the mouth gave her a chill.

"He's watching us," Tunney said, his voice low.

"How do you know it's a he?"

"It's at least a fifteen-footer. Has to be a male. And the only one. They're very territorial." Tunney couldn't help but think of Agent Branch.

"Well, he smells bad," Olivia said, trying not to think what kind of things might be in the water with the creature.

Tunney didn't smell anything. "You, okay?" he asked as they headed back. "You look kind of pale."

"It's hot." Olivia handed him her water bottle as she slipped off the button-down. She tied it around her waist, but not before he caught a glimpse of her weapon.

Tunney tried keeping his eyes on hers and not her hips as he passed her water back.

Olivia dumped water in her hand and applied it to

the back of her neck.

"I heard you tell the guy from Justice you're not an agent anymore."

"Consultant," Olivia clarified.

"Is it because of those special skills we talked about?"

"Doesn't mean I don't know how to use a gun," Olivia told him.

"Ever had to?"

"I've only ever shot one living thing," Olivia said, feeling better. The water definitely helped. The heat had come over her in a flash.

"How'd that work out?"

"He lived." But it wasn't because she was a bad shot.

Chapter Eleven

Olivia stopped under the trees with the tendrils of weeping moss. "This is the spot." It was the halfway mark between the crocodile pond and the new dumpsite.

There was no cross, no dried flowers, nothing to memorialize what happened here. Just a sad, empty place where two girls who had lived just around the corner took their last breath.

"Pittman shot them while sitting behind the wheel of his car. He never even bothered to get out." Olivia tried not to flinch as the muffled sound of rapid-fire gunshots echoed in the trees as she witnessed the deaths from Pittman's point of view. For the first time, she felt nothing from the victims. It was a strange perspective. Something was off with her connection. Was the interference coming from the trees or somewhere else? A low-level hum radiated from the crocodile pond. It was almost mournful or longing. Olivia couldn't help but think they were all connected.

Tunney studied the spot with a slow look back to the pond. "Why leave them in the open? Tossing them to the crocs would have been the easiest disposal ever. Same goes for the gravesite up the road. Why not bring the body down and throw it in the pond?"

"Dead bodies are heavy." It was a suggestion. Not a question.

"Had to be someone familiar. You would have to know the area. Did Pittman live around here?"

"Silver Springs. Ten miles or so, I think."

"How did he know about this place?" Tunney asked.

"He and Terry McCleary are cousins." It also made Pittman a cousin to the girls he killed.

"Damn. That's cold."

"I've seen worse," Olivia said.

"McCleary ever try to come after Pittman?"

Olivia shook her head. "He never said a word." Terry McCleary seemed resigned to the fate of his daughter. She hadn't realized it until now.

"I read the report last night. The girls were shot multiple times. Both with different weapons. Both recovered from Pittman. A third was loaded and waiting in the car. Why all the guns for two little kids? Seems like overkill to me. What was he expecting? Zombies?" Tunney rubbed his head. He could feel the heat creeping up on him. Used to, he could have spent hours outside without the effect, but he had grown used to an air-conditioned office. "This is all kinds of wrong."

Olivia watched the other agent, gauging the emotions filling his face. There was nothing she could say that would make it better. The truth was always best. "Pittman said he wanted to make sure they were dead."

"Well, I guess there's that," Tunney commented. "It sounds like it was a job or something to scratch off the to-do list."

Tunney sensed she was distracted. Her gaze was back up the trail in the direction of the gravesite. "Do you think they'll find a bullet hole in the one found up there?"

"If they do and it matches the McCleary girls, then Pittman will go down for that one, too," Olivia said.

Tunney recalled their conversation the night before. She didn't believe Pittman did the other girls. "And if they don't?"

"Then I'd say we have another perpetrator on our hands. Killers are ritualistic. Different methodologies, means different killers."

It was a creepy thought. "Is Pittman crazy?" Tunney asked as they resumed their trek back towards their vehicle.

"Not clinically."

"Doesn't killing two defenseless little girls without provocation seem crazy to you?" Tunney was frustrated and looking for some insight. Dr. Osborne was the expert.

"There's a difference between mentally unstable and criminally responsible. According to the McNaughton Rule, a person may be mentally ill but still know the difference between right and wrong. Pittman was declared criminally responsible because he demonstrated he knew what he did was wrong."

They needed kill'n. Pittman's words came back to her in a rush. "That's why Pittman is spending his days inside a prison and not a psychiatric facility," Olivia explained. She knew all along something wasn't right, but there was nothing she could do. They had a confessed killer and the forensic evidence to back it up. She wanted another pass at Pittman, and it had nothing to do with the Justice Department.

"That's why I couldn't do what you do." Tunney

shook his head. "I bet Pittman's a popular guy inside." In a place that housed bad guys, child killers ranked at the bottom of the food chain.

"He didn't molest them, but I doubt his fellow inmates cut him any slack for it. At least that's something. For the family anyway," Olivia said.

As they neared the car, Olivia tossed her empty water bottle inside and eyed the boulder again. She untied the shirt at her waist and removed her gun, stashing them both inside the car with her purse. "I want to check it out before we go," she said, bypassing Tunney.

It was an easy climb for her. The side of the rock was jagged, the crevices easy access for her small hands. Realizing what she had in mind, Tunney rushed to take the spotter position.

"I could have given you a boost."

"I'm good," Olivia assured him. A couple of reaches, and she was at the top.

"Rock climb at the gym?" Tunney asked, impressed with her scaling ability.

"As matter of fact we do." Silas was gradually coaxing her out of her shell. He said she needed some variety from yoga.

Olivia stood up, taking a moment to enjoy the height advantage. She was never taller than anyone. From up here, she had a great view of the area.

"See anything?" Tunney asked her.

Olivia looked down to answer him when she heard it. Not a scream, but a screech, high-pitched and frantic. Terror echoed in those sounds. Olivia clamped her hands over her ears to make it stop. It was a death scream. The blow came from above. Olivia tried to focus on Tunney, but tears pooled in her eyes, causing her vision to swim. She saw movement in her periphery, swept away by a falling sensation. The scene ended with a crushing thud followed by blackness.

Tunney watched her teeter. "Oh, God, no." He hoisted himself up, rushing to keep her from falling. He grabbed both her hands and gently steadied her into a sitting position. "Put your head between your knees or something. Just don't pass out on me."

Olivia slowly lowered herself to a sitting position, breathing deeply with each movement. "I'm not sick," she insisted. She opened her eyes and looked to the canopy above. The sky was black with crows as they scattered them from their perch. They heard the screams too.

Olivia looked down, seeing Tunney clearly this time. Now that she was steady, she took her hands back.

"Don't fall off that rock or your husband will make sure I'm working mall security for the rest of my career. *If* he lets me live." Tunney noted the smirk on her face. "You think I'm kidding?" He blew out his breath and tried to breathe normally. "What the hell just happened?"

"I'm guessing you didn't hear anything?"

"Just you gasping. I thought you were gonna yak or faint or something. You looked like you were somewhere else."

Olivia nodded. She scanned the ground below, plotting a course to get herself off the rock. That's when she saw them. "What are those?"

Tunney turned to see the mounds of twigs bound together in small bundles. They were lined up in a pattern of neat little rows. At ground level, they would go unnoticed. He started to step down from the rock to get a closer look.

Olivia stopped him. They could be evidence. "Get a picture first." She pulled out her own phone and snapped a picture from her vantage point. She scrolled through her photos, looking for the aerial views from the drone. She had them all along. She had tried downloading them last night at the hotel, but they were taking so long she had eventually given up. She passed Tunney the phone. "Look familiar?"

He looked closely at the screen and back down to the ground. The resemblance was too close for coincidence. "Yea. They do."

Olivia nodded and pushed the last number on her phone. Silas answered on the first ring.

"I found something you're going to want to see."

****

Barry had not been back to the neighborhood since the last time he was at Wendy Florren's house, the night he found Mark. The word murder didn't do it justice. His friend had been flayed—alive. Sometime during the process, Jamie Lynne Smythe stopped long enough to remove his tongue. The coroner's report said Mark was alive for that too. The demon inside of Smythe told Barry it was because Mark was the one who told him about Olivia. It was another item on a very long list of things Barry tried not to think about.

Barry wasn't going back to Wendy Florren's. His destination was a few blocks over, but like her house, this one too was uninhabitable. It was the childhood home of Jamie Lynne Smythe. Barry wondered what occurred within those walls that shaped and molded him into the sadistic killer he became. Sergeant Mark Austin may have been his last victim, but that was only because fate intervened. Olivia Osborne had been his next target. As far as Barry was concerned, she still was.

Barry checked in at the door and donned the obligatory booties while the one assigned to door duty added his name to the list. "Who's in charge?" An officer Barry recognized as Brad Harris stepped up to greet him.

"I caught the call. I thought I might see you here, Lieutenant." The last time Barry saw Officer Harris, he was a new academy graduate. More than a year later, the fresh face was gone. Smythe's killing spree had seasoned him. Harris was the one who found the third victim's car in nearby McAllister Park. His first big case, and almost eighteen months later he was still working it.

Barry stepped off to the side. The crime scene had garnered a fair amount of foot traffic for a break-in. "What do you know so far?"

"The guy mowing the lawn called it in. Keeping up appearances is part of the deal living here."

Barry saw the signs of change as he drove in. A homeowner's association made sense. Economically this was a struggling, barely middle-class neighborhood perfect for the first-time homebuyer, but a murder in the lush greenbelt where kids played ruined it for everyone. Since leaving wasn't an easy option, banding together was the smarter thing to do.

Barry was curious. "Is lawn service included in the home owner fees?"

"No, but for this place a few guys on the block

pitch in cutting the grass at least once a month. This month's lucky guy noticed the curtains blowing in the wind and knew something was wrong."

"I'm assuming no one is paying the HOA fees either." Barry remarked. It didn't seem fair Smythe was the one who caused all the trouble, and he was the only one not paying. Eventually, the taxes would come due, and the city would have to decide what to do with the property. All mundane realities no one thought about when serial killers went on the run.

"Actually, the fees have been paid in full."

"Really?" It had been an off-the-cuff remark, one Barry certainly didn't expect answered. "Who?"

"Smythe's attorney," Officer Harris told him. "Mr. Kaine foots the bill with something extra for the lawn service since there's no one else do it." The house was owned by Smythe's spinster aunts. Olivia theorized it was their absence in his life that was the catalyst behind his killing spree. With no one watching, the budding killer found the freedom to explore who he really was. Barry wondered if Olivia amended her profile when the demon showed up.

"The lawn guy says Mr. Kaine is a very generous man."

Barry wondered if the generosity was supposed to make up for defending murderers. Brennon Kaine was a fancy Long Island attorney gun-for-hire.

"He gave me Kaine's number. Said it was in case the house ever needed anything. I'm guessing someone should give the counselor a call about the broken window," Harris suggested.

Barry dragged a hand over his face. The day just kept getting better and better. As the lieutenant in charge of the scene, the notification was on him. "I suppose so," Barry relented. Like him, Kaine was just doing his job, but Barry didn't like him. If he was honest with himself, it was probably more about the attorney's previous, intimate relationship with Olivia than Kaine's clientele. Another thing on his *not to think about list.*

"Kind of surprising it's the first time we've been called out here," Officer Harris said and what Barry had been thinking from the start.

Gating the neighborhood had helped, but likely it was the nature of Smythe's killings that kept people away. Smythe was a regular Jack the Ripper with his female victims. For his male victims, he liked to take body parts. With Mark it was the tongue, with the other it was the penis.

"What do the other neighbors have to say? Anyone report seeing anything suspicious?" Barry asked.

"Most of them are still at work, but the elderly lady across the street thought she saw a light inside the house two nights ago," Harris reported.

Barry nodded, digesting. "Flashlight?"

"She said it looked like somebody was home. I checked. The utilities are still on."

"Kaine pay for those, too?" Barry asked.

"You got it," Harris assured him.

Barry decided he would need to ask the attorney about that as well. "Canvass the area again this evening. Call me with an update. Check recent bills. See if there's been an uptick in usage." Barry figured it was a long shot, but every little bit helped.

Harris nodded as he and Barry parted ways.

Inside the house, the motif was forever stuck in the

eighties. Brik a'brac, complete with doilies and heavy curtains, adorned the place. Lots of flowery wallpaper. It was clean, relatively, considering it had been abandoned for over a year, but glass crunched with Barry's every step.

"What've we got?" Barry asked, announcing his presence. The one who turned to look at him was Katie Morgan. She, too, had worked the Wendy Florren scene. She was a newbie then, but today it looked like she was in charge. The wheels of time ground slowly forward.

"Looks like vandals." Katie stepped closer and lowered her voice. "Glad you could make it." The two of them had formed a bond. First with the Florren scene and then unexpectedly after Mark's passing. It was a long story Barry had shared with no one. The story was Katie's to tell. She was still contemplating what to tell Mark's parents.

"Thanks for the head's up." Barry would have gotten the call eventually. He was the SAPD officer still assigned to work with the FBI on the open Smythe case, but Katie wanted him here sooner, not later.

On the way over Barry notified Lieutenant Renard. The call should have gone to him, but Barry offered to handle it. Once the other officer found out who they were talking about, there was no argument from him. "Don't want to touch that one with a ten-foot pole," were Renard's exact words.

"Vandals, huh?" Barry's voice brought everyone to attention. His direct approach had earned him a reputation for being hard-nosed, but it paid off. He had one of the highest clearance rates in the department, and whether he wanted to or not, Zavalla was pushing him to take the captain's exam.

"Lots of glass breakage, but then again," Katie opened her arms up to the room. "Who could blame them? There are only so many precious moments you can stand." The little glass statues were popular back in the 1970s and 80s. It appeared as if Smythe's aunts had owned most of them.

"Is that what I'm stepping on?" Barry knew all that glass couldn't be from the window.

Katie beckoned him down the hallway to the bedrooms. "There's this." Random graffiti adorned the walls. Crudely drawn pentagrams were sporadic. During the media storm, word leaked that some believed Jamie Smythe was possessed by a demon. Skepticism was kept at a minimum mainly due to the support of the local Archdiocese. In a city full of Catholics, their endorsement went a long way. Olivia's name didn't come up, not in that story anyway. Also, probably due to the Church. Besides, she was a hero for shooting Smythe and the only one of his victims to escape with her life.

Barry followed Katie to one of the bedrooms. More figurines and doilies accompanied by a strong odor of musty roses. The closet doors stood open, still full of clothes. They had been pushed to the sides, leaving a clear path inside.

Even with electricity, it was murky inside the confined space. Katie clicked her penlight and pointed to the floor. "Looks like someone was looking for something."

Katie handed over her light, and Barry bent down to probe further. There was a slice in the blue carpet revealing the original floor beneath. Scuff marks on either side of the wood showed it had been pried open. Someone tried to put the pieces back, but they didn't fit the same. The space was small, the opening giving way to blackness.

"There's another one, across the hall, in Smythe's room."

Barry followed, pausing at the threshold, taking it all in. It was a stark contrast to the rest of the house. It wasn't stuck in any time frame. It was devoid of life. The walls looked like they were bare even before the forensics team arrived. Jamie Smythe displayed no hero worship. The desk was empty, but it had once housed a computer. Barry could still see the dust pattern, but everything on the bookshelves was seized after Smythe's arrest. Apparently, inquiring minds wanted to know the reading habits of serial killers.

"Does this room seem odd to you?" Barry asked.

"Aside from the obvious?" Katie asked him. "It creeps me out just being in here." The bitterness in her voice matched his. Katie felt his stare and answered the question. "It's undamaged."

Barry nodded, thinking the same thing.

"Except for this."

The closet was as sparse as the rest of the room. Certainly not as cluttered as the one across the hall. This one was home to only a few pairs of jeans and non-descript t-shirts, a pair of old sneakers shoved in the back. What was missing were scrubs. Before his arrest, Jamie had worked as a medical assistant caring for the elderly. Scrubs were part of the kid's daily attire. Barry wondered where they were now.

Katie cleared her throat, regaining his attention. She pointed to more shredded carpet and loose floorboards. "My guess is there's only one person left alive who knows what was down there."

Chapter Twelve

The road trip to speak with the drone owners was canceled as Silas dispatched a team of forensic techs to the scene. Olivia suggested she and Tunney grab something to eat while they had time. It would be a while before the techs got to the good stuff.

Instead of heading back to Ocala, Tunney cut their trip in half and stopped in Silver Springs. According to the billboards, the town's main attraction was glass-bottom boat rides. Under any other circumstance, it might sound appealing, but Olivia had seen enough of the local wildlife for one day, and Tunney was only interested in seeing the place Pittman had called home. At the time of the killings, Pittman had lived and worked as a maintenance man in a nondescript apartment building that looked just like one that could be found in any other small town. On a whim, Tunney stopped in the leasing office but got nowhere. The employees were as transient as the residents. No one was working there at the same time as Pittman.

Finally, they stopped for lunch. Olivia caught Tunney eyeing her attack on the nachos they ordered as an appetizer. "What? You promised me lunch an hour ago. I'm starving." Wading into residual energies left her feeling depleted. Even though the event she experienced back on the rock was brief, it was intense. Given she could trip into another pool of some unforeseen energy when they returned, she took the opportunity to refuel.

"At least you're feeling better," Tunney commented. The mounds of sour cream and cheese, laced with jalapeños piled on her plate, took him from his doodling on the kid's menu accidentally left on their table. For someone so petite, she sure could put it away. Maybe she didn't have time for breakfast.

"The comment you made about my husband," Olivia said, finally deciding to shove the plate aside and reach for her soda. The caffeine provided more fuel.

Tunney held up his hands. "I meant no disrespect," he was quick to assure her.

Olivia waved him off. "That's not where I was going. I get how humor is a great shield against anxiety, after all, you did think I was going to throw up on you." Olivia really did think his crack about working mall security for the rest of his career was funny. She would have said so at the time if she hadn't been caught in the middle of a murder scream.

Tunney chuckled, glad there was no grudge-holding. Seeing her with the guy from Justice this morning he had decided she wasn't someone he wanted to piss off.

"But I suspect there was also a kernel of truth in there somewhere."

"I was scared," Tunney admitted with a grin. "I had no idea how I was gonna catch you if you fell. Not to mention I was in the direct line of fire if things went south."

Olivia smiled. "What is it about him?" She coaxed. Olivia was seeking a different perspective on the man she had known for almost a decade.

Tunney shifted in his seat, an uncomfortable reminder of his previous behavior. He owed her an explanation after last night. She and the big guy might have worked together for years, but the marriage thing seemed new. "I think wary is a good description. Cautious."

Olivia's expression encouraged him to continue.

"You know us male, law enforcement types. Add in the FBI, factor in the BAU." *Mix in an attractive female.* "It all adds up. He's an alpha male among alpha males. An alpha-alpha."

Olivia smiled at the description.

"I fully intend to apologize to him when I see him," Tunney assured her.

Olivia nodded. "That's not what I was looking for either, but an apology will go a long way with Silas."

Tunney guessed as much. Agent Branch was old school. Probably military-raised.

As soon as the waitress deposited their food, Olivia began tossing jalapeños on her mushroom burger. She noticed Tunney eyeing her choice. "I'm missing home. In San Antonio, we put jalapeños on everything."

Tunney shrugged and eyed his own lunch. He had ordered shark.

****

By the time they made it back, a tent was up, and a grid was in place. Inside was a long folding table laden with tools and buckets waiting for evidence to be collected.

The lead tech beckoned Olivia to follow him as soon as they returned. With a gloved hand, he held up a diamond-shaped object constructed of twigs. It was held together with pieces of vine and moss. It was one of many Olivia spied from her perch on the rock. "I was told to show you this. Any idea what it is?"

Olivia stared at it, knowing it was left by a killer.

"It looks like a God's eye to me," the tech said.

Olivia reached out and righted his hand, changing the shape. Now it looked like the drone pictures. "God has nothing to do with this."

Tunney stepped up. "You were right. It's familiar." He saw it on the kid's menu at the restaurant. "It's a tic-tac-toe board."

"Juvenile," Olivia muttered.

The tech was relieved he was wrong. "One of the least disturbing things I've found at a crime scene." Less scary than a God's eye would have been.

"Now that you've seen it, follow me. The agent in charge suggested you might be interested in this as well."

Olivia and Tunney donned the appropriate footwear and followed. "We've counted nine mounds so far. Now, maybe I see the significance."

"The same as in a tic-tac-toe board," Tunney said.

"Now that I've removed the covering from the first one, let's see what's below."

Olivia squatted next to the tech while Tunney remained standing, surveying the area. The tech pulled out a soil probe and looked at Olivia. "Agent Branch seemed to think you would have an idea what we might find down there." He looked at her, waiting for a guess.

"I don't know if all of these are hiding something that was once alive or not," she told him. "But all of them mean something to whoever put them there."

The tech nodded at her cryptic prediction and slipped the probe under the dirt. The results didn't take long. "There's definitely something dead down there."

"Not likely human," Tunney said. "At least not from the size of these soil depressions. My guess would be animal, a small one."

"Maybe *parts* of humans," Olivia suggested.

The tech smiled at Olivia. "Nice." Coming from the head doctor, he expected nothing less. "I'm Josh, by the way. I'm looking forward to working with you Dr. Osborne."

Olivia returned the smile. "You can skip the doctor part. Agent is fine."

Josh nodded. "It's going to be a little while before we know what we've got." Olivia backed out of his way. "I get the impression you and the agent in charge have worked together before. Should I call him now or later?"

"Let's wait until we have more to tell him. Right now, we don't know if we need the medical examiner, a vet, or an anthropologist."

"Or a priest," Tunney suggested.

****

On foot, Olivia and Tunney followed the road back the way they came in.

"Not up for what they might pull out of the ground?" Tunney asked. The longer they were out here, the more creeped out he became. He had the feeling they were being watched through the trees.

"I'm not squeamish, I'm just not feeling the waiting game today." Olivia thought she detected echoes of the scream she had heard earlier trapped in the rustle of the wind. Crows watched from above. Something clung to the trees, pinging her psyche. The other missing girls all died here. What Olivia felt was more than residual energy, but what it was, she wasn't sure. All she knew for sure was she needed to keep moving rather than standing still.

"So, where are we headed?" Tunney thought he might know based on her earlier conversation with Bauman.

"If we continue straight ahead and take a right, we'll end up on the road where the McClearys live." And another one of the missing, Ashley Knowles. The McCleary residence was on a direct path from where they found the body.

"I want to take a look and see how things are holding up." Olivia was curious to see if the family was still intact but didn't want to disturb them. Silas made it clear he didn't want the locals to know the FBI was back in town. Sixteen months ago, the murders turned this place upside down. The return of the FBI would stir up memories and questions no one was prepared to answer.

"Did the McCleary girls come down here often? Being so close and all?"

"Apparently it was their favorite thing to do," Olivia said.

"This place is creepy. I'll say it again. I can't imagine letting adolescent girls wander out here alone. You could scream and nobody would hear you."

Except for the crows....

"I tell myself people like you and I have a perverse view of the world. Then again, people become comfortable with what they see every day. With spotty internet and cable TV a luxury, these girls had little else except nature and each other."

"Can't imagine raising kids these days." Tunney

caught himself and looked over at her. "You and Agent Branch?"

"No. Maybe someday. Maybe not. You?"

Tunney had guessed right; the marriage must be a new thing. Given their ages, statistically, they should have had kids by now. "Not that I know of," Tunney smiled. "My sister has three. All boys. That works for me. And keeps my parents off my back."

They turned on the road where the McClearys lived. Calling it a neighborhood was a kind description. In reality, it was a row of wooden dwellings with small porches, all in need of a good paint job. Air conditioner units, called swamp coolers, sagged from rickety window frames propped up by spindly wooden legs. Unfenced, untended lawns overlapped one another. A dog was tied to a tree in front of one of them. At least there was a bucket of water nearby. The pooch barely raised its head as they passed. The place was a ghost town in the middle of the afternoon.

"These all look the same. Broken down and depressing," Tunny observed.

"My Gran used to say it's amazing what a good paint job will do for a woman or a house."

"Do you read minds, too?" Tunney asked. It was meant to be a joke, but something out here was messing with his head. He guessed it was the heat, but he wasn't sure anymore. This was a strange place, like the land that time forgot.

"Maybe it was an echo from the past. This started out as small community of circus personnel in the late 50's and 1960s. This is where they came to spend the winter months."

From the sound of things, this place was getting to

her too. "Doesn't look like there's been an upgrade since, Tunney muttered."

Olivia stopped at the McCleary's house. It was the next to last one. Another season in the sun hadn't done the place any favors. "Looks empty."

The grass in the yards was taller than the others. The lack of water dripping from the window unit in front added to her theory.

"Let's go around back just to make sure. I don't want to have to explain myself if someone is home."

Tunney trotted around back while Olivia studied the house next door. She thought she saw a curtain pull to the side but wasn't sure. She was tired, working her way toward grumpy. Olivia wasn't sure what the feeling was in the pit of her stomach, but she felt like feeding it would help. This place was sucking the energy out of her.

Tunney reappeared at the edge of the house and beckoned her over. The screen door in the back was standing open. "Least we could do is check it for squatters," he suggested and drew his gun. "Crocs and gators aren't the only wildlife around here."

Olivia removed her weapon and scanned the yard. It looked as abandoned as the house. There was an empty shed in the back. The door to it was open too, hanging loosely, clinging to one side. An abandoned animal cage stood off to the side on more rickety stilts. Olivia spied a clothesline that served as a dryer.

With the perimeter clear, she turned and followed where Tunney had gone. The scattered assortment of trash collected on the small screened porch reminded her of the cramped little room back at the San Antonio hospital. Fortunately, this place lacked the same ambiance. The air was devoid of emotion. Maybe abandonment had wiped it all away. In the corner was a banged-up washing machine that had seen better days.

Tunney waited for her. With her arrival, he called out, announcing their presence. A hollow echo was their answer. He stepped through the open door into a small kitchen populated by a half stove and a rusted refrigerator. The inside was empty inside, minus some brown goo. The cabinets were bare as well; beer cans littered the sink. There were no signs of life, human or otherwise.

"This place has seen better days,"

"It didn't look much better when it was occupied." Olivia had visited once to interview the parents.

"What did the parents do?" Tunney wondered.

"Dad worked at one of the nearby horse farms. Mom worked at the park where they have those glass-bottom boats."

The kitchen bled into a hallway. Straight ahead was an empty living room. They turned down the hall, stepping on glass as they went. "That's some bad luck," Tunney observed, careful to side-step the mess. Olivia noted the empty frame on the wall.

They stopped in front of the bathroom, the only one in the house. The mirror above the sink was also shattered. "That's another seven years."

Olivia brushed past him to what was the master bedroom. More shards of glass, remnants of a mirror mounted to a dresser. A pillowcase was bunched up in the corner.

Tunney joined her, surveying the damage. "Damn vandals."

"I don't think it was vandals."

Tunney looked confused.

"These people didn't have a lot."

"So why leave the dresser behind?"

"It's the mirrors. If it was just the one in the bathroom and the one in the hall, I'd think vandals too, but not this," Olivia said with an eye on the dresser. It didn't look like the mirror was removable. Breaking it was the only alternative.

"Who's afraid of mirrors?"

Olivia gave Tunney the same spiel she gave Silas. "Many cultures have superstitions attached to mirrors. Witches use them to communicate with the spirit world. Some believe the glass is a portal to the past or somewhere else. Either way, once you open the door, you never know what's going to come through the other side."

Her prediction sounded ominous. "People really believe that stuff?" Tunney asked.

"We don't all live in the same world, Agent."

Tunney nodded. He should have known. She seemed so normal, but if she could read death, she probably wasn't. "Were the McCleary's those type of people?"

"What do you mean *those type*?"

"The superstitious kind." Tunney clarified. He had touched a nerve.

"I don't know. The only time I met them we were discussing their dead daughter."

Olivia moved down the narrow hallway. She hadn't made it this far into the house before. She had barely been invited in. Currently, this was the only room in the house keeping out the rest of the world. It must have belonged to the girls.

Tunney wedged his way past her. "Let me," he offered.

Olivia laid her hand on the frame. It hadn't been closed gently. The sound of a slam echoed down the hall. Olivia severed the connection before it could reach her thoughts.

Tunney struggled with the knob. Leaning in with his shoulder, he managed to force the door open. Olivia caught a rush of adolescent perfume, sickly sweet. She gagged but swallowed it down and resorted to breathing through her mouth. A throwback to her nursing days.

"Holy, shit," Tunney said. "Why?"

Olivia squeezed past him. Inside were twin beds with a small bedside table pushed in between them. Textbooks still sat on top, collecting dust. Clothes were in a pile in the corner where they had been discarded. Backpacks and a soda can were in the corner. The room was stuck in time.

"It looks like they just left," Tunney said.

"It was a Saturday morning. The girls took a walk like they always did. They didn't come home for lunch, but according to Melanie, Ava's mom, that wasn't unusual. They could have taken a snack with them for all she knew. When they weren't home by the time she had to go to work, she went looking. She was the one who found them."

Olivia watched as the old green Chevrolet crept up to them. The girls approached the car without fear. Pittman was the only one afraid. It was why he didn't get out.

"Jesus," Tunney muttered, aching to leave the cramped little room. Hands on his hips, he stood and scanned the opposite wall. There was a dresser with the top drawer still half-open. Next to it a sheet covered something on the wall. Beneath the folds was something shaped like an oval.

Olivia saw Tunney step forward. She stopped him before temptation could set in. She didn't want to see what was on the other side. She reached out and grabbed his arm, stopping him before he could make contact. "You don't want to do that."

Chapter Thirteen

Barry spent his afternoon at the Smythe house. While Katie and the team worked, he wandered. Feeling claustrophobic, Barry patrolled the neighborhood. He took another slow crawl past the Florren place. On his second pass, he noticed a construction vehicle. The inside of the house definitely needed new paint and carpet.

The house next door was absent a car in the driveway. He wondered if Gail Wallace and her son Billy still lived there. Billy was the one who found Smythe's bike. Wanting to keep it for himself, Billy hid it by the house next door, leading the killer straight to Wendy Florren. Barry's survey continued to the backyard. The thatched roof of the treehouse was visible. He wondered if Billy and his friend still went up there. Maybe it had lost its appeal since Billy witnessed the attack in the greenbelt. Barry would make sure someone canvased the Wallace house despite the fact they were blocks away. Given what she had been through, Ms. Wallace was probably more vigilant than most about what was going on in the neighborhood. Barry pondered coming back to break the news himself.

Killing time, Barry found himself at the drive-up fast-food joint with the carhops. He wasn't hungry, but he could go for something to drink. It was the place where Olivia identified Smythe. He was a regular when he lived in the neighborhood. Barry wondered if his subconscious led him there for a reason, or maybe it was just convenient. It had been for Smythe. It was also cheap. A good choice for a boy on a budget. For Barry, it was fast and easy. He drove away with a diet coke, thinking there was something else he should be remembering.

Back at the house, he stayed out of the way but kept finding himself staring into the black hole in the floor of the closet. Barry got down on his hands and knees and tried to reach inside but got nowhere. His arm was too big, and the space too small. Someone opened the floor for a reason, and he wanted to know what it was. He passed along his suggestion to Katie but had to get back downtown before seeing it through. Zavalla wanted an update, and it wasn't a phone conversation. On the way, Barry texted Olivia, asking if she knew when she would be back. She told him things had taken a turn in Florida which told him she didn't know. When she asked if everything was okay, he assured her it was under control.

****

"You have to tell him." Those were the first words out of the captain's mouth.

"Right now, there's nothing to tell. Last I heard vandalism was still our jurisdiction not the purview of the US government," Barry argued.

Anthony Zavalla knew Bartholomew was correct, but it was a dicey play. The move pushed intradepartmental pleasantries to the very edge. If Bartholomew was going to make the climb to captain, he had to learn to play nice in the sandbox.

"Then solve it and give the local FBI station chief a

courtesy call. It's not a suggestion," Zavalla told him.

"I have time," Barry assured him. "Agent Branch and Dr. Osborne are out of town on another case."

"Silas Branch isn't the only FBI agent in town."

"Tell him that," Barry shot back before he could stop himself.

The lieutenant was still carrying the torch for Dr. Osborne. Zavalla had hoped the marriage would have helped him move on. "I know the look in your eye," Zavalla baited him.

Barry ran a hand across his head. The captain wasn't as easily appeased as Amanda. "Did it set off some perimeter alerts? Yea, it did. I mean why now after all this time? What changed? The neighborhood is locked up tight."

"Summertime. Bored kids?" Zavalla suggested.

The captain had a point. Barry thought the same thing about the vandal cases near the hospital.

"If you think it's Smythe, you have to tell Agent Branch now," Zavalla cautioned, quickly realizing his words were lost. "You don't believe Smythe ever left, do you?" Zavalla knew Bartholomew's secret obsession. There were whispers about the map occupying a wall in his office. Bartholomew was supposedly plotting suspected Smythe sightings.

"Why would he? He didn't get what he came for."

"At least call Smythe's attorney and give him the news. I hear Mr. Kaine hasn't been stingy with the resources. He wants Smythe taken care of."

"Uh, huh," Barry grunted the acknowledgment. After he and Brennon Kaine had a face-to-face with the demon in Smythe, Barry hoped Kaine kept with Olivia's suggestion the kid never be allowed to go free.

"And keep me in the loop," Zavalla said as Barry exited. He should be going home, but Zavalla knew the lieutenant was headed back to his pit of an office.

****

Olivia knelt beside the field tech.

Josh brushed the soil from the white remnants clustered in the shallow hole in front of them. They had unearthed three mounds so far. To the untrained eye, the finds all looked pretty much the same. "They're small and there's more hair than I would expect. I'm hoping it's an animal. The anthropologist and Agent Branch are tied up with the dentist. Luckily, the ME was readily available. He's on his way now. I really hope they're not human."

Olivia hoped Silas' absence meant they were close to an ID. "It would have to be a pretty small human," she said, sliding her arm across her midsection. She felt nothing from the bones. It had to mean they were animals. She retreated to where Tunney was waiting by the car. He handed her a soda and offered a variety of snacks.

"I suggested the peanut butter crackers. The protein will keep you full longer. I also grabbed some energy bars. I'm thinking of having one myself. Must be the heat."

Tunney had gone all the way back to I-75 to find a convenience store. There was a closer one, just a little way from the McCleary house, but it was the only one in Eden. Tunney would stick out like a sore thumb among the natives. "I also picked up a cooler and plenty of waters. Looks like we could be here awhile."

Olivia was grateful. Tunney was starting to grow on her despite the rocky start. While she munched, she rifled through the email box on her phone, looking for something from the state hospital. She saw both of Vines' emails. It must have been the one about residents claiming they saw someone they didn't know that piqued Barry's interest. Still, she was curious about what made Barry want to know when she would be home, but she couldn't think about it right now. She was more interested in quieting the rumble in her stomach.

Olivia and Tunney hadn't finished their snacks when a chorus of text messages swept through the crowd. Dental records confirmed the remains found across the road belonged to Ashley Knowles.

****

Zavalla was right. He should have left already. Staying late wasn't going to win him any points with Amanda. She had taken the rest of the week off in preparation for the housewarming party on Saturday. Tonight, she wanted to go out for drinks and dinner, or in other words, a real date. Barry debated on how to get out of it, then decided to blame it on the FBI. He felt obligated to see her through the housewarming party this weekend, then he planned to break it off for good.

Barry passed Norma's desk. He spied her purse sitting out in the open, signaling him she was leaving for the day. There was a stack of pink phone slips waiting for him, piled neatly next to it. Given his location, she knew better than to disturb him in the field. Barry quickly thumbed through the notes confirming his original hypothesis. None of them required his immediate attention. He deposited the bulk of them in the wastebasket, saving Norma from attaching them to the clip outside his door. She rarely came into his office. The last time had been to rescue a plant he had neglected to water.

Barry raised his head just in time to avoid a collision with the lanky boy exiting his office.

"Oh, hey, lieutenant. I'm Andy, the intern. You weren't here. Miss Norma said it was okay if I go in."

Barry wondered how old one had to be to earn an intern spot. Andy looked twelve.

"I tried to get you a map like you requested, but I was having trouble locating one then someone told me you already had one." Andy offered a shaky smile, the silence feeding his anxiety.

Barry rushed past him, making a beeline to the wall. Barry stood, hands on his hips, staring at what Andy had done. New pins stood out, clustered near old ones.

Andy followed as far as the lieutenant's desk. "I plotted the locations from the spreadsheet you sent back this morning. The one with the break-ins. I used different colored pins so not to interfere with whatever you already had going on."

The tingle began at the base of Barry's neck as the realization took hold. He had been looking for a pattern, and now with Andy's additions, he had one. Between two unrelated events.

With an eye on the lieutenant, Andy reached for the spreadsheet he had left on the desk. Every available space was occupied. Norma assured him if he left it on top of the laptop the lieutenant would find it—only because he would have to move it to open the computer. Andy started reading the street names. Just in case the lieutenant wanted to check his work.

Barry had only been looking for missing items, not

addresses. A sense of urgency sent him back to his desk. He slammed the chair out of his way, causing Andy to jump. He wanted to run but didn't.

Outside the office, Norma heard the clatter. She poked her head inside to see what was wrong. Barry was working his cell phone and squinting at the screen.

Barry stared at the photo. It was of the receipt he found in the dingy little room in the place no one should be. It was the thing he should have remembered.

"What's in the 'other' column?" Barry asked. It was part of the spreadsheet he hadn't gotten to.

Andy quickly flipped pages of the printout he made. He had heard the lieutenant was old-school. "Reports of some strange guy hanging around the neighborhood."

"Is there a description?" Barry watched Andy scan what was in front of him. "Read it to me," Barry snapped, the pit in his stomach growing larger.

Andy was glad he didn't have to summarize. They all sounded the same. "Thin male, twenty to twenty-five years of age, slight in stature with a scar on his head."

Barry's eyes wandered to the evidence bag still sitting on his window sill.

Norma finally decided it was safe to speak. "Is everything okay?"

Barry shook his head. "No. No, it's not."

Chapter Fourteen

Olivia and Tunney stayed onsite long enough for the ME to tell them he couldn't help them. They needed another kind of doctor.

With the fading light, Tunney suggested they head back. They weren't going to catch a killer tonight. Back in Ocala, Olivia passed on a sit-down dinner. Exhaustion won over hunger, and she opted for fast food instead. Tunney deposited her back at the hotel. With food in hand, they parted ways in the lobby.

Olivia stripped off her clothes and headed straight for the bath. Water was her solace. It soothed her mind, but tonight, it wasn't her mind that needed refuge, but her body. Something was siphoning her energy.

Olivia wrapped herself in her robe and polished off her drive-thru cuisine even if it was cold. Popping it in the microwave for a quick zap would take too much energy. A salad would have been the healthier choice than the fried chicken and gravy, but something green and leafy wouldn't satisfy the hunger raging inside of her. Exhausted, she fell asleep on top of the covers.

****

Tunney didn't venture far. Olivia wasn't the only one feeling tapped from their day in the backwoods. A shower revived him enough to make it as far as the hotel restaurant. He was still there when Agent Branch arrived. The suit and tie looked as fresh now as they did when he left that morning, but his face told a different story. The agent in charge had his own rough day.

Silas loosened his tie and headed for the bar. "Two shots of your best bourbon."

Tunney watched Silas swirl his drink and get a quick sip in before approaching. When he wasn't staring off into space, he was checking his phone. If he was waiting for his wife to join him, Tunney could tell him it wasn't happening. She was down for the count hours ago.

Silas' gaze finally made its way over to Tunney. Silas saw him when he came in but needed a moment to regroup. Silas indicated the empty spot next to him. Tunney accepted the invitation and said what he needed to say.

****

Olivia didn't stir when he came in. By the time Silas got out of the shower, she had shed her robe and migrated beneath the covers. Without turning on the light, Silas slid in behind her and pulled her close. Silas buried his nose in her hair, drinking in the scent of vanilla and honey.

"Rough day?" Olivia asked, her voice husky with sleep.

"You could say that. You?"

"Not as much as yours. Want to talk about it?" Olivia asked, even though she knew the answer.

"Nope." All Silas needed was the warmth of her. She quieted his mind and chased away his monsters.

Olivia linked her fingers through his and brought them to her lips.

"I saw Agent Tunney downstairs. He said you had a tiring day. Everything alright?"

Olivia knew what he was really asking. "I didn't bring the test," she reminded him.

"Anything you want to talk about?" Silas felt she was holding back on him. He was trying to be supportive, but he wasn't sure what she needed.

"I'd rather not," Olivia whispered as she turned over to face him. Her lips found him, and there was no more talking.

****

Their first meeting of the morning was a private show for the new Ocala District Attorney. Travis Hobbs won the position after securing a conviction for Larry Wayne Pittman in record time. He was the youngest district attorney ever elected in Marion County. He looked like he was ready for more.

Silas recapped the events leading to the discovery of the remains. His words mirrored the statement he gave the press the night before after he notified the family. Ashley Knowles was eleven years old and the third girl to go missing. During the original investigation, no one even realized she was gone until after the McCleary girls were murdered. The timing had always bothered Silas.

"I put in a request to see Larry Pittman in Gainesville," Travis Hobbs interjected. With a killer in hand, the DA's office decided Pittman was responsible for Ashley Knowles as well as the other two missing girls despite the lack of proof.

"Perhaps you should hear the facts of this case first," Silas cautioned. Instead of turning to Dr. Sheppard, the anthropologist who examined Ashley's remains, Silas looked across the room to Olivia. They still hadn't talked about what she and Tunney found.

"It is imperative we investigate this case with no preconceived ideas about the guilt or innocence of any one person," Silas warned. "Our victim deserves that much."

The DA didn't look happy with the suggestion, but he didn't interrupt Silas a second time. He was too busy looking down at his phone.

"Yesterday Dr. Osborne and Agent Tunney from our Tampa field office surveyed the location where Ashley's remains were found. Dr. Osborne, would you please share with us your findings?"

"According to witness statements, after school on what was to be the last afternoon of her life, Ashley Knowles walked to the Eden convenience store where her mother worked. She left with a candy bar and a can of soda. According to her mother, Ashley said she was heading home. When she arrived, Ashley told her grandmother she was going to spend the night with Ava McCleary. She went to her room, dropped off her backpack, and changed her clothes. That is the last confirmed sighting we have of her."

The story matched the same one the family gave Silas last night when he joined local law enforcement to give them the news.

"What did the McCleary mother have to say about Ashley?" Hobbs wanted to know.

Olivia's response was interrupted by the door of the conference room. She recognized the visitor as Marc Singer, from Justice. He flashed quick credentials Silas' way and took a seat. Silas' eyes shifted quickly between Singer and Hobbs only to land back on Olivia.

Olivia ignored everyone but Hobbs. "Melanie McCleary's previous statement says Ava didn't ask about having a sleepover and she hadn't seen Ashley in a while. She went on to say that after school Ava and Dorcas went outside and didn't return until she called them for dinner."

"No one questioned Ms. McCleary about Ashley until after her own daughter and niece were found murdered. Given the circumstances, who can say how clear her memory is," Hobbs suggested.

"Losing a loved one is a traumatic event. It has been my professional experience when dealing with these families that the time leading up to the event is clearly stuck in their minds. In my professional experience, I have no reason not to believe Melanie McCleary. Furthermore, I believe, unfortunately, given what happened to the McCleary girls, Ashley Knowles slipped through the cracks." If Hobbs was looking for a reason to shut down a new investigation, he was going to have to try harder. The Bureau wagons had already circled.

Hobbs remained undaunted.

"Dr. Osborne, why don't you tell us what you discovered happened to Ashley?" Silas asked what Hobbs would not.

"According to Ashley's grandmother, Ashley arrived home from the convenience store in the amount of time it would have taken her to walk with no stops. I believe on her way she ran into Ava McCleary. The girls would have taken the same route home from school. I believe it was then Ava issued the invitation, since Ashley didn't mention the sleep over to her mother, but she did to her grandmother. I believe Ashley planned to spend the night with her friend Ava, but unknown to little Ashley Knowles she had already spent her last night on earth."

An eerie silence hung in the room at the declaration. Hobbs looked like he wanted to ask a question but thought better of it, and Olivia pushed forward. "She didn't get far. Ashley was killed very close to where she was buried. If one knew where to look you could see it from the front room of her house."

"How can you possibly know that?" Hobbs finally found his voice.

"There's a big rock across the road from where Ashley's remains were found. It was a pivotal point, bound to be well known to the children in the area and could have been a meeting place. Ashley's grave was discovered just across the road. The shallowness of the grave says to me it was an improvisation. Meaning it wasn't planned or something went wrong."

Hobbs took a deep breath. As far as he was concerned Olivia Osborne was nothing more than a hack, playing for whichever team paid her a fee. The fact the FBI had taken her back after she worked with criminal defense attorneys was something he didn't understand. All she did was muddy the waters, which was exactly what he did not want.

"Why are we even talking about this? Pittman told me he put Ashley in the crocodile pond. Considering that wasn't where she was found, it means he knew where she was all the time and was trying to mislead us. He didn't want us to look for her."

For the first time, Olivia consulted the notes in front of her before speaking. She wanted to know the answer before she asked the question. "Did you look for Ashley? In the crocodile pond or anywhere else?"

Hobbs squirmed for the first time. As the local hero

for putting a child murderer away, he wasn't accustomed to being on the receiving end of what sounded like an accusation.

Olivia didn't wait for him to answer because she knew what he did—nothing. "I have Mr. Pittman's statement in front of me. Mr. Pittman's reply to your question regarding Ashley's whereabouts was that she was *probably* in the pond. That sounds like a suggestion, not an answer. Certainly not the detailed confession he gave of Ava and Dorcas." If Pittman had made a formal declaration, Hobbs would have added that to his win column as well. "At no time, according to this transcript, did Mr. Pittman say he *put* Ashley in the pond."

"Then what did he do to her, Agent?" Hobbs asked, attempting to diminish her competence by calling her agent instead of doctor.

"In his previous statements, Pittman claimed he didn't even know who Ashley Knowles was. I have found nothing to convince me otherwise."

"No surprise there," Hobbs muttered.

Silas shifted in his chair, catching Olivia's attention. Hobbs was getting to him, or rather Hobbs' attitude toward her. She was used to the sentiment. She had dealt with types like Hobbs her entire career, mainly from the FBI. Discounting her was easier than believing her.

"There's no reason to believe Mr. Pittman knew Ashely. He did not live in the neighborhood. He confessed only to the murders of Ava and Dorcas. Mr. Pittman had a day job. Did you pull his employment records from that day?"

Hobbs' silence told Silas there were no such

records in the folder Olivia was holding.

"Perhaps Dr. Banigo can share with us what he found adjacent to the rock Dr. Osborne just mentioned," Silas suggested, hoping to diffuse the situation. Hobbs could go at her all morning long, and Olivia could dish it back in heaps. She didn't need or want his help. Olivia was as good with lawyers as she was with killers. Maybe she should have been the one to go to law school.

Salazar Banigo cleared his throat, not expecting to be called so soon. He had been enjoying the show. "I examined three small burial sites last night. The remains I examined were animal, not human. All of them had their skulls crushed. It looked like someone's private pet cemetery to me."

"Serial killers often start with animals, don't they?" Hobbs asserted. "Sounds like we have our guy. We have his confession to the McCleary girls, and he tried to kill his girlfriend."

"We have no evidence about who is responsible for the animal killings. The findings are still being logged and processed," Silas cautioned.

"Choking your partner during consensual sex doesn't qualify," Olivia clarified. She had reread Pittman's background last night.

"Pittman is sick and twisted. If, as you say, Ashley never spent the night with the McCleary girls, maybe Pittman wanted some *special* time alone with her," Hobbs suggested.

Olivia did nothing to hide the look of disgust on her face as Hobbs searched the room for the only unfamiliar face. "Are you the anthropologist? Can you tell me if the Knowles girl was molested?" the DA asked.

Dr. Juliya Sheppard spent most days as a professor of forensic anthropology at the University of Miami. Occasionally, she lent her services to the Bureau. As a woman of science, she was accustomed to academia. She had no patience for the theatrics the attorney seemed to crave. "Due to the soft tissue breakdown of the body, I can't tell you if she was molested or not. However, I can tell you what her bones say. During non-consensual sex, choking often occurs. Subduing a victim puts strain on the small u-shaped bone in the neck, the hyoid, causing it to break. In Miss Knowles case, her hyoid bone was intact, telling me she wasn't strangled. Derive from that what you will."

Hobbs swung his attention back to Olivia. "Agent Osborne, you don't mind speculating."

"In my *expert* opinion," Olivia clarified. "We should consider whoever killed the animals, also murdered Ashley Knowles."

The late visitor spoke for the first time, cutting off whatever remark Hobbs was going to make next. "Marc Singer," he said to the room with a glance toward Silas Branch. Singer had heard his star was on the rise with the Bureau, but Olivia Osborne was and always had been his Achilles heel. Singer gave the agent in charge a chance to interrupt him, but he didn't. That told Singer Dr. Osborne must not have told him about their encounter. If so, he would have garnered more of Branch's attention.

"Doctor Osborne, if you could share your opinion with us. The Justice Department is keenly interested in hearing it."

"The animal graves, as well as Ashley's Knowles

resting place, were covered with stick figures woven together. They weren't random."

"Dr. Banigo just called it a cemetery. Are you sure they weren't crosses, signs of respect?" Hobbs asked.

"What Dr. Banigo didn't tell you is the animals had their heads bashed in. My suspicion would be the same of Ashley Knowles. To do that, you have to look into the eyes of the person whose life you intend to end or attack from behind. Either way, it is a calculated endeavor, not a demonstration of respect. It is a cold-blooded, brutal act, performed with intent and purpose."

Even Silas felt the chill at such a suggestion. Olivia didn't mince her words. It was one of the things he liked about working with her.

"The graves don't indicate a sign of remorse?" Singer asked.

"In this case, I'd say no. The graves were for the killer. A place to store their trophies."

"Forensic evidence?" Hobbs wanted to know.

"We have aerial footage from the grave site," Silas answered.

"This is a picture of the pet cemetery Dr. Osborne and I discovered yesterday," Tunney spoke. He slid his phone across the table at anyone who wanted to see it. "I took that photo before the techs arrived. The figures aren't crosses. They are tic-tac-toe boards."

Singer stared until the picture faded from sight "Tic-tac-toe. That's a game."

"Juvenile," Olivia clarified.

Tunney noted it was the same word she used the day before. He wondered if it was a substitute for a child.

"There were nine graves. The same number of

squares on a tic-tac-toe board," Olivia continued.

A look from Silas prompted Dr. Sheppard to lean forward in her chair, indicating she had something to say. Her instructions had been to wait for Dr. Osborne's theory before sharing her findings. Olivia had already given her an opening.

"I can confirm forensically, Dr. Osborne is correct. After examining the remains of Ashley Knowles, I determined the cause of death to be blunt force trauma to the back of the head. The blow was delivered from above by someone with a significant height advantage. She also had a broken nose. I would suspect it occurred when she hit the ground after the blow from behind. The clothes found with the body match the description of the clothes she was wearing when she left her house. There was blood on her shirt, consistent with a nose bleed."

Olivia swallowed as she listened to the description of the vision she witnessed yesterday. What she saw in her peripheral vision was another person standing beside Ashley. Ashley wasn't supposed to see what was coming. Except she had. She screamed at the moment of realization. It was too late to save herself. But her scream still lingered in the trees.

"When you say significant height advantage, how significant are we talking?" Singer wanted to know.

Dr. Sheppard reviewed the notes in front of her, taking her time. "Agent Branch, how tall are you?"

"Six three."

"At least as tall as Agent Branch."

"You can tell us that right here, right now?" Hobbs didn't like where this was going.

"Ashley Knowles was a big girl for her age. I

calculated her to be five foot five to five foot six."

"Mr. Pittman is five foot nine," Olivia added, consulting her own folder.

Hobbs opened his mouth to protest again, but Sheppard cut him off. "According to school records Ashley weighed one hundred and forty-two pounds two weeks into the school year, seven months prior to her death. It gives credence to what Dr. Osborne said earlier about a shallow grave and improvisation. That could be what went wrong. Her killer underestimated what it would take to dispose of the body."

"Dead bodies are heavy."

Again, Tunney noted Olivia used the same description as yesterday. She probably had this whole thing figured out. Maybe that was what concerned Hobbs. The DA was definitely out of his league.

"Again, two methods of killing and two different methods of disposal. Meaning at least two different killers," Olivia surmised.

"At least *two* different?" Singer repeated, sounding as distressed as Hobbs.

"Pittman already confessed. I don't believe he killed Ashley. Do you really think she would stand there patiently while someone bashed her on the head from behind, in broad day light? Someone else was there to distract her. Now that we know when she was killed and where she was dumped, we should re-interview Melanie McCleary."

"Why?" Hobbs was quick to object. "Why not leave the poor woman alone?"

"Dr. Osborne already told us why." Silas decided to take the hit on this one and deliver the news no one wanted to hear. "Ms. McCleary's statement says Ava and Dorcas left the house immediately after arriving home from school. Given the time and place Ashley Knowles was killed, the McCleary girls would have been outside in close proximity to her murder."

"There you have it," Hobbs said. "They saw what Pittman did, and he killed them for it."

For Olivia, the question was simple. "Then why did he wait?"

Hobbs shook his head at her suggestion. "Why do you not want it to be him?" he demanded.

"It's not about Mr. Pittman. It's about getting it right. It's about finding a killer."

"We got it right the first time," Hobbs said with confidence. "There hasn't been a murder since I put Pittman away." Hobbs would not let this woman stand in his way of convicting a confessed child murderer a second time. FBI or not. "One reason serial killers stop killing is they're incarcerated."

"There are two reasons they stop, Mr. Hobbs. The other is they're dead."

Chapter Fifteen

Will Ibarra found Barry in his office, staring at his computer. If Will had to guess, he was looking at photos of Smythe's house. News of the break-in traveled fast. Will rapped softly on the door frame rousing the lieutenant's attention.

"I think I have something you've been looking for," Will said, sticking his head in Bartholomew's office.

"And I was just starting to get used to you," Barry deadpanned, his attention not wavering from his screen.

Will was glad to see his boss was in a joking mood. Maybe that meant he had missed him while he was away attending Agent Branch's class. Will had been interested in joining the FBI even before he left his teaching position at the Academy. Leaving SAPD would mean Will would miss the man who had quickly become a mentor and a friend. It was a rough gig at first. Seeing Jamie Smythe in full demon mode forged a bond between the newbie and the crusty lieutenant most people couldn't begin to understand. Will was one of the few who knew there was more to Bartholomew than his firm game face. He wasn't invincible. He had feelings. About the job, the victims, but most of all, the ones he held close.

Will waved a brown paper bag in front of him. He ran into Norma in the break room, and she mentioned their boss probably needed to eat. At the suggestion, Will headed outside to the nearby food truck before she beat him to it. Sometimes it took a village with the lieutenant.

"Chorizo and egg, just like you like." The spicy Mexican pork was Barry's favorite. Will spied a mug of coffee nearby but had brought an extra one anyway. He had also learned the lieutenant couldn't have too much. Will noted the damp hair and the shirt that didn't look like it had been slept in. Both positive signs he at least made it home long enough for a shower.

The mention of food broke Barry's connection with the screen. "I am accepting donations, thanks." Barry swiveled himself so he could take full advantage of the taco. He had grabbed food sometime last night, but it was the fast kind. "So, you skipping class today?" he asked between bites.

Will gave him a half-smile and slid into the one empty chair across from the desk. The other one was full of files. What was in them, Will had no idea. They seemed to live there, or maybe they were strategically placed to discourage visitors. "Agent Branch is still in Florida and Agent Sharpe canceled. The teaching gig is more Silas' thing anyway."

Barry noted the use of the agent's first name but was relieved to hear Silas was still gone. It gave him more time to investigate his theory before the agent swooped in and took over again. More importantly, it meant Olivia was out of harm's way.

"Why didn't you call me last night?" Will wanted to know.

Barry shook his head. "Didn't want to interrupt." Not only was Will spending his days away from the office rethinking his career, but he had also recently made significant changes in his personal life.

Will waved him off. "Jess gets the job." He and Jessica Tate, the *News You Need to Know* reporter started dating not long after the Atascosa County case. After a year together, they agreed to take their relationship to the next level and cohabitate. "I appreciate the consideration."

Will waited until Barry plowed through the first taco and moved on to the second before launching his assault. "So, you wanna tell me why you think it was Smythe who broke into his own house?" Will had run into Katie from forensics on his way in this morning. She looked beat. Katie had an infant at home and no baby daddy. Still, she stayed the night, her hopes pinned on whatever story Bartholomew believed.

Barry took Will through what he found at the state hospital, and the surrounding neighborhood, and linked it all the way back to the break-in at Smythe's house.

"That's some story. Have you shared this with the FBI?"

Barry shook his head. "Not yet. I can't. I have no evidence. Right now, all I have is a theory. I'm waiting for forensics. Frank Tobias is cutting his fishing trip short but can't make it back until tomorrow. He would have come back today but was about to step on a charter in search of some elusive fish when I called. He's personally going to handle the stuff I bagged from the hospital. How long is your instructor out of town?"

"Don't know. You might want to give Agent Sharpe a call about the break-in. That way there's no surprises. He can run interference between you and Silas."

Barry appreciated what the sergeant was trying to do. He and Silas didn't have the easiest of relationships. If it had been just about work, they could have stayed out of each other's way, but it was never about work. They only pretended that it was. "On a first name basis, huh?" Barry tried to make it sound like a joke but doubted it did.

Will grinned. "Jess and I've been spending a lot of time with Kimmy and the baby, lately. Those times include Dr. Osborne and the agent."

"How is Kimmy?" Barry genuinely wanted to know. Amanda didn't often talk about her work, but she had expressed concern over Kimmy's decision to terminate her therapy sessions. The girl survived eight months of captivity at the hands of Andre Roche. She came out of it with a baby—luckily not Roche's. The pregnancy had been part of the reason she ran away in the first place.

"She's putting her life back on track. She starts nursing school in the fall. Jess credits Olivia for that. She's really taken Kimmy and Addy under her wing."

Andre Roche targeted Kimmy because of her gifts. He did the same with Olivia. Kimmy's family had every right to be encouraged by her progress to take back control of her life. It appeared whatever assistance Olivia had to offer suited Kimmy's healing needs far better than more traditional ones. Barry tried not to wonder what those were.

"Why after all this time would Smythe go back to his house?" Will wanted to know.

Barry spent the better part of the night asking himself the same thing. He looked across the room at the map. "Smythe's been lucky. The hospital would have been perfect cover. He knows how to blend." Having worked as a nurse's aide Smythe was comfortable in a medical setting. Barry was reminded of the lack of scrubs in Smythe's closet. He could have dressed the part, like when he played the role of victim while he lured his own. "With the changes at the state hospital, access was getting harder. The hospital kept him sheltered. The vandalism kept him in money but got him noticed. He kept the items small enough not to arouse suspicion, but just enough to eat."

Will looked down at the spreadsheet Barry had shared. It was plausible. "Except the last item—the bike. Was he looking for a payday to make a move because something spooked him? Was he missing home and thus the break in?"

Barry thought about the food receipt from one of Jamie's old haunts. "I think you're half right. Smythe didn't pawn the bike. He needs it for transportation. To get back to the house, he would have had to take the VIA bus which means several exchanges, and he didn't want to risk the visibility. Cut off from being able to make his own way, it came down to what makes the world go round...money."

"And he found that in the house?"

"I think that's why he finally went back. It may have been hidden under the floorboards in the closets."

Will recalled Katie mentioning them. It must have been bothering the lieutenant as well. "It's a solid theory, but how are you going to prove that one?"

"I'm going to suck it up and call Brennon Kaine."

Will recalled having to pull his boss off the fancy attorney the day they interviewed Smythe. "And you think he'll tell you?"

"I think he wants Smythe locked away as much as I do."

If all else failed, Barry could always get Dr. Osborne to make the call for him. Will thought it but didn't say it. "You've done a lot of thinking about this. Did you work this all out in your car in front of Smythe's house last night?"

"You following me, sergeant?"

Will smiled. "No. I wasn't sure if you did until just now."

"I didn't spend the whole night," Barry conceded. Just until about three or so. He figured Smythe would have made an appearance by then, and if Amanda had stopped by his place, she would have given up and gone home. He gave her a key for a purely legitimate reason, not a personal one, and he had yet to get it back. Barry asked her a few times, but she always had an excuse for why she didn't have it with her. He should have been paying more attention.

"Are you avoiding home?" Will asked, figuring now was as good a time as any to ask. Scuttlebutt around the office was that Bartholomew was broodier than usual, even before the Smythe thing. It could mean it was personal. "I know it's none of my business and you can tell me so, but are things alright with, you know?" Will meant Amanda Greene. She was the woman in Barry's life, but deep down, even Will knew she wasn't the one he wanted.

Barry leaned back in his chair. Used to, Mark would have been the one he talked to about these things if he talked about them at all. Letting someone new in was hard for him.

"Jess and I saw Dr. Greene at the 707 last night,"

Will confessed, hoping some sharing would do the trick. It was one of the places Will and his police academy buddies liked to hang out. Last night they gathered to hear Will's thoughts on the FBI. "It looked like a work thing," Will explained even though Barry didn't ask. "Jess ran into her in the bathroom. She seemed disappointed you weren't there." Jess described her as a slobbering mess, but Will decided not to share that much. For Dr. Greene's sake, Will hoped that meant she knew it was coming.

For someone who had planned a date night, Amanda wasted no time finding something else to do. Barry hoped it was a sign she was tired of waiting around for him. "You and Jessica are coming to the housewarming, right?"

Will smiled. "Sure. We got you." It wasn't much of a confession, but it was enough for Will to know things didn't look good for Amanda. He knew Jess would be glad to hear it.

Barry raked a hand over his face. "Good. You can't leave me hanging. That's how it's going."

It was the most Will was going to get out of him. He switched back to what brought him to the lieutenant's office in the first place. "You have Frank in the lab, but you need boots on the ground tracking Smythe," Will suggested.

"I'll email you everything I've got on the neighborhood incidents as well as the photos from Smythe's house," Barry told him. "I'm heading over to canvass the hospital neighborhood. I want to talk to the residents who included a description with their complaints. Also, if you hear your buddy, Silas is on his way back home, you let me know," Barry said with a smirk. He hoped to hear from Olivia before then but didn't want to count on it.

"Will do." Will didn't mind the research, and he knew Barry had to keep moving. It's how he felt useful. "Now that Smythe has his hands on some cash, why not just skip town? Why stay where everyone's looking for him?" Will wanted to know.

"This is his home. He'll never leave. More than that, what he wants is still here."

"What does he want?"

"The one he came for, Dr. Osborne."

****

The tension level in the room dropped considerably once the DA and Marc Singer departed. Silas wondered about the timing but decided he would handle Singer later. He had two school photos to add to the whiteboard of their missing victims. Their introductions were brief. Brittany Hoffman and Kelsey Rowe, both age twelve. Brittany was the first to go missing in August, followed by Kelsey two months later in October. All victims knew one another. They attended the same school and lived in the same neighborhood.

"Without bodies, we were always at a disadvantage. Finding Ashley Knowles gained us some ground. Now, we start over. We do what needs to be done. We canvass. We ask the questions that should have been asked the first time. We focus on these three. Even without all the bodies, we know the victims. The victim type tells us about the offender. The geographic area is small. Specific and isolated. Whoever killed Ashley Knowles was comfortable there."

Silas looked at Olivia and wondered about their attempt to bring children into this world. These girls were betrayed by someone they trusted. No matter how long he had been doing this, Silas still could not reconcile what humans did to one another, especially the defenseless. "I believe we have established Ashley Knowles knew her killer."

"I would like to request Dr. Sheppard accompany me to interview Ashley's mother and grandmother," Olivia asked. "After that, Agent Tunney and I should head up to the school to interview the girl's teachers. I read online the school will be open today with staff available to speak with the kids now that word is out about Ashley. We should use that opportunity to our advantage. You should also know that during our visit to the dumpsite yesterday, Agent Tunney and I went by the McCleary house. The place is abandoned, but the girls' room looks just as they left it. I think forensically it could be of benefit."

Silas found himself caught in her words. For a brief moment in time, they were the only ones in the room. She had a theory, but she didn't share it. And not because she was unsure. As far as Silas knew, the only thing Olivia had ever been unsure of in her life was him.

"Agent Tunney should take lead on the house," Olivia suggested.

Silas nodded his agreement. "Now that we located one body, we need another walking search and recovery of the entire area. Hopefully, our next meeting will supply us with the manpower we need." Silas checked his watch. They had about ten minutes before other members of local law enforcement arrived.

Silas changed his seat, putting himself next to Olivia, but she took the lead. "I should have told you already, but Singer was waiting for me in the hotel lobby yesterday. He wanted to talk about Pittman. I finally got around to finishing the file Singer sent me. There's nothing in there that adds to my profile. I can't give him the slam dunk that the DOJ and Hobbs want. Since Pittman was asking to see me before we found Ashley's body, I can only assume whatever he has to say is new information. He won't share it if Singer is there."

Silas understood. He had to get to Pittman's lawyer before Hobbs.

"You didn't correct me when I talked about Ashley knowing her killer. As usual, you are way ahead of me on this, aren't you?"

Olivia reached under the table to squeeze his knee, prompting Silas to lean in closer. "You're on a path you don't want to take, aren't you?"

"Have you always wanted to go where you were called?" she asked softly.

Silas was reminded how glad he was he didn't live with what was inside her head. He moved his hand down to cover hers. "You don't think we're going to find those other two girls, do you?" he asked as others began to fill the room.

Olivia thought about it. Her eyes stared across the room at something he couldn't see. "I doubt it. But I won't know that until I see their school records. I want to know how much they weighed."

Chapter Sixteen

Dr. Sheppard followed Tunney and Olivia to the Knowles' house. While the two doctors talked to the Knowles family, Tunney talked to anyone in the neighborhood he could find regarding missing pets, missing girls, or anything else interesting they might remember. It had been over a year since they were last questioned. Time sometimes made people more willing to talk. The forensics team was finishing up at the pet cemetery and probably wouldn't get to the house until tomorrow. The only thing left was to join Olivia at the middle school when they were both done.

"Why me, Dr. Osborne?" Juliya Sheppard asked after Agent Tunney left them. Sheppard worked with the dead. Sometimes those she uncovered had family waiting for them, but most times not. She was curious about the request.

"Ashley's family may have questions about how she died. I can't speak to that." Olivia had seen the horror of Ashley's death. What she meant was the family needed to hear Dr. Sheppard's clinical view. "They will seek comfort in what you tell them. And at the risk of sounding sexist, because you're a woman."

Dr. Sheppard smiled at the comment. This woman was practical and direct. Two dying personality traits as far as Sheppard was concerned.

"From reviewing Ashley's background, the women

in her life have been on their own for a long time. Trust me. They will prefer speaking to us over any man who sat in that room with us today."

Juliya nodded. She didn't meet many women she liked. Most of them were intimidated by her, or by her title. She had no time to soothe such concerns. With Dr. Osborne, it wasn't necessary. She wasn't easily intimidated, least of all by another woman. This woman swam comfortably among the sharks.

"You're used to being the only woman in the board room, aren't you?" Sheppard asked. She belonged to a heavily populated boys club herself. They just didn't carry guns or ooze testosterone like the law enforcement types.

"More times than not," Olivia said with a smile.

"You seem to handle yourself just fine," Sheppard assured her. "And then there's Agent Branch. He's a whole different breed, isn't he?"

****

The floor plan was almost identical to the McCleary house. Olivia was glad when Sherrie Knowles suggested they talk outside on the enclosed porch where the air was fresh. Inside, the tiny home was stifling, filled with the odor of the salves and ointments Ashley's grandmother used to ease her aching joints. The aroma caused Olivia to rethink her choice of fish for lunch more than once.

Sherrie's first questions were for Dr. Sheppard. Olivia was glad she brought her along. The woman did an excellent job easing the young mother's concerns about what might have been her daughter's last moments. Dr. Sheppard performed admirably, doing just as Olivia asked, and providing comfort. It had been quick, Sheppard assured her.

Olivia sat quietly and relived the vision Dr. Sheppard's forensics couldn't possibly tell. It was a surprise attack, but still, Ashley ran. Not far and not for long, but she experienced minutes of blind terror. When she fell for the last time, it was quick, the darkness moving swiftly to swallow her. Olivia could see it as a black shroud coming to claim its prize. Ashley's death was an offering.

"Did you find a necklace?"

The question snapped Olivia back to reality. Her fingers were twisted in the silver chain around her neck that housed the little cross from Gran. Andre Roche broke the original chain when he took it from her. She had since lengthened it, so it was easier to reach. Taking it from her had gotten Roche killed.

"It was a gift from my mom for Ashley's eleventh birthday. She never took it off."

"What kind of necklace?" Olivia asked.

"It was a tree of life. It was a reminder how important family is and that we are stronger together."

Ashley would not have lied to her grandmother. She was telling the truth when she said Ava asked her to spend the night.

Olivia looked at Sheppard. The look in the other doctor's eye told her there was no necklace. Neither was prepared to share the news with Sherrie Knowles, not until they had no other choice.

"Anything of Ashley's that we find, will be returned to you once the examination is complete," Olivia assured her. Dr. Sheppard would go back and look for it. If it wasn't there, they would scour the dump site again.

"Sherrie, I'm sorry, but I need to hear in your own words what happened the last time you saw your daughter." Olivia watched the broken women sit straighter in the tattered chair and steel herself the best she could.

Sherrie Knowles focused on some unseen spot just over Olivia's shoulder and began. "Ash stopped by the store after school, just like she always did on Fridays. My boss let me slip her stuff sometimes, no charge." Sherrie tried to smile, but her eyes were too tired and too sad to pull it off. "She was trying to be good. You know, because of her weight. She took a candy bar and a diet soda. We used to say they cancelled each other out. Ash liked the lemon-lime drinks. She said it was because they didn't taste like diet."

Olivia nodded, wondering where Ashley got her weight problem. Both her mom and grandma were rail-thin. Grandma from some insidious disease process, no doubt. Sherrie's lack of weight was due to the cigarettes she smoked. She wanted one now. Olivia was relieved when Sherrie opted for what was left of her thumbnail instead of reaching for one.

"Did being overweight cause problems with the other kids?" Considering what Sherrie said about the candy and the diet soda, Olivia was curious if Ashley was the only one watching her weight.

"Ash knew she wasn't skinny and petite like the others," Sherrie said, her eyes moving outside to the tattered backyard. "Kids can be so cruel. Girls especially."

"Cruel, how?" Olivia asked.

"The usual. They said things."

"Anyone in particular?" Olivia pressed.

"Ash was overweight most of her life. She stopped telling me. I told her she'd grow out of it."

"Did she spend the night with the McCleary girls often?" Maybe being next-door neighbors, Ava was different.

"Ashley and Ava were pretty close."

"So, Ashley telling your mother she was spending the night with Ava wasn't unusual?" Olivia resisted pushing the grandmother. She sensed the woman carried a tremendous amount of guilt about the last encounter with her granddaughter. She couldn't help but wonder if the burden was part of her failing health.

"When Dorcas came, things changed. Ash hadn't been over there in months."

"Changed how?"

Sherrie shrugged like it was a long-dead subject. "Two girls together are fine. Add another one, and there's always an odd one out. That was Ash."

Olivia nodded. Growing up with few playmates, she knew all about the odds. Having one friend and then losing them would have been hard on the already self-conscious Ashley. If there was an invitation to spend the night, she would have taken it. "When did Dorcas come to live with Ava?"

"Two summers ago, not long before school started. The last year of their lives." For a moment, Olivia thought she was going to shed a tear for all the school years her daughter would never attend, but Sherrie chased away the thought with a shake of her head.

"Any idea why? Where were her parents?" Olivia probed deeper. Right now, Sherrie Knowles was her only source of information.

"Dorcas's mom, Debbie, is Terry's sister. From

what Melanie said, Debbie was always one step ahead of social services. Melanie and Terry took Dorcas in because I think they were afraid of what would happen if they didn't."

Olivia made a note to review whatever they had on Dorcas's mother. She remembered Terry and Melanie, but no one else. This case had not been her typical. She usually worked with the accused, but when Silas called her to join the case, it was to interview the family. Silas knew something wasn't right, but even he couldn't say what. Instincts were hard to describe. He needed her to find them, yet all she could offer him was a withdrawn, secretive family who had suffered a great tragedy. Her explanation to Silas at the time was that everyone responded to grief differently.

"Do you know what happened to the McClearys?" Olivia asked.

Sherrie shook her head. "No, sorry, I don't. All I know is Terry left first. Melanie not long after. I don't even know if they stayed together. None of us talked after." With thoughts of the past, Sherrie moved to another fingernail. "They didn't give notice to Sanderson, the guy we rent from because he kept asking me about her. Since what happened he hasn't been able to rent the place. Sometimes I think I see a light inside the girl's room at night. I don't know if it's real or just a memory."

Sherrie ushered them toward the door. Ashley's grandmother appeared to be sleeping in her rocking chair. A gnarled hand snuck out from underneath the covers to grab Olivia's hand as she passed.

"Ash was a good girl."

Olivia bent down so she could be on the woman's

level. As she looked into her pale blue eyes, she could see the life leaking out of them. She saw this woman die in this chair, mourning her granddaughter. The moon would be shining through the window when she took her last breath. Olivia resisted the urge to take back her hand.

"Ash wouldn't go down that road by herself. We told her to stay close after those other girls went missing. She did what we told her. She wouldn't lie to me."

Olivia concentrated on breathing through her mouth. Up close, the smell of the salves was different. Maybe it was the woman's future she smelled. "What would make Ashley go down that road? What reason would she have to go to the place you told her not to go?"

"If Ash thought Ava was going to be there, she would go. Ash missed her friend. Or if she thought she would find Dolly." The old lady let go of Olivia's hand and retreated back under the blanket.

Olivia waited until they were outside to ask, "Who is Dolly?"

"Ash's dog. Mr. Baker down the road gave her one of his pups when things started to go bad between her and Ava. I thought it might help," Sherrie explained.

"Where's the dog now?"

Sherrie shook her head. "Disappeared with all the other animals in the neighborhood. Ash was pretty broken up about it."

****

Tunney gathered records from the school nurse on the two remaining girls, while Olivia met with the teachers. Some were teary-eyed when they spoke about

Ashley. On the surface, they had nothing new to add. They played together and lived within walking distance of one another. The girls all knew each other, having attended school together since kindergarten. All except Dorcus. Dorcas changed everything.

Olivia skirted questions about Larry Wayne Pittman, like if she believed he had anything to do with Ashley. When she said they were keeping all possibilities open, the two youngest teachers offered Albert Kniffen as a possible person of interest. He was part of the janitorial team for both the elementary and middle schools. He also had a part-time job at the same convenience store where Ashley's mother worked. They described him as a "lurker."

With papers in hand, Agent Tunney slipped quietly into the corner and listened. Olivia couldn't help but notice the constant eye shift the six grade English teacher kept giving him. After the interview, Olivia was out the door first to find a bathroom, leaving Tunney on his own. Maybe he could learn something she couldn't. The oldest of the three teachers, Mrs. Snively, was waiting for her outside the stall when she was finished.

"I know the other two would never say this, but there were a lot more people upset today over Ashley Knowles than the two that were shot."

Olivia didn't know what to say. She let the silence do the work for her. Most people didn't want to be alone with their thoughts, especially when they had something to share. It didn't take long.

"I've seen a lot of kids in my forty years of teaching and that Dorcas, she was a problem."

The woman had been teaching almost as long as Olivia had been alive. That was a lot of kids. The teacher must have seen Olivia doing the math in her head.

"An average of twenty-five kids per school year over forty years, that's about a thousand, give or take a couple of hundred," Ms. Snively answered for her.

"Always middle school?"

"I spent a couple years in first grade, but decided I could relate better to the older ones."

"What do you mean by Dorcas was a problem?" Olivia wanted to know.

Ms. Snively didn't hesitate. "Not nice."

As the quiet, shy girl at school, Olivia encountered her fair share of bullies. Girls could be cruel, but all that stopped once word got around about how bright her green eyes turned when she got upset. After that, the other girls ignored her, while Olivia kept her eyes buried in books. Gran taught her that was a better choice. "How? Was she mean?" Olivia asked.

"Not mean. Worse. Devious. *Shrewd.*"

"Interesting choice of words for a thirteen-year-old."

"Dorcas had what you would call an *old soul.*"

The term conjured images of something sinister.

"I'm sure you've come across one or two of those types in your line of work."

Olivia recognized this woman for what she was, an observer. The teacher had profiled more people than she had.

"Dorcas wasn't a fan of Brittany or Kelsey either. She used to bully Brittany on the playground for some little bracelet the girl wore. And she didn't shed a tear over the girls when they went missing, not like her classmates."

Olivia found the revelation interesting. "Would Dorcas' reaction have been any different with Ashley?"

Ms. Snively didn't hesitate. "No, it wouldn't. Dorcas probably disliked Ashley the most. She was jealous of her friendship with Ava. She busted that up as soon as she got here."

Olivia nodded, digesting the information. "Any thoughts on Albert Kniffen the janitor?"

Ms. Snively snickered. "More people wanted to talk about him than they ever wanted to talk about Dorcas."

"You spoke up about Dorcas before?" Silas had suspected certain aspects of the case were withheld during the initial investigation.

"Sure did. But no one wants to talk about the deviousness of little girls. She was sure a lot sharper than Albert Kniffen. He's harmless. Keeps to himself. Doesn't even drive. I doubt he would have the courage to talk to those girls or any other ones. He's not a toucher. The other two don't like him because he likes to look. But no more so than Miss Lee checking out your partner. Tell him he should watch himself with that one."

Chapter Seventeen

Tunney and Olivia compared notes on their way back to the hotel. "I talked to a neighbor who lives a couple of doors down from the McCleary house. His name's Mr. Baker. He's the one with the dog tied to the tree. Today she was on the porch with him. He said he only tied her up when he had to go somewhere, which considering his age, he rarely does. He claims he doesn't go farther than the convenience store where Sherrie Knowles works. He described Sherrie and her mom as 'good people.' He told me his dog had eight pups last summer. None of the pups he gave to the neighborhood kids are still around. They were all gone before the girls."

Olivia listened as she gazed at the passing cars on I-75. It was after work hours, and traffic was heavier than she'd seen it. "Sherrie Knowles said a neighbor gave Ashley a puppy."

"He still has the mom. Says he keeps her tied up because he doesn't want to lose her too."

"I think she's safe," Olivia remarked. "After killing humans, killing animals probably isn't nearly as much fun. Since the killings have stopped, I'd say his dog is safe."

The comment reminded Tunney of her discussion with Hobbs that morning. "So, you're convinced the killer stopped?"

"A true serial doesn't stop on their own," Olivia corrected him.

"You mentioned there were two reasons, incarceration or death. There have been no more killings here, but what if after Pittman confessed, the freak who did the others packed up his little circus and relocated?" Tunney suggested.

Tunney had a point. One she had not considered, but maybe she should. "What are you thinking?"

"Interviewing the locals today, I found out a good majority of the low-income population, like the McClearys, are as migratory as the tourists. The McClearys might have lived here, but Terry worked elsewhere, doing seasonal travel. So did Ashley Knowles' father. He was a carpenter. One year he took up with the carnival and never came back."

"Terry McCleary left shortly after Ava and Dorcas' deaths," Olivia told him.

"I heard that, too. No one seems to know where," Tunney said. "I thought I might do some research, see if I can get a hit on any other missing cases that seem similar."

"Sounds like a plan," Olivia agreed. "Is that going to be before or after you talk to Ms. Lee?" Olivia asked about the googly-eyed teacher. "She didn't happen to tell you anything interesting, did she?"

"She was more interested in knowing if I had a badge."

"What did you tell her?"

"That all I had was laminate," he admitted, and Olivia laughed out loud. "She seemed disappointed. As for the girls, she said she shouldn't speak ill of the dead."

"Translated that means if you can't say something nice, then don't say anything at all. That's what my Gran used to say."

Tunney pulled up to the hotel, letting her out at the entrance.

It told Olivia he had somewhere else to go.

Before she got out, Tunney reached into the console between them. "I almost forgot. Here are the nurse's notes on the girls' first check-up of the school year."

Olivia took the papers and shoved them in her purse for later. Right now, all she wanted was dinner with her husband. Silas was leaving the forensics lab and heading to rendezvous with her for dinner. They had notes to compare.

"Thanks for suggesting I take lead on the McCleary house. I'm meeting forensics there first thing in the morning." Getting in the good graces of the special agent in charge couldn't hurt. Especially if he wanted to get out of Tampa.

"You were there. You saw it. Not to mention your concern for me went over well."

"He told you about that, huh?"

"Best not to tell him anything you don't want me to know," Olivia warned with a smile.

"Good to know. What do you want me to do about the mirror?" Tunney hadn't forgotten how she reacted when he wanted to uncover it.

Olivia paused. "I suggest leaving it as is until I can talk to the McClearys. Someone in that house has a particular set of beliefs. There's power in belief. Whoever covered the mirror did it for a reason. I want to know why, before we unleash something we know nothing about." She didn't want to have to chase it back to whatever dark corner it came from.

Tunney pulled away, wondering if Agent Branch had learned what questions not to ask.

Silas was waiting for Olivia in the lobby. At her request, they headed to the nearest restaurant they could find.

"So, were you able to get a hold of Pittman's attorney?" Olivia asked once they ordered. With Tunney tied up with forensics tomorrow, she was hoping for a road trip.

"Pittman's in the infirmary. Apparently, he had some kind of altercation in the exercise yard. He's having nasal surgery tomorrow and won't be available for questioning until Tuesday. His attorney said his client would be more than happy to speak with you then."

"So, what are we doing tomorrow?"

"I'm spending more time at the pet cemetery and coordinating with local law enforcement for our walking recovery on Saturday. It's gone out to local media, and I have more agents coming in to assist."

"Any luck locating the McClearys?"

"Not so far. Looks like they split up so we're tracking the two of them separately. I've also got feelers out on Dorcas' mother. Agent Dunn found her last time. She was somewhere near Winter Haven in court ordered rehab which is why she wasn't here."

"You might want to run down some info on an Albert Kniffen, a janitor at the girls' school. He also works at the same convenience store as Ashley's mom." Olivia spied their waitress, weaving her way through the tables. She really hoped the plates she was carrying were for them.

"We did. Dunn cleared him last time. Kniffen lived in a half-way house at the time due to some repeated petty larceny charges, nothing serious. He had regular curfew times. Between those and his jobs we eliminated him. Do we need to take another look?"

"No. It was just follow-up from my talk with the teachers today," Olivia explained.

"I'd like to hear. You owe me some insight into that brain of yours," Silas reminded her.

"You probably don't want to go there. Not at the table," Olivia said. They were in luck. The plates of food were for them, and they had a rule they didn't talk about work at dinner.

Back at the hotel, they headed to the bar, avoiding their room for the remainder of their conversation. It was another self-imposed rule. They went to great lengths to draw a line between work and personal time. Given the kinds of humans they hunted, they wanted something untainted by the horrors they encountered professionally. In a profession where fear was not something they showed, they reserved it for each other, but they had also learned how to turn it all off and submerge themselves in normalcy. They cherished their downtime and guarded it closely. They went to the gym. They worked in the yard, and they discovered Sunday afternoons were perfect for binge-watching other people cook.

Silas snagged a beer for himself and some fruity non-alcoholic drink for Olivia at her request. He wandered outside on the patio, where she had found them a table away from others. It was a beautiful night with a bright moon high in the sky. They would continue the discussion of their day before going back inside for some private time. Intimacy was also important, emotional as well as physical. Silas was more than surprised, not to mention pleased, to learn his demure wife's sexual appetite rivaled his own. Lately, however, he felt himself struggling to keep up with her. Given the robust nature of his single years, Silas would take that secret to his grave.

"I'm hopeful that you have some idea where we're going with this case because I don't," Silas led with the confession. He mulled over her requests from the morning, profiling her ideas like the actions of a suspect.

Olivia looked across the table at him as she took a sip of the fruity concoction. The look on her face told him she wasn't sure she liked it. "Too much coconut," she said with a wrinkle in her nose.

"I thought you liked coconut."

"Not today."

Silas nodded and watched her push the drink away. "Want something else?"

"Give me a minute," she said. "Just keep talking."

Silas took a sip of his beer. "Okay, then I have to tell you, before Pittman came forward with his confession, we had no suspects. Zero. Zilch. So, if he's out of the running, who's up?"

"Remind me what bothered you about this case the last time."

"Do I have to narrow it down to one thing?" Silas asked. The pull on his beer was longer this time. It went down like he was going to need another. "I felt reluctance, and not just from the McClearys. I honestly think the sheriff's office attributed the first two girls to an animal. Not unlikely, but also easy. I don't think they wanted to entertain the fact one of their own could have done it. Or that they were going to have to ask for help. It's a small place and yet those girls vanished into thin air."

"What did the parents say?" Olivia was curious if their stories matched those of the teachers.

"All the parents worked. Ashley Knowles was the only one who had anyone at home waiting for her after school. The girls went missing in broad daylight, all of them at a time when no adults were around. It made it hard to pinpoint the last sighting when the interview pool consisted of kids the same age."

"Did any of them have anything to say?"

"Nothing helpful. They were scared." Silas tried to catch the eye of a passing waitress to indicate he wanted another beer, but the place was packed. It was a Thursday night. Most business travelers had returned home only to be replaced by the summer crowd.

Olivia could feel the frustration roll off of him. She reached across the table for his hand.

"The McClearys were different than the other parents," Silas shook his head, taking a moment to put into words what he felt. "They didn't want to talk about it. But not like parents of most murdered children. It's like they were resigned to the fact it happened. That their girls were next."

"They weren't surprised." It was a statement, not a question.

"That's the best way I can describe it."

"Did you suspect Pittman for the other girls?" Olivia asked.

"Of course we did, after the fact. If Pittman hadn't

come forward this thing would still be unsolved. After what you said this morning to Hobbs, I went back and checked Pittman's work schedule. You were right. The afternoon Ashley Knowles went missing, he was working. Then there's the manner of the kill and the disposal. Doesn't make sense he would flip the script like that. As sick as he makes me, just like you, I believed him when he said he didn't kill the others," Silas confessed.

"What reason did he give you for killing Ava and Dorcas?" Olivia knew what Pittman told her. She wondered if his story had changed by the time she arrived.

The description was still stuck in Silas' head. "They needed kill'n."

Silas drained the last of his beer and looked to Olivia, but she was lost in thought.

"Hey, this was supposed to be you sharing with me. Not the other way around," he reminded her.

At least Pittman's story was consistent. Still, she was missing something. "Why two guns?"

Silas shrugged. "He never said." The truth was no one ever asked. A confessed murderer off the street was all anyone wanted.

"According to Melanie McCleary, she was home that morning. She didn't go looking for the girls until it was time for her to go to work. How did she not hear the gun shots?" And why wasn't one gun enough? Seeing the scene from Tunney's viewpoint changed Olivia's perspective.

"We need to find the McClearys." Olivia urged. "Tunney and I learned they split up. Terry left soon after Ava and Dorcas' death."

Olivia was way ahead of him. They hadn't discussed the details, but Silas had known just the same. It's what she did. "Hobbs will latch on to Terry's disappearance," Silas theorized, draining his beer.

"I saw what happened," Olivia confessed. "Ashley wasn't alone. There were two people. One to distract her and the other to deliver the blow."

Silas filled in the blanks. "According to Sheppard the injury to the skull came from behind. Terry McCleary would be the obvious choice for an accomplice."

"It came from above," Olivia corrected him. "From the top of the big rock where we found the pet cemetery. Ashley never saw it coming."

Silas was skipping ahead, back on the hunt for another killer. Now it made sense why Terry McCleary never went after his cousin for killing his daughter. Silas didn't know why, but Terry was in on it. "Sheppard said Ashley was dead before she hit the ground."

"She wasn't. She was screaming," Olivia told him.

Her words sobered him, stopping Silas in his tracks.

"Terry McCleary wouldn't need the height advantage of the rock. No one tried to stop Ashley from running away. She fell exactly where she was found. With two grown men, why a shallow grave? Why a grave at all when there's the crocodile pond?"

The revelation sent a chill up his spine, prompting Silas to reach for Olivia's hand this time. It was a comfort measure for both of them. His throat felt raw. Silas went back to his beer, hoping to wash away the scene she had just painted, but it was as dry as his mouth.

"According to the grandmother, Ashley told her she was going to be with Ava. I believe the grandmother as much as I believe Pittman. If that's true, it means Ava and Dorcas knew what happened to Ashley."

The knot in Silas' stomach grew tighter, like a noose. "We're processing their room tomorrow."

"There were beliefs of some kind in that house, something involving mirrors. There's one covered in the girls' bedroom. I told Agent Tunney to leave it the way we found it until I know more."

"Mirrors, again?" Silas asked.

"They can be a conduit. I told you that. There's something in those woods. Something very old. I can hear whispers in the trees, but I can't make them out. The language is different."

"Is it threatening?" Silas needed to know.

Olivia took a pause. "It's just different, and I'm not familiar." If it was demonic, she would know. It wouldn't hesitate to make contact. They spoke the same language. "Whatever it is, it's obscure. It's been here a very long time. It thinks of this place as its own."

Silas looked at her with tired eyes. "Tell me, what else you know. In this world. And then I'm going to go get that other drink I need."

"I think it would be easy to throw puppies in the crocodile pond. And little girls, too." Olivia saw the pain in his eyes at the realization. "You asked."

Silas squeezed her hand. He should have known the answer. It was in the questions she had asked him that morning. "I'm going to get that drink now."

Chapter Eighteen

Leaving the cocoon she shared with Silas, the room came alive. Alcohol-infused adults with lowered inhibitions buzzed inside her head. As soon as Silas returned with his drink, Olivia planned on encouraging him to take his beer and follow her upstairs to their room. She preferred the quietness of his mind and yearned for his warmth. Alone in the dark with him, Olivia could free some of her own inhibitions. But not yet. She had picked up a traveler on her way back from the bathroom. She returned to the table on the patio with Marc Singer in tow.

"Ignoring me isn't going to make me go away," the lawyer said.

Olivia slid into her seat undaunted just as Silas arrived. He handed Olivia the sparkling water she requested. They even had the ginger she asked for. Silas glanced between his wife and the lawyer, unsure what he might have missed. Olivia's face was passive, while Singer looked poised for a fight. Silas set his beer on the table and remained standing.

"I need to speak to Dr. Osborne, alone," Singer said, never looking Silas' way.

"I'm the special agent in charge," Silas reminded him.

Singer peered down at Olivia. "I'm aware, Agent Branch, but this is between the doctor and the

Department of Justice."

"Agent Branch stays, or I go." Olivia's tone was smooth but icy. "If the Justice Department wants to talk to me, now is your chance."

"We could compel you," Singer threatened.

"You could, but I don't work for you," Olivia reminded him.

Silas saw the first hint of fire in her eyes. "There's no need for this," Silas chimed in, glaring at Singer.

Neither Olivia nor Singer listened.

"I didn't say I wouldn't talk to you—I gave you a condition. Instead of considering it, you're trying to bully me. I don't respond well to bullies," Olivia told him.

"Like Andre Roche. You said he was a bully. Is that why he's dead?"

"Andre Roche was a known rapist and a murderer. He got what he deserved." Her words were measured and firm, keeping Silas and Singer both in their place.

Silas couldn't remember the last time he had seen her so angry or her eyes so green.

Olivia sipped her water and watched Singer. Her stare never wavered until he had to look away.

"I'm going to be there for Pittman's interview," Singer finally said.

"You're not invited," Olivia told him.

"You can't keep me out."

"Really?"

Silas heard the challenger in her words as he watched Singer's hand go to his head. He looked like he had the beginnings of a headache.

Olivia leaned forward in her chair. "*Compel.* Such an interesting word." She flashed Singer a slight smile.

"Mr. Pittman will talk to me and only me. If you boys from Justice want something from him, you're going to have to sit back and wait for me to give it to you. From now on, that's how this works."

Singer didn't move. Silas wondered if he could. Maybe he was revving up to go at her again. Either way, Silas didn't think that was the smart move. People standing around them were slowly starting to move away.

"Don't make me force you to leave," Silas said.

"You're not invited here, either," Olivia told Singer.

Finally, Singer snapped out of his trance. The bravado was gone, but not the threats. "This isn't over," Singer threatened.

"Yes, it is." Olivia was matter of fact.

Silas watched Singer shuffle away, wondering if the lawyer didn't have one too many. Maybe he needed the liquid courage to take her on. Silas took a long swig of his own drink and focused on Olivia. The lightning storm inside her eyes had faded, returning them to their usual shade of green.

"Singer was right about Roche. It's my fault he's dead," Olivia confessed. "I traded him and Ana on the condition *Alleracsap* release the boy. Jamie is free because of me."

****

The box was waiting for her in the bathroom. Olivia walked back to the bedroom with it in her hand. "What is this?"

Silas tried to find a smile because she looked like she wanted to cry.

"I just told you I'm a demon dealer. How could

168

you even think about having a baby with me?"

Silas offered his hand, coaxing Olivia to sit next to him on the bed. "What I heard you say was you saved a man's life with no concern for your own."

Silas was right, at least about part of it. She had saved Barry's life. She knew now hers was never in danger. She had the power all along, just like *Alleracsap* said. Sensing the demon was so much easier now. She opened something between them that night in the barn, something she couldn't put back even if she wanted to. It had always been there, waiting for her.

"You said the demon's name. You told me doing that gave It power. But I think the stakes have changed."

Olivia trusted Silas more than anyone in her life, yet still, she kept things from him. She told herself it was to protect him. Maybe it was to protect herself.

"The demon isn't the one with the power," Silas said. "Not anymore. Maybe not ever. You told me your ancestors were there, watching over you. You did what you had to do, and no one, including you, should second guess what you did. How could I want anything more than that from the mother of my children?"

Silas reached over and covered her hand still holding the box. "I want you to take this in the morning before you go."

Olivia looked at him, just now realizing she wasn't included in tomorrow's agenda. They had only talked about what Tunney was doing.

"I took the liberty of booking you on a flight back to San Antonio. It's going to be an awful weekend here. You don't believe we are going to find those little girls, and you can't see Pittman until Tuesday. Amanda's party is this weekend, and you should be there. You'll be coming back to this shit storm soon enough, I promise."

"But,"

"I know. I'll miss you too," Silas told her. He squeezed her hand, reminding her of the box still between them. "I want this for you. You need it. You're stuck again. Between the knowing and the not knowing. You're caught up in the wondering and the hoping and you're driving yourself crazy. You need to know."

Silas caught a glimpse of tears building. She couldn't blink them all away.

"This is about you. Not me. Not even us. This is for you." As the tears began to fall, he pulled her into him. "I'll always be here. The before. The after. I'll love you all the way through it."

****

For the second time in a week, a phone call took Silas away in the middle of the night. Something about the Knowles house. Something with the grandmother.

The test was waiting on the bathroom counter, strategically placed directly in front of her make-up bag so she couldn't miss it. No excuses. Olivia glanced at herself in the mirror. Inside that little box could be the last pregnancy test she ever took.

Olivia did what she had to do and shoved the stick back inside the box without waiting for the results. She showered. She dressed. She packed. She ate. She slipped the box into her purse on her way out the door. She and Silas would learn the results together. It's what they would have done if the phone call hadn't interrupted their plans.

Silas was in full work mode by the time she arrived

at police headquarters. He'd been at it for hours, preparing the conference room. Sign-in sheets littered the table in preparation for tomorrow's search. For now, they had the room to themselves. Olivia asked about the phone call first.

"Ashley's grandmother passed away last night. In her sleep. She went peacefully," he said solemnly.

Olivia thought about the woman and what she saw. "The moon was shining on her through the window. She was in her recliner in the living room, wasn't she?"

"How did you know?"

"I saw it. Yesterday when I held her hand."

They had spent years working together. Silas was comfortable with her gifts, but this was a new one. She had never seen the future before. "That's different," he said carefully.

"I'd say so." Olivia looked up at him. "I said something to Agent Tunney the other day about sharks. It was off-handed, but the expression on his face told me I was dredging up memories." The look on Silas' face told her she was on to something. "Something happened, didn't it? Something in his past."

Silas would never have mentioned it. It was something he learned when he called the Tampa field office inquiring about the agent. "Tunney began his career as an agent with Florida Parks and Wildlife. On one of his last cases, a surfer got attacked by a shark. Tunney pulled him to shore, but the guy bled out before help could arrive. He died in Tunney's arms."

Olivia felt sick, like she was drowning.

Silas saved her. "Livie? Why are you asking?" He stepped closer, his hands gliding down her arms, bringing her back from wherever she had gone.

"I saw that too," she said. "I saw the past."

Silas didn't know what to say. Maybe she had too much on her mind. Maybe it was the stress of what they were trying to create. "Did you do it? Did you take the test?"

Olivia nodded and turned to look at him with tears in her eyes.

"Are you okay?" *What was he thinking, sending her away?*

"I took it, but I didn't look." Olivia felt around in her purse until she found the box. She reached inside and pulled out the stick, her fingers wrapped tightly around it, so neither could see. A plus or minus sign was going to define their life. "I brought it so we could do it together." Her eyes searched Silas'. "Either way, I think I'm done. Are you good with that?"

Silas reached for her hand. "Yes." He had decided that was the answer a long time ago.

"We're in this together, right?" she whispered.

Nothing had been more right in his life. "This is good. This is for real," Silas repeated the words Olivia said to him the night she told him she loved him.

Olivia opened her hand.

****

"This changes everything."

Olivia looked up at him, barely seeing him through the veil of tears in her eyes as Silas placed his hand on her belly. She laid her hand over his.

It was changing her already.

Chapter Nineteen

Desperate to think about something other than what he had just done, Silas headed to the morgue. According to Doctors Banigo and Sheppard, they had something he needed to see.

Silas met them in a cramped little room not much bigger than a closet. Most of the space was consumed by a large table that served as ground zero for the evidence gathered at the pet cemetery.

Dr. Banigo took the lead. "We identified nine graves in total. Based on the ground pattern and animal remains, we arranged our findings in what we believe to be the most likely chronological order." Dr. Banigo pointed Silas to where he should start.

Silas studied the items in front of him. Dr. Banigo was correct when he described the site to the DA, saying it looked like a private memorial. It began with animal remains, but among them were brightly colored tags and small collars. They looked like animal mementos. None of them were big enough to fit either of Olivia's dogs back home. Silas wondered if he wasn't looking at the puppies that once belonged to the old man Tunney interviewed. The one who gave them away to the neighborhood kids.

Dr. Banigo moved on, pushing Silas to the final items. "The last mounds contained pieces of jewelry. Based on information given to the sheriff, I believe they belong to our first two victims. Brittany Hoffman was wearing a bracelet the day she went missing, and Kelsey Rowe a locket necklace. We found it in the last mound."

"I'll have someone get a hold of the parents so they can come down for a positive ID." Verification should be easy enough. The parents would have provided photos. Silas shook his head at the conversations to come. "I was hoping for good news."

"All the bones were animal," Dr. Banigo reminded him. "In our business this might be as good as it gets. At least these parents will get something back of their daughters."

Silas knew Dr. Banigo meant well. Not everyone's definition of good was the same. The medical examiner once cared for the living in his native land of Nigeria until he realized his patients were just waiting to die. Salazar Banigo chose to escape his country and come to this one to look after those who had already made the transition.

"There's more," Dr. Sheppard spoke up. "Yesterday, Ms. Knowles asked me if I found a necklace. She claimed Ashley never took it off. I didn't find it. There was nothing on her except the clothes she was wearing. I had some techs go back to the site, but still nothing." Dr. Sheppard had crossed her T's and dotted her I's before telling him because she knew the special agent in charge wouldn't have it any other way.

Ava, Dorcas, and Ashley were all dead within twenty-four hours. It meant everything stopped at once. Silas sighed at the implication. The necklace wasn't there because whoever killed her didn't have time to bury it. The DA would want to tie that piece of information to Pittman. Still, Silas knew they didn't find any of the girl's personal items in Pittman's possession. He wasn't a trophy keeper which meant he had killed for another reason.

"Do you think we're going to find the other girls tomorrow?" Silas asked no one in particular.

"In my opinion, separating the jewelry from the victim says no. But that would be more Dr. Osborne's area of expertise," Dr. Banigo replied.

"After listening to her requests yesterday, I reviewed the descriptions of the other two missing girls," Dr. Sheppard told him. "Dr. Osborne suggested burying the Knowles girl could have been an improvisation. The other two girls were average height and weight. My point being they are much smaller, comparatively to Ashley Knowles."

"Meaning it would be easier to bury them?" Silas theorized. He would take that story over what Livie said about little girls and puppies.

"On the contrary, since Ashley was found just across the road, Dr. Osborne could be right. Ashley was a big girl. Burying her might have been easier. The other missing girls were small, throwing or pushing them in the crocodile pond would have been much easier."

The forensics matched what Olivia had been trying to tell him last night.

Dammit.

****

Action was the only remedy to the chaos bubbling inside of her. With two long hours on the road, Olivia occupied herself with a to-do list and implemented it as soon as she reached the airport. She called her doctor and made an appointment for prenatal labs first thing Monday morning. Until the blood results were back, Olivia wanted to keep their pregnancy news between her and Silas.

She also texted Amanda about the dogs. Olivia knew she should be grateful for the help, but she dreaded having to see her. All Olivia wanted to do was stay inside the bubble she left behind with Silas. Relief came quickly when Amanda replied that the dogs were already home, something to do with lawn preparations for the party. Amanda asked if she wanted to meet later for drinks, but Olivia lied and said she was flying standby. Free of obligations, Olivia settled in for the direct flight home and let her mind lapse into baby overdrive.

Back in San Antonio, her fur babies eagerly greeted her as she let herself in the back gate. Not wanting the reunion to end, she brought them inside with her. Daisy ran to her bed, inspecting all her toys before laying down to watch her mistress while Alvin sniffed at something on the floor. Olivia was going to investigate when she heard a car pull up outside. Relieved to see it was Agent Jon Sharpe and not Amanda, Olivia greeted him on the porch.

"Do you know why I'm here?"

"I can only imagine," Olivia smiled.

"Silas let us know you were home alone."

"And he wants you to keep an eye on me." Silas had his reasons. Olivia didn't always understand them, but the *Good Samaritan* case changed both of their lives. She wondered if the case would ever be over.

"Something like that," Jon agreed. "Just wanted you to know someone will be passing through from time to time."

"Thanks for the head's up."

"Just yell if you need something. My cell is the same."

Her move back home to San Antonio had concerned the FBI enough that someone decided they wanted to keep tabs on her. Jon Sharpe was the one who lurked outside her house. It was a minor annoyance, but Olivia didn't protest. It came in handy the day she locked herself out of her house. She called Silas and demanded he give her the agent's number. Olivia still didn't know if it was the fit she threw about having a babysitter or because she used the word "handsome" when describing him. Either way, it got her what she wanted.

For Jon Sharpe, it was the easiest assignment of his career. Before the call from Silas Branch, Agent Sharpe had never heard of Olivia Osborne. Other than her excursions to horrific crime scenes at the behest of the BAU, Dr. Osborne lived a pretty solitary life. No close friends, except a cop Sharpe thought at first might be a boyfriend and an older black gentleman who dressed like a priest minus the collar. Despite minimal outside contact, Dr. Osborne didn't seem unhappy. Jon found himself hoping she wasn't lonely.

Jon remained a silent watcher until one day, his assignment called him. He expected her to be mad. Instead, she embarrassingly asked for help.

"I suppose I could have called a locksmith, but considering your training, your breaking and entering skills are probably better anyway."

Jon couldn't help but ask if his surveillance skills were that bad. Olivia spared his ego by letting him know she was pretty good at surveillance herself.

"I hunt monsters. Sometimes they hunt back."

****

Olivia closed the front door to find Alvin still standing by the old mail slot. Olivia kept it for nostalgia purposes despite the renovations. She bent down to assure him she wasn't going away again when she noticed the business card. Someone must have slipped it inside while she was out of town. It was an old-school line of communication, accompanied by a shiny black card. Silver stenciling said *Samael Knight - Collections and Acquisitions.* On the back, written in elegant script was the only form of contact. A handwritten phone number with two words. *Call me.*

Olivia couldn't process what it meant before Jon was back at her door.

"I just got a call from Lieutenant Bartholomew with SAPD."

****

"So, what have we got to work with?" Silas asked Tunney.

It was their end-of-day regroup. Tunney spent his day in the field processing and canvassing. After his trip to the morgue, Silas played organizer for tomorrow's event. The plan was to walk the narrow strip of land between the convenience store where Sherrie Knowles worked and where Ashley was found. Once the sun went down, a candlelight vigil was scheduled in Ashley's honor. Silas hoped with hundreds of volunteers, they would find something. He had one more appearance in front of the camera before the day was through. It was his final plea for volunteers before tomorrow. Since Silas had been out of the action, he hoped Tunney had something worth sharing. It would help in the update he had to give Patrick later. FBI academy students were arriving in the morning to assist with the canvass.

"The girls' room was a treasure trove, like a time capsule of their last day on earth. Their unfinished homework was still sitting on the bedside table, empty soda cans, candy wrappers," Tunney was venting, upset by what he saw. He slid Silas an itemized list from the girls' room.

Silas barely glanced at the list. He was struggling to concentrate. Other than a text to let him know she was home Silas hadn't talked to Livie since she left. He was looking forward to some face-to-face time with her later, but that was still hours away. Silas spent the day counting the minutes until her return. He just needed to find the dead in between.

"Hit the highlights for me. What items do you need to get to the head of the line for the lab?" Silas asked.

"A pile of dirty clothes in the corner might give us a good hit if Dorcas or Ava met up with Ashley. She had pretty long hair from the recent photos her mother provided. Maybe we have a transfer."

"Shoes?" Silas asked.

"Two pairs in the closet, one for each girl, something they might wear to church. Nothing else. No sneakers. I'm sure they were wearing the only other pair they had the day of..." Tunney trailed off. "They may still be in an evidence locker somewhere." With little Ashley on his mind, it was easy to forget the room he was processing belonged to two dead girls. "The bedsheets were dirty as well, so maybe something from there. And we found a necklace under one of the girls' pillows."

"The graves in the pet cemetery contained trinkets. There are a lot of keepsakes floating around," Silas mused. "Make sure we have a photo of the necklace you found in their room. I want Ashley's mom to have a look at it. She said Ashley's was missing, and we didn't find it at the gravesite."

Tunney had gone quiet. Silas followed his gaze to the murder board. Ashley Knowles' school picture had been added to the whiteboard over the column with her specifics. Tunney got out of the chair and moved closer. He pointed to the necklace around Ashley's neck. "That's it. This is the one. I remember it because of the tree."

"What you just said, doesn't leave this room." Silas cautioned. He indicated to the pile of boxes in the corner. They were slowly taking over the conference room. The chief was currently looking for an empty office. "There should be a sketch or something from the last case, indicating whose bed was whose. It should be in Agent Dunn's things," Silas told him. He rubbed his eyes and avoided looking at Tunney.

"Dr. Osborne figured this out already, didn't she?" Tunney knew it.

"I'm sure she has. But even she and I haven't discussed it. Not fully. We have to find the evidence first. Then she will fill in the blanks," Silas assured him.

Tunney nodded the slow realization of what Dr. Osborne carried around in her brain made his head hurt. "Has she always been this way? Known things she shouldn't?"

"As long as she can remember."

Tunney didn't know the agent well, but he could tell Silas wasn't himself. He thought he knew why. "Where is Dr. Osborne? Is she going to be onsite tomorrow?"

Silas shook his head and shoved the list Tunney gave him into the folder he'd been carrying around all day. It was a collection of everything he needed to review later. "I sent her home for the weekend. We're going to see Pittman on Tuesday. I'll need you to hold down the fort here. You up to it?"

"Yes, sir," Tunney assured him. "How is she feeling?"

"She's fine. It was me. I wanted her to have a break. Thank you for asking."

Tunney didn't doubt she was. It was the agent he wondered about.

Chapter Twenty

Barry showed up outside her house before Jon Sharpe left. Being the good hostess Gran taught her to be, Olivia offered them iced tea while she tried not to guzzle her vanilla soda. She had promised herself a power nap, but since sleep wasn't currently an option, she had to combat her fatigue with something. Caffeine and sugar were easy substitutes.

"So, what are you thinking?" Sharpe asked the lieutenant.

Olivia was positive Sharpe had already asked Barry the question, but Agent Sharpe was suspicious, wondering if the lieutenant would change his answer with her in the room. Sharpe's instincts were dead on, but Olivia was sure whatever Barry told him wouldn't be the whole story.

"As I said on the phone, it looks like vandalism, probably neighborhood kids. I wanted to tell Dr. Osborne myself, in person, as a courtesy," Barry explained with a glance toward Olivia, accompanied by a polite smile back to the agent. "I didn't want her to worry."

The last thing Barry expected to find was Jon Sharpe parked in front of her house, but once Barry started down her street, he couldn't bail. Amanda had been the one to tell him Olivia was back in town. He should have texted her first.

"How did you hear the chief was out of town?" Sharpe asked.

"My sergeant, Will Ibarra, is taking your class at the Academy. He told me you gave them the day off because Agent Branch was still in Florida. That's how I knew to call you," Barry clarified.

Only because she knew him did Olivia know Barry was on his way to being annoyed.

Sharpe was satisfied with the story of the break-in. Vandalism made sense. What didn't was Bartholomew's visit. Was the lieutenant going above and beyond considering what happened to his partner, or was there more to it? Like, Dr. Osborne? Sharpe stared at the SAPD officer searching for an answer.

"Vandalism is still SAPD's jurisdiction even on this one," Barry reminded him.

"That may be, but this is Smythe we're talking about. I have to inform the chief." Sharpe's tone was conciliatory but firm. "I've already arranged for surveillance on Dr. Osborne."

Seeing the potential for a testosterone-fueled turn, Olivia interceded, shifting the focus to Silas. She briefly explained what he was dealing with in Florida. "I just wanted you to be aware," Olivia said, looking at Sharpe. She knew the assistant special agent in charge was not what he had hoped for his next career move. Before Silas came along, Jon Sharpe believed the station chief job was his.

"As for SAPD, they did their job informing the FBI. I see no reason why Silas has to hear any of this right now. Agent Sharpe, you have it covered. I feel safe." Olivia flashed him a smile. Appealing to his ego would get her what she wanted. It had worked before when she needed inside her house. Today it was to get him out of her house so she could learn what really had Barry spooked.

"SAPD has someone sitting on Smythe's house for the next few nights just to make sure we don't have a repeat performance. If something happens, you will be the first to know," Barry assured the agent.

Given the plan of action, Sharpe had no valid argument. Other than his gut. He should file the visit away as none of his business. Silas could handle the lieutenant if it was more than that.

"I've got to give it to you Lieutenant Bartholomew, I thought you sounded convincing," Olivia said as she watched through the window. Barry looked like he was on his way to a smile until she showed him the text Sharpe sent her before he pulled away from her house.

—Call me if you need me.—

"Sweet. It was the smile that did it." The comment earned Barry an eye roll. "He was being a prick. I didn't like his tone."

"And I thought it was just Silas you didn't like. Or is it all FBI agents?" The caffeine had worked its magic, but the increased energy was quickly giving way to hunger. "Agent Sharpe was only protecting me. I would like to think you would do the same."

"Of course, *I* would." The answer was automatic. Barry finally looked at her, allowing himself to really see her now that they were alone. The glow she radiated the other day at the hospital was gone. Olivia looked tired. It must be the case in Florida.

Without asking, Olivia went to the kitchen to refill their drinks. She also dug out a package of cookies left over from the plane. When the flight attendant came by with extra, she didn't hesitate. Olivia offered to share, but Barry passed. She was just being polite. Nothing about her said she wanted to share.

"Now that we're alone, do you want to tell me what's really going on?"

"I don't think it was neighborhood kids," he began.

"Good. That makes two of us. So, why are you here?"

"It was Smythe."

Olivia's breath caught in her throat as she wrapped an arm protectively around her waist.

"I know it, just like you know things," Barry told her.

"You have evidence of that?"

"No. Not exactly."

Olivia took a deep breath, managing not to let go of the scream clawing its way up her throat, looking for an escape. "Then get some. I can't do this. I can't be hiding from every shadow in the corner. I'm trying to make a life here. It's not just me." She squeezed herself tighter.

"Believe me, I'm aware," Barry heard himself snap. Being back in this house reminded him all over again that someone else was sharing it with her. "I need you to hear me out. I'm only trying to look out for you."

"And you don't think I can do that?"

"I have no doubt what you can do. I've seen you in action. I was there, remember?" His words were gentle this time.

Mention of the barn shut her down. Olivia took a sip of her soda and untangled herself. Barry wondered if she was talking about something other than Jamie.

There was a demon to consider, but that wasn't his purview.

"Tell me why. What's the precipitating factor? What changed? What would drive him home now?" Olivia wanted to know what he was thinking.

Barry started with the house first. "I think he was after cash."

"What's he been doing before now?"

"I wouldn't have known if you hadn't asked me to take a look at the neighborhood around the state hospital."

Olivia's eyes narrowed, not seeing the connection. "What does that have to do with Jamie?"

"You were right about a spike in reports of stolen property. All within blocks of the hospital. The locations correspond with where we've received the most sightings since his escape. Pawning here and there got him by. I wondered who would be crazy enough to break into a mental hospital. Smythe is. He's the most wanted man in the city. Hiding there was perfect cover. And you can't deny to me, of all people, what I know you felt inside that room. I felt it, too. He was there." Barry saw the wave of realization wash over her.

"Then he got locked out," Olivia said. "He lost access to food and shelter." She had predicted the why, just not the who. Barry's summation made sense.

"You always said he was clever. He didn't even choose his own victims." Smythe was a stranger killer, one of the most challenging offenders to catch because there was nothing to link the victim and perpetrator.

"They chose him," Olivia repeated the words from her original profile. It's how Smythe earned the name the *Good Samaritan Killer*. He killed those who helped him.

Raised by spinster aunts who believed children should be seen and not heard, Jamie learned to avoid detection by retreating into role play. Only then was he the one in control. Parks were his escape before they became his hunting grounds. Free to roam, Jamie could create any fantasy world he wanted. He knew how to blend in, playing the role of a cyclist complete with the upscale bike he couldn't afford, and his special shoes. Shaving his body completed the image of a bike enthusiast and minimized forensic evidence. His small size and quiet demeanor made him appear non-threatening, but he compensated for it with a blitz-krige attack to overpower his victims. Except for the dead bodies he left behind, Jamie was a ghost. Without interference from the FBI, he could have kept killing for a very long time.

"I followed up with the homeowners who reported sightings or made calls about a homeless man sleeping on their property," Barry explained. "He was clever enough to change his appearance. His hair is growing, yet their descriptions match Smythe, right down to the scar on his head no amount of hair can cover up."

It was a testament to the accident Smythe suffered as a child. The injury left him prone to seizures and prevented him from obtaining a driver's license. A bike was his only means of transportation. It transitioned seamlessly into his dreamscape, just like the scar. Shaving his head was in style and didn't call so much attention to the mark that changed his life.

As an adult, Jamie had worked as a nurse's aide. "Hiding out in the hospital must have felt like coming home," Olivia concluded. It was how he was able to walk so calmly out of University Hospital, wearing a pair of stolen scrubs, easily accessible to someone who knew where to look.

Olivia caught Barry staring down at the phone in his hand. He didn't look happy.

"Problem?"

"No," Barry said and returned it to where it lived on his hip. "Not important."

"How would Jamie get home? Would he risk a trip on a VIA bus? I also don't see him calling for a ride."

"A bike was stolen a week or so ago. The biggest ticket item yet." Barry reached for his phone again.

"Dammit." Barry dismissed the message. It never made it back to his hip before it buzzed with a call. This one, he answered. "No. I'm not returning to the office," he said with a glance at Olivia. "Go home, Norma and have a good weekend." Barry put the phone away and turned back to Olivia.

"Do you want to tell me what that's about?" Olivia guessed it was Amanda, but his girlfriend wasn't any of her business.

"No. Do you want to tell me what you're going to tell Silas?" Barry countered.

"I won't go to him without evidence. The FBI kind. I cannot live my life on lock-down. You know that better than anyone."

"I don't have evidence, not yet," Barry reminded her. "I don't know if you've read your emails, but Vines confirmed there are no cameras in that area of the facility. They've been ordered, but that doesn't help us. I bagged the stuff we found in the room. It goes to forensics tomorrow when Frank Tobias gets back. I already filled him in on what I'm looking for. That's it.

That's all I've got."

"Then, for now, there's nothing to tell Silas except there was a break-in." Olivia reached for her glass only to find it empty. The package of cookies was only crumbs. She stirred and looked outside. It was still light out, but her stomach told her it was time for dinner.

"Hungry?" Barry asked.

"Starving." She craved something deep-fried and bad for her.

"Want to get out of here and go grab something to eat?" Before she could answer, Barry remembered something he had forgotten. He reached for his phone again and scrolled until he found what he was looking for.

"*Tater tots, corn dogs and a large vanilla soda*," Barry said, reading from his phone.

"I was thinking of something we couldn't get at a drive-thru, but those are some of my favorites," Olivia mused.

The look on his face sapped her smile. Barry slid her the phone so she could see. "That's the fast-food receipt from that dingy little room at the hospital. Apparently, those aren't just your favorites."

Olivia pushed the phone back his way. Even without the demon inside of him, Jamie was still obsessed with her. Just like coming home, it was something Smythe couldn't leave alone.

She wondered if it was a lingering effect. "It's not evidence, not the kind ordinary people look for."

"So, does that mean you're not telling Silas?" Barry had to know. He couldn't leave her life to chance.

"Not now. Not with him this far away." It was her way of protecting the man she loved, and the father of her children. After she saved Barry's life, Silas asked her where he fit in her life. That was when she told him she loved him, and she wanted to be with him. But she also needed Barry for the role he was meant to play. Now was his time, because she wasn't the only one he was protecting.

"Until Silas gets back, it's all on you."

Chapter Twenty-One

Silas watched from behind the cover of sunglasses. The search and recovery teams were underway, and the turnout was more than he hoped for. So far, they had a generous supply of volunteers scouring the path he'd mapped out with local law enforcement. Silas elected to stay behind at the sign-in tent and provide oversite while administrative staff from the Ocala police department entered data from the volunteer sign-in sheets. Today's participants would be compared to those who walked the area with the local sheriff's department almost two years ago after the first two girls went missing. It wasn't uncommon for a perpetrator to insert themselves into an investigation or return to the scene of the crime. Silas felt they were merely going through the motions, but it was a box that needed checking.

"I heard Dr. Osborne has a meeting scheduled with Pittman." It was DA Hobbs. Silas noticed the only walking he did was to the nearest camera. The scuttlebutt around town was the DA planned on running for a seat in the Florida statehouse. The news of this case had spread across the state and was slowly gaining nationwide attention. Pinning more murders on Pittman would win votes.

"I'm gonna want a full report. Unlike what I received yesterday. Imagine my surprise when I found out your guys were at the McCleary house."

Silas didn't even lift his shades. "Dr. Osborne does not report to you. Nor do I."

"I can and will call the BAU, Agent Branch," Hobbs threatened.

Silas smiled. "If someone isn't complaining, I'm not doing my job."

"I want answers. The good voters of Marion County want resolution."

"Save it for the campaign trail, Counselor," Silas cut him off. He had neither the time nor the patience for a stump speech.

"I want to know what you were looking for at the McCleary house."

"I told you, this is a new and independent investigation. The last time anyone saw Ashley Knowles alive, her plans were to spend the night with Ava McCleary. We're looking for forensic answers," Silas assured him.

The look on Hobbs' face said he thought it was a waste of time. He was so determined all roads led to Pittman that he was willing to bypass every other one.

"I want to know what Pittman says to Dr. Osborne," Hobbs said, sounding just like Singer without the barbs of Roche.

The confessed killer was well within his rights to refuse the DA's request for a visit. Without something worthy of a warrant, the killer didn't have to talk to Hobbs. "Since evidence will get you your own audience with Pittman, why don't you make yourself useful and track down Terry McCleary?" The school teacher who had an eye for Tunney had passed on information that said Melanie McCleary moved to Gainesville, but Terry dropped off the grid. As Ava's dad and Pittman's cousin, he could have something interesting to say. "He's a missing piece of this puzzle. It would free up some of my resources with your assistance. With a little quid pro quo, maybe Dr. Osborne will be more inclined to speak with you."

Hobbs walked away without comment, just as Silas' phone buzzed with a text from home.

—I must be pregnant. I just threw up. Remind me never to drink orange juice again.—

****

Pregnancy throw-up wasn't as bad as stomach-flu throw-up. Olivia immediately felt better, like it had never happened. She brushed her teeth and went on about her business. Olivia gathered the dogs and took them for a mid-morning walk, but it wasn't the same without Silas. She missed the small, mundane things she never thought about when she lived alone. They were spoiled. Since deciding to be together, they had spent little time apart. It had been a whirlwind romance culminating in marriage three months later. Once they started, they never looked back. The face-time last night helped, but it wasn't the same.

The fresh air was good for her psyche. It kept her mind from wandering back to Florida or to Jamie. She needed to stay on track. She had been struggling to concentrate even before Barry dropped his bombshell. Maybe it was the increased blood flow to her uterus.

Olivia revisited her plans for the day. Shower, nap, and a quick trip to the grocery store for comfort food. Considering key lime pie was currently at the top of her wish list, she should probably start at the store. She also needed to pick up a bottle of wine for Amanda's party.

Olivia was almost home when she felt a sudden pull from Alvin. Lily was standing on the curb, waiting for them. The nubby-tailed schnauzer headed straight for her, sniffing her hand, looking for the treat she usually slipped him. Her hand was empty, but he licked anyway. He might be demanding, but at least he was polite.

"I had no idea you were back already."

"I'm sorry, Lily, I should have checked in with you. I'm just home for the weekend," Olivia explained. Barry's news last night had imploded her whole evening.

"It's not necessary, really." Lily shifted from one foot to the other, her body language in direct conflict with her words. "I've been thinking a lot about what you said. I was wondering why you asked Ross what he heard first, the moaning or the alarm."

"Just curious. I was trying to establish a timeline, his state of consciousness," Olivia answered carefully.

"Like me accusing him of seeing his own reflection in the mirror?" Lily tried to laugh but failed.

"Something like that."

"The alarm company came out yesterday and gave us a clean bill of health. I read somewhere electrical disturbances can signal the presence of ghosts. Can you check out the house and give me an impression of what you think is going on?"

Olivia's hesitance must have shown through to her face.

Lily dismissed the thought with a wave. "Obviously, not right now, but maybe later?"

"I will, I promise," Olivia assured her.

"I know you're busy. Ross is gone this weekend

and I'm," Lily's eyes wandered to her upstairs windows. "On edge."

Olivia nodded. "I completely understand. Today's just—"

"You don't have to explain."

"You're safe, Lily," Olivia assured her. The middle of the street wasn't the place for a discussion on hauntings, especially those associated with her family's questionable past. "Stay off the internet. Electric disturbances are also common in old houses undergoing renovations."

"That's what the alarm guy said." Lily finally let go of her hands. The fear was gone, replaced by something that looked like loneliness.

"Let's get together tomorrow," Olivia promised.

****

A local restaurant provided tents and food. Donations were accepted and pledged toward the cost of Ashley Knowles' funeral expenses. After refueling, Silas headed back to Ocala police headquarters. He had a meeting with Brittany Hoffman's mother and Kelsey Rowe's parents. Silas had discouraged them from attending the day's walk. He didn't want them there just in case something was found. Sherrie Knowles was also waiting.

One by one, he took the other parents into a room and showed them photos. As expected, the items belonged to their missing daughters. The only comfort Silas could offer them was that they would eventually get their personal items back. This part of his job sucked.

"What does it mean, you finding Ash's necklace at the McCleary house?" Sherrie asked.

Silas had saved her for last because he had anticipated the question. If he could have spared telling her where they found the necklace, he would have, but he needed her insight. "I'm not sure yet, but let me and Dr. Osborne worry about that. You take care of yourself."

"Ash wouldn't have given up the necklace. You know it and I know it." It was Sherrie's sister, Tina. "It's those girls. They're responsible for all of this."

"You don't know that," Sherrie told her. "Ava was a sweet girl." Tina responded by stomping out of the room. "You'll have to excuse her. With Mom and everything, she's on edge."

Silas wondered how much one woman could endure. The loss of a child. The loss of a parent. Yet, Sherrie Knowles was stoic, almost without emotion. Maybe she had already spent all of hers.

"When can I get it back? The necklace?" Sherrie asked.

"It'll be a while, but I promise, I will see that you get it," Silas assured her. "I want Dr. Osborne to take a look. She'll want to talk to you again."

Sherrie nodded. "She's a nice lady. She's the only one who didn't make me feel guilty for not knowing where my girl was every minute of the day. I did the best I could, you know."

"I think that's all any of us can do."

As Silas led her out, he found Hobbs and the other families gathered in the conference room, with Tina leading the charge. "It's that family, those girls. They are at the root of all of this."

Hobbs stood at the front of the room, calmly listening to their concerns before assuring them they would all have their say. The Marion DA's office would get to the bottom of it. The consensus of the room was it had to be someone the girls knew. Someone close to them. Someone they trusted. It was a small place. They spent their whole lives here, all except Dorcas.

"Agent Branch, do you have anything to add on behalf of the FBI—some assurance to these good people that there will be justice for their little girls?" Hobbs asked.

Hobbs appeared to extend the olive branch, but he would snatch it back just as quickly and blame the FBI if things didn't go well, or they didn't find a solution to his liking. Silas didn't have time for this man's needs. His focus was on the families, not votes.

"As I discussed with the DA, this is a new and independent investigation. We at the BAU will leave no stone unturned. We want what you want—to bring your daughters home."

"They could be right," Hobbs said after the last of them filed out the door. The attorney seemed more subdued than earlier in the day. "My office found Terry McCleary. Unfortunately, he won't be speaking to anyone. He's dead."

****

When Silas returned to the search area, Tunney was waiting for him. "What's going on?" Silas asked, seeing they were heading toward the crocodile pond.

"A group of yahoos were throwing their leftovers into the water and a croc lunged up the bank. One guy slid down, but luckily his buddies were there to catch him. Otherwise, he would have been lunch."

"Stupid," Silas muttered under his breath.

"You think? The croc Dr. Osborne and I saw the other day was at least a fifteen-footer. I'm sure it was the same one, even though the guy claims it was bigger. I'm sure it looked that way up close. They are big and they are faster than people think. Are we sure the crocs aren't responsible for the other two girls?" Tunney asked. So far, their grid search had turned up nothing.

"Not unless the crocs have a penchant for keepsakes. The trinkets found in the pet cemetery belonged to Brittany Hoffman and Kelsey Rowe. Their families made a positive ID. Both girls were wearing them at the time they went missing. The necklace you found yesterday was definitely Ashley's. Did you find out whose pillow it was under?"

Tunney looked at him. He was struggling to keep up. They were power walking down the dirt road where a crowd was still gathered. "I studied Dunn's notes last night. It was Ava's bed."

Silas headed toward the truck bearing the Fish and Wildlife insignia, but a couple intercepted Tunney and him before they could get there.

"Are you the agent in charge?" The woman had fiery red hair and wore a camera around her neck. A guy with a man bun hovered at her side, willing to let her take the lead.

"I am," Silas said. "How can I help you?"

"I'm Valerie Toshi. I'm the one whose dog was eaten here a couple of years ago."

Silas remembered hearing the story. It was what led to the Halloween tale.

"Those crocs in that pond act like they are used to being fed. I think someone treated them like pets. My Rosie didn't get close, but that croc just jumped up and took her. Just like it came for those guys earlier."

Silas turned to Tunney. He was the wildlife expert.

Tunney shrugged. "It's possible."

Silas turned back to the couple. The owner of the man bun took a tentative step forward.

"My name is Jonas Cole. I wrote *The Monster of Eden*. I think that croc over there is why you can't find those other two girls. He ate them or they were offered as some kind of sacrifice. Either way, the croc got them."

Tunney had to walk away before the look on his face got him in trouble. SSA Branch was on his own. The agent was adaptable, whether it was the crazies or the argumentative attorney. Silas Branch might be a pain in the ass to his fellow agents, but he had the patience of a saint with civilians, and he was popular with the public. He had already garnered more TV time than the local DA. He could also be the reason for the number of female volunteers who showed up on a hot and muggy Saturday morning. Tunney saw how they looked at him. To his credit, Agent Branch ignored every one of them. He was also wearing his wedding ring. It came on when Dr. Osborne left.

"The guy posed an interesting theory," Silas confessed once the couple was out of earshot. "The writer said the story goes someone from a traveling carnival brought the crocs here back in the thirties. Makes sense, they're not usually native to here, are they?"

"It's not typical but given the Florida coastlines it could happen—in theory. But to be here, this far inland, someone would have to bring it," Tunney conceded. He recalled what the trooper, Bauman said about migration, but transportation seemed much more reasonable.

"I never read the monster article. I left that to Dunn," Silas said. "Have you run across any notes about that?"

"Agent Dunn thought it was full of shit." Tunney told him.

"Maybe. Maybe not," Silas said, thinking it was something Olivia might want to know. "Why don't you read it for yourself. Consider it homework," Silas suggested as he approached the Fish and Wildlife guys. Silas watched them hammer danger signs and stakes with plastic, orange netting on the side of the pond closest to the road. It made Silas think of something he would find at a construction site meant to keep people out. "Makes me wonder why these weren't up already," he commented.

"Exercise in futility. They never stay up." From the weathered face, Silas pegged him as the veteran of the two. The patch on his shirt identified him as Dale. The other guy, the younger one, was posting another 'no swimming' sign closer to the road.

"Why do you think that is?" Silas asked.

"The people back in here like to keep to themselves. It's always been that way, even after the old timers died off and the younger ones moved in."

"How long have these crocs been here?" Silas asked.

"They're a legend. I've been hearing about them or their ancestors my whole life and I'm pushing fifty."

"So, there is more than one?" Tunney asked.

"Sure. There's at least a thirteen-footer, probably the female. But there's another one in there. I've only seen its snout, but from the looks of it, he's much larger."

"How big do they get?" Silas asked. He was watching the water but couldn't make out anything. It was too murky, dangerously deceptive of what lurked just below the surface.

"They can grow up to twenty-three, twenty-five feet, but not typically this far north," Dale said.

"How do you think they got here?" Tunney asked.

"I'd say someone brought them. Lots of stories about the people who used to live up here. Carnie types that stayed here during the winter."

Chapter Twenty-Two

Barry felt like an imposter, with Amanda's family and her work colleagues. It was worse with his own coworkers. Barry wondered what they were even doing there. He didn't invite them. What was he missing?

As for Amanda, they had hardly spoken. She was icy. He had brushed her off again last night. They hadn't seen each other since the night they picked up the dogs. Why would she have been driving by Olivia's house?

Maybe he should face the facts. The ones he had ignored. Dr. Amanda Greene had a thing for cops. She set her sights on him the day they met. Barry debated if he should share his growing suspicions with someone else. More importantly, what would he tell someone if they came to him with this story?

Get out while you still can.

Barry found himself some whiskey and slipped away into a corner. He had ignored all the signs of an obsessive woman because he had been so desperate to forget Olivia. What had it gotten him? He was still walking a tightrope with his feelings for her. Worse than that, had he unknowingly placed Olivia in danger?

Across the room, he saw Olivia with Will and Jessica. She looked better than yesterday. The glow from earlier in the week was back. She looked relaxed even though he knew the intimate social gathering was trespassing on her psyche. Was that his role in her life—to watch? At least that's what the whispers of a dead woman told him. According to Ana Lutz, in ancient times, when angels and humans roamed the world together, the term *Watcher* was synonymous with sentry or protector. It was ironic that was the role he adopted the moment they met.

In a flash, Barry was back to their first visit to Wendy Florren's house—his hand darting in front of Olivia, shielding her as they entered the backyard. Even with no danger in sight, he felt something—the need to protect her. Was it just cop instinct or the residual left behind by the demon?

Barry put down his drink. He should probably talk to someone about the thoughts floating around inside his head. Barry envisioned someone with robes. Father Dominic might be a good start.

****

Eventually, Barry saw her alone and followed Olivia outside to the porch. It overlooked the backyard, away from the party. Olivia stood with her back to the door, gazing into the dark, staring at something only she could see.

"You shouldn't have followed me," Olivia said softly. "If you don't know it yet, you're in trouble with Amanda."

Despite her warning, Barry moved closer, joining her at the railing. It wasn't a conscious decision but instinct. "What? Did she say something"

"She hasn't spoken to me, but her thoughts are screaming at me from across the room."

Barry heaved a sigh of relief. "I needed to know that you are alright."

Olivia stared at him as if assessing what he was saying. When she was satisfied, she turned back to the yard. A mist was starting to form. Olivia heard a low rumble of thunder in the background. "I was thinking of another party. One I should have attended but didn't. Mark's housewarming."

Barry's breath slowed at the mention of their friend. They hadn't talked about Mark. Silas had been the one to tell her he was dead. Barry also left Silas to deliver the news that it was Madeline, Mark's sister, who tried to kill Daisy. Barry couldn't bring himself to have either of those conversations.

"Mark was so proud of the deck he and a friend had built in the back."

Barry swallowed hard at the memory.

"You were the friend, weren't you?"

The party was six months before they met. If she had only been there. Barry told himself not to think of what that could have meant. Maybe everything, maybe nothing at all.

"Was Mark seeing anyone?" Olivia asked, her gaze wandering back across the empty yard.

Mark had his own feelings for Olivia. It was those old feelings that drove a stake between the two friends as soon as Barry met her. He and Mark weren't as close the last week of his life as they had been, but Barry did know something most didn't. "He had a couple of dates with Katie in his last days. She was pretty sweet on him." Maybe Mark could have turned a corner.

"Katie, the crime scene tech?" Olivia remembered her from Wendy Florren's house. She volunteered for the Travis Ames crime scene as well.

"She had a baby a few months back." It was a

reminder of how much time had passed.

"A boy, right?"

Barry said nothing. He had said too much already.

"You need to let go," Olivia said softly.

Barry opened his mouth to say something and then stopped himself. She didn't need to hear any of it. She already knew.

"We are all where we are supposed to be. All except you," Olivia said and slipped quietly into the night, followed by the rain.

****

"So, did you talk to her?" Amanda asked.

It was just the two of them in the kitchen.

Barry ignored her and concentrated on pouring himself a drink. The conversation with Olivia pushed him to replace the one he had discarded earlier.

"Don't pretend you don't hear me or you don't know who I'm talking about." Amanda moved closer, the smell of alcohol coming with her. She had started drinking long before the party.

Barry wasn't sure if she wanted an answer or attention. He kept his eyes on the glass, letting her lead the way.

"I saw you," Amanda said, making it sound like an accusation.

Barry sighed before speaking. Wondering who else was left in the house. The last downpour chased everyone away but family who'd stayed behind to help clean up. It was the first time they'd been alone all night.

"You invited her. She's your friend. She saved my life," Barry concentrated on remaining passive. "Was I not supposed to talk to her?"

"No," Amanda snapped. "I'm talking about last night." This wasn't an accusation. It was the truth.

Anger, like alcohol, had a way of igniting the tongue. Barry struggled to hold both. He had to be careful what bridges he burned. "You followed me?"

Despite her alcohol consumption, Amanda was calculating. She lifted her chin in defiance. "Some people wanted to go out after work. I picked the place."

Barry almost reminded Amanda she didn't work yesterday, but he let her talk, curious where this was going.

"I know your haunts. I saw the two of you having dinner. If it makes you feel any better, I called her too, because I knew she was home alone, but I guess she wasn't. Home or alone."

"I told you I was working a case."

"With her?"

Outside Barry heard a clap of thunder and the sound of approaching footsteps. Barry lowered his voice, hoping Amanda would do the same. "Let's not do this. Not now."

Amanda crumbled under the edge of his tone. She wasn't so far gone she couldn't see the end was near. "I just want to know. Why am I not enough?"

Amanda was in tears by the time her sister-in-law Yesenia walked in "Javier's in the garage. I've got this," Yesenia whispered, giving Barry the out he needed.

Family played a pivotal role in Amanda's life. When her husband, Eric, a former cop, committed suicide, Amanda took a sabbatical from helping others and moved back home. She said reuniting with her parents and four brothers reminded her of the importance of family. Buying a house was one step closer to planning for the future. If he had paid better attention, Barry would have seen his part in the new life Amanda wanted.

On autopilot, Barry retreated to the garage and out of the way. Javier was there as promised. He worked patrol on the west side of the city. There was a police scanner on low in the background.

"When my sister gets something in her head there's no stopping her, you know that, right?" Javier said, with a tip of his own glass of whiskey. Barry was still sitting in the kitchen somewhere. He had never taken a sip. Amanda was drinking enough for both of them. Both of them drunk wasn't a good combination.

"I'm starting to get that," Barry said. He liked Javie and Javie, like the rest of Amanda's family, liked him. Even more than the house.

"She's a lot sometimes."

Was it so obvious things were falling apart between them that her big brother felt the need to step in? Luckily, Javie seemed to run out of words.

"I care about what happens to Amanda," Barry assured him.

Javie smiled and toasted Barry again. "Then I trust you'll do the right thing when the time comes."

Barry raised an imaginary glass, not sure Javie would be toasting him if he knew how he really felt. Luckily, Javie looked down for the count. Barry found himself listening to reports of traffic accidents and random electrical outages. He was looking for a connection to somewhere other than here when Javie pulled him back.

"Just so you know, that whole business with Eric is

finally over. She was cleared."

Barry didn't have time to process the comment before the police scanner interrupted again. This time with a report of shots fired.

Barry was out the door without so much as a goodbye.

****

Two SAPD cruisers and an ambulance were on the scene by the time he arrived. He could see Olivia in the back of the ambulance. A flash of his badge got Barry to the head of the line. "What's going on?"

The nearest officer nodded toward the ambulance. "The home owner said she heard something. She got up to investigate and claims she saw something in the bathroom. From there she proceeded to shoot up the place."

"Is she hurt?"

The officer shook his head. "She stepped on some glass, cut her feet up in a couple of places. Nothing that can't be fixed on scene. They're stitching her up now. Her neighbor is with her. She says she can take her in for the night. Oh, yea, and the FBI is here."

Barry felt him before he saw him. He turned around to find Agent Jon Sharpe.

"Lieutenant," the agent nodded. Barry nodded back.

"Were you in the neighborhood?" Sharpe asked.

"I was. Were you?"

"We keep an eye on our own."

Barry looked next door and saw two government-issued cars parked in front of Olivia's house.

"There's someone securing her house now, if that's what you're wondering," Sharpe said. Whatever suspicions he had about the lieutenant were confirmed by his presence.

"If he's securing the house, then what are you doing?"

"Waiting on Dr. Osborne. She asked me to walk Ms. Forester's house with her," Sharpe said, nodding toward the one looming over them.

"SAPD can do that," Barry told him. He knew he sounded argumentative, but he didn't want this man here. It would be just fine with him if he left now. He would see that Olivia got home safely.

"They already have. Dr. Osborne wants a look for herself."

They both looked up to see Olivia emerge from the back of the ambulance. She saw them but quickly turned the opposite way, towards the front of the vehicle. By the time they got to her, she was on the ground in front of the bumper. Her head was between her knees, her mouth open, sucking in gulps of air. Jon Sharpe rushed to get an ambulance attendant as Barry knelt down next to her.

"You should move, I may throw up on you." Olivia closed her eyes and concentrated.

Sharpe returned with an EMT in tow who came armed with a bottle of water, and a blood pressure cuff. The emergency technician knelt on the other side of her.

Olivia took the water but waved away the cuff and the stethoscope the EMT had untangled from his neck.

"You looked a little pale in there," the tech said. "Don't you think you should at least let me take your blood pressure or something, just to see what's going on?"

"I know what's going on," Olivia insisted. She sat up and leaned back against the bumper. The feeling of cool metal helped clear her head.

"Then do you mind sharing that with me? Because you look a little sick." The EMT smiled. He was doing his best with a potential patient who didn't think she needed him. He wanted to be accommodating, but he absolutely did not need this FBI doctor, sick or not, to keel over on his shift. An incident like that would require too much paperwork. Not to mention, he didn't like the looks of the two men hovering over her. They were both armed and looked like they could be real pains in the ass.

"I'm not sick," Olivia insisted. Her nausea was gone and now all she felt was embarrassment. Since when did she get sick at the sight of blood? "I'm pregnant. Give me a minute and I'll be fine, or I'll throw up on your shoes. It could go either way. This is all kind of new to me so I'm still not sure." Olivia pushed herself to a standing position. She felt a head rush come on and leaned against the ambulance to compensate.

The technician smiled for real this time. "Okay," he said, rising with her. "That explains it." He gave her another once over. "Pregnancy, especially in the early stages, will do that to you. If you're fine with it, then so am I." He looked back at the two men flanking him. "You heard that right, officers?" With nods from everyone, the EMT made a hasty exit. He would gladly take the crazy lady in the ambulance over this one.

Olivia finally looked up at Barry and Jon. Both were staring back at her. "Don't worry. I'm not having a baby tonight." She took a big gulp of water and screwed the cap back on. She looked at Jon. "You ready to walk the house now?"

"Absolutely," Sharpe said, trying not to grin.

"I'll wait here," Barry said, looking like he wanted to throw up.

"Of course, you will," Olivia said. "Here, hold my water."

Chapter Twenty-Three

The SAPD officer spied the gun in Agent Sharpe's hand. "The scene is secure, sir. No signs of forced entry," the young patrolman assured him as they approached the house.

"Thank you, officer," Sharpe said but didn't holster his weapon as he followed Olivia up the stairs and inside the dark house.

"We don't need the gun," Olivia told him once they were alone. "You can't shoot what I'm looking for."

Sharpe started to ask something but stopped himself. Having never worked with her, he suffered a momentary lapse. Resigned to his fate, Sharpe slid the gun back into its holster. He probably didn't want to know what she was looking for.

Olivia tried the switch on the wall with no luck. Lily said the power went out just as she got to the master bath.

Sharpe snapped on his flashlight. "The front porch light is still on. Must be a breaker."

"It's a haunting. Maybe a poltergeist," Olivia explained. The lack of light added to the ambiance.

It unnerved Sharpe how casually she threw out the words like a haunting and a poltergeist were everyday occurrences.

"Take the hallway to your right. It will lead you to

the laundry room. The breaker box should be in there." Olivia gave directions as if she'd been there before. She had never seen the breaker box, but Sharpe didn't need to know that. She wondered if the familiarity was familial. Alone, she moved to the center of the room and closed her eyes.

Sharpe hesitated. "You okay in the dark?" He sounded unsure.

"I got this," Olivia assured him.

As his footsteps faded, Olivia took a deep breath and let the house seep into her senses.

No matter how many times the house changed hands, this room had always been the center. It stood witness to marriage proposals and birth announcements. Life and death flowed through here and spanned generations. There was laughter and tears, dancing and sitting, standing guard and waiting for the dark to pass. Her relatives watched over their dead in this room. Olivia caught a brief glimpse into the past as black shrouds covered the mirrors. It kept the Travelers away. This might have started with a lost one, but she felt the tug of something else.

"Think I got it," Sharpe called from the other room. He sounded relieved. Light chasing away the dark was one of man's greatest accomplishments. Controlling his environment fed his need for safety.

Olivia tuned him out and waded through what was waiting for her. *She wondered if Lily knew her daughter was thinking about getting married or that Ross was...* The light snapped on, severing her connection.

"The ones marked master bedroom and bathroom were off, too. They should be working now," Sharpe told her.

With a cleansing breath, Olivia followed him up the stairs.

Inside the master bedroom, only one of the bedside table lamps was on. The bathroom was still bathed in blackness. Sharpe tried the switch, but there was no light. "This doesn't make any damn sense."

"If you're looking for logic, you've come to the wrong place," Olivia said gently. "Go back downstairs and check again. Turn the breaker off and back on. Think positive thoughts, like how you know what you're doing is going to work. Just for good measure." She smiled up at him.

Sharpe looked like he wanted to ask a question or argue with her, probably about leaving her alone, but he gave up and offered her the flashlight instead.

"No thanks, I'm good," Olivia told him.

Sharpe looked into the darkened room and nodded. "Watch the glass," he cautioned, casting a splash of light across the floor. "You don't want to slip and fall."

Olivia waited until he was gone before entering. It was decidedly colder in the bathroom. She avoided looking at the mirror for the same reason she refused the flashlight. She didn't want it bouncing off the mirror and awaking whatever was lurking there. A flicker of light was a beacon to the malingering spirits lining up behind the glass, waiting for her to notice them. Her connection with the house alerted the lingering ones of her presence. Their energy was pinging on the edge of her periphery. Olivia felt the gathering but was reluctant to open herself wide enough to know how many were attached to this house. Their energy barely registered as a mere hum in the background. They wanted an audience that she refused to give. Passing through the rooms, she sensed at least three already. Their deaths were old, but one of them was still screaming. It was muffled and full of gurgles, but still a scream. That was the only one that interested her.

The floor in the bathroom was tile. The glass from the shower was scattered beneath her feet. The shower walls were gone, no match for the high-velocity shots Lily fired. The pieces of lead shattered the glass into a million jagged pieces. In the ambulance, Lily was unable to articulate what she saw. Olivia knew it had nothing to do with the drugs coursing through her veins. What Lily experienced was inanimate, without form, but it filled her with fear. Menacing was the exact word she used. Olivia resisted the temptation to feel the same thing even though it beckoned her.

Her nostrils flared while a faint prickle formed in the back of her throat. A viscous woodsy scent filled the air, similar to sandalwood or amber. Slowly her hand moved to the cross at her neck. The smell evaporated, leaving a lingering fragment in its retreat, allowing Olivia to focus her sights on the open shower. The ambient light from the bedroom had reached its limit, but she had excellent night vision. There was a small window in the bathroom. Outside wispy clouds obscured the full moon. Something passed across it once, then twice, swinging like a pendulum. There was once a tree outside the same height as the window before someone chopped it down. Whatever she was seeing belonged in the missing tree.

As her vision of the past faded, something slithered across into her space, invading her senses. Olivia spotted a dark mass huddled in the corner of the shower. It lurked just on the periphery of this side of here. She could *feel* the darkness, soft like a blanket.

There was another tug from the other side, this one more powerful than the one downstairs. Once, the other side had the power to pull her where it wanted her to go, but no more. Those days were gone. The power of the darkness was just an illusion. She was the one in charge. She always had been. The energy was hers to command. She just hadn't known it—not until the night in the barn. Maybe it was her consolation prize for feeding a bad man to a demon.

Olivia could travel to that shadowy place with the purple and gray sky all on her own. It was dry, acidic, and smelled of the past. The thing in the corner shouldn't be able to get here from there, but someone had opened a door. *It* couldn't enter without invitation, or maybe it had been lingering much like the specters in the mirrors waiting for just the right time. Removal of the St. Benedict medals freed the blessing, and now this thing was free to roam. Its origin was familiar but not its essence.

Her senses quickly caught up with her. This was demonic in nature, but not *Alleracsap*. He no longer required a vessel to speak to her. Olivia had paid her family debt. *Alleracsap* released Jamie from his possession as a token to her. Now she and the demon communicated as equals. He no longer lingered just in her dreams.

Olivia's fingers traveled back to her neck, clasping the cross. "This place is not for you. You are not welcome here," she commanded to the darkness.

The air in the room responded, producing a swirl of hot breeze at her feet. It shouldn't be sharing space with the cold. *Alleracsap*? Her thoughts searched for him, thinking his name. The power of her voice wasn't necessary. Not anymore. Their connection was that strong.

Olivia's skin prickled and her breathing accelerated. The smell of amber ignited the room like liquid fire. The mass stirred and started to take form. The room flooded with the pungent smell of sulphur. It clogged her nostrils and produced an involuntary cough she feared would morph into a gag. *Alleracsap*!

"She is mine!" The words came from behind her in a hiss loud enough to fill her ears. A blanket of warmth encased her shoulders.

A low growl of protest emanated from the huddled mass. It did not retreat. In response, Olivia clutched her cross, thrusting it forward as far as the chain would allow. Thoughts transformed into commands. Under her breath, she mumbled the prayers of St. Benedict in Latin, the words flowing off her tongue with ease.

"Crux sacra sit mihi lux! Vade retro Satana! Nunquam suade mihi vana! Sunt mala quae libas." *May the holy cross be my light. Begone Satan! Never tempt me with your vanities! What you offer me is evil.*

Outside the darkened room, a burst of energy ignited. The bedside lamp exploded with a pop.

"Dr. Osborne!"

It was Agent Sharpe.

Olivia heard the crunch of glass and knew he was near. The darkness slithered away, but her eyes never left the place it left behind. The wobbly bounce of Sharpe's flashlight played across her feet.

Olivia took a quick step back, sliding on the shards of glass beneath the slick soles of her shoes. In a flash, she saw what would have happened had he not been there. She would have hit the back of her head on the corner of the vanity. Death would have caught her before she hit the floor, but Jon Sharpe got there first.

"Keep your light on the floor," Olivia told him, but she was too late.

****

"What the fuck was that?" Sharpe asked once they were downstairs in the light. He was pacing the living room, sucking in air like she'd done earlier in the driveway.

"Tell me what you saw," Olivia encouraged him.

"What? You didn't see it?"

"I'm asking what you saw." She remained calm; her words measured, in agent mode.

Sharpe shook his head as if that would make it go away. But it wouldn't, and neither would she. He looked at her to find her looking at him like he was a witness. "Young, female, stringy hair covering her face. Standing in the shower. She was wearing something white and flowy. Maybe a gown of some kind."

Olivia nodded. It was supposed to be an encouraging sign, but it wasn't.

"You didn't see her?" Sharpe asked again.

Olivia shook her head. "No. But that doesn't mean you didn't. I believe you."

"What the hell was it?" He took a seat on the Forester's couch. He needed a moment. "I think her hands were moving, forward like she wanted to touch me." Sharpe reacted with a visible shiver.

"It's a haunting. A manifestation. It will stay with the house," she assured him. *Or wander down the street*, but he didn't need to know that.

"No wonder your neighbor shot up her bathroom," Sharpe said. "Let's get the hell out of here before that thing decides to come back." He vacated the couch and headed for the door. Gripping the door handle, he stopped and steadied himself, slipping back into the agent he was. "Talk to me about something normal. Like how long have you known?"

"Known? That there was a haunting?"

"No. How far along are you? If there's a baby bump somewhere, you're hiding it well. Silas hasn't said a thing."

"We just found out yesterday. I didn't mean to blurt it out. I seem to be having a problem with impulse control," Olivia confessed.

Sharpe smiled. "Pregnancy can do that. Kat and I have one you know. And another on the way. Your secret is safe with me."

Outside the driveway was empty. All that was left was the officer who let them in. "Lieutenant Bartholomew took Mrs. Forester next door."

"Am I going to have to ask him to leave?" Sharpe asked as they headed to Olivia's. He really didn't want to ask the lieutenant to do anything, but he would do whatever she needed.

Olivia just looked at him.

"You got this too, am I right?"

"I do. But thanks for the offer."

"Anytime," Sharpe said as they reached the steps to her front porch.

The other agent leaned against the tree in the front yard. Olivia wondered if the spot was his choice or Barry's. Either way, he looked ready to go. It was midnight on a Saturday night. Olivia was sure he would rather be anywhere but here. "The house is locked up tight," he told them.

Sharpe waved him off. He peeked over Olivia's head to see inside the house. The lights were on. The lieutenant was waiting.

"It's okay. Really," Olivia assured Sharpe.

Sharpe nodded. "Call me if you need anything. And congratulations. Kat is really into the whole Mommy group thing. I could arrange an invite if you like."

"Thank you. I'll think about it." Olivia meant it. She was definitely out of her element, and she had no one to ask even the simplest of questions. "About tonight. Please don't feel the need to tell Silas. Let me do it. He has enough to worry about."

Sharpe nodded. He wouldn't say it out loud, but their history put his loyalty to her over that of his boss—at least on this. He wasn't sure he could describe it even if he wanted to. "I heard it's a nasty case. Missing kids. It's never easy. Especially when you have one of your own."

****

His visit was unexpected, but she didn't stop him. She didn't mean for it to happen, not like last time. It was just supposed to be once.

As soon as he touched her his hands were everywhere at once. In her hair, gliding along her neck, finding their way inside the folds of her neckline. A moan escaped when he squeezed her. He pushed her against the wall, pressing himself into her. One hand left her breast to slide down to her hip. He was slowly gathering the folds of her dress, pushing them out of way, kissing her harder as he went.

She didn't remember how they got to the bedroom, but before she knew it, she could feel his bare chest on hers. The length of his body stretched over hers. He looked down at her with such need in his eyes. She hadn't felt needed like that in a long time. There was no way she was stopping him.

Chapter Twenty-Four

Olivia stuck her head inside the downstairs bedroom to check on Lily.

"Don't worry. She's asleep," Barry assured her. The room was original to the house. It still housed her grandmother's antique bed. Barry tried not to dwell on his own memories spent there.

"I went to get her a bottle of water and when I got back, she was out like a light. The EMT told me they gave her something to calm her down and pain meds for her cuts. He said she should sleep for a while. I'm just glad I got her here before she passed out."

Olivia nodded, eyeing him carefully. They'd seen more of each other in the last week than they had in a year. How could they spend so much time apart and come back together so easily?

Barry followed her outside to the front porch. The rain had cooled the mid-summer air. Olivia turned off the porch light, and they sat with the lights on behind them. They had spent time together on her quaint little front porch before. It only seemed right they go there now.

"Thank you for taking care of Lily. You didn't have to do that."

"You had other things you needed to do. Besides, she'd had a pretty rough night. I feel bad for her," Barry said, keeping his eyes on the empty street in front of them. It was better than looking at Olivia.

"Just like you didn't have to come here. Why did you? We both know you have somewhere else you should be."

Barry finally turned to look at her. She wasn't angry. She looked sad more than anything. "The party was over," he offered lamely.

"You weren't planning on staying?" Olivia was genuinely curious. Since she and Silas decided to be together, they spent very few nights apart. The distance between them had been geographic. Not personal.

Barry shrugged. The subject matter made him uncomfortable, but if Olivia kept pressing, he knew he would tell her. "I guess we both need our space."

"*You* need your space," Olivia corrected him.

"*I* need my space," Barry repeated.

"She would want you to stay." Olivia watched him for a reaction and got none. "Unless she asked you to leave." Her words hung there. She was probing. Amanda had been comfortably numb when she left, but before that, Olivia saw no interaction between them all evening. A man she didn't know spent more time with Amanda than anyone else. The implication pinged somewhere in the background, like white noise. Olivia couldn't think about what Amanda might be doing right now. Not with Barry in front of her, commanding her full attention.

Barry shook his head. "She didn't ask me to leave. Her brother and I were together, trying to stay out of the way. When I heard your address come across the scanner I couldn't not come. I had to make sure you were safe."

Olivia nodded. "Are you worried about Jamie?"

"I heard *shots fired* and started driving."

Olivia sat with the words for a moment. He had a point. "Do you have proof yet it was really him in that room?"

"No. Frank just got back today. Forensics is doing what it does."

Olivia nodded. "Jamie doesn't take chances unless he has a very good reason. Getting kicked out of the hospital would have made him desperate. I think you're right about the cash. His aunts died months before he started killing. Surely, they left him something, which means there has to be a money trail."

Barry nodded at the suggestion. He wondered what the DA knew. There was a team of people gearing up for a trial, but everything stopped when the prisoner disappeared. Barry looked across at her again. "Where do we start?"

"I'll talk to Brennon." Brennon Kaine, the high-priced defense attorney Jamie could never afford, but the one who wanted the case anyway. "He needs to be told about the break-in. As a courtesy."

"I already made that call," Barry assured her. Luckily, he only had to leave a message. The attorney was probably just as relieved at avoiding a conversation. They hadn't spoken, not since the standoff they shared at the jail infirmary when Smythe went all Linda Blair on them. "Good, then I'll put a bug in his ear about the cash. Given the circumstances, Brennon will share."

Meaning Brennon was as loyal as he was.

"I know you're worried about me," Olivia conceded.

"You're damn right I am." The answer was more

growl than anything else.

It took her a moment to find her voice again, steeling herself against the torrent of emotions raging inside of him. "Once I see Silas, I'll tell him what happened. I promise."

Barry held her gaze before looking away again. Silas loved her, but that was a choice. With him, it was something else. More whispers from the dead, real or imagined, told Barry his place in her life was not a choice. It was some kind of doctrine, set in motion by events he didn't understand.

"You don't need to worry about me." Her words were useless, but she said them anyway.

"I will find the bastard," Barry assured her. If Silas were here, he would put her on lockdown. Her husband was probably very content that she spent her days consulting for hospitals instead of the Bureau. Advising hospital bureaucrats wasn't her passion or talent, nor would it stop the monsters from coming.

For Barry, keeping her safe didn't mean he had to lock her away or clip her wings. He couldn't do that to her. Olivia would eventually find a way to set herself free.

"He won't hurt me," Olivia said, meaning Jamie.

Barry studied her. She was an immovable force. He could only imagine how protective she would be of the children she would bear. "I think you're wrong," Barry told her, the conviction in his eyes matching her own. "Smythe kills those who help him. No one has helped him more than you." She freed him of a demon. Most people would be appreciative, but Smythe wasn't like most people. Barry wondered if Smythe hadn't gone in search of the demon—just like Roche.

Olivia held his gaze for a long time. The determination in her eyes ultimately surrendered to resolve. "Do whatever makes you feel like I'm safe."

Barry nodded. "Jamie I can help with. But what about that thing in your bathroom? That's outside of my skillset." Changing direction was what he did in the interrogation room to keep his suspects off balance. This time he did it to redirect himself. They had been heading down a dangerous path. One that ended with him telling her things she didn't want to hear.

Olivia responded in kind. "What thing in my bathroom?" she asked, her words measured. She would give nothing away. Not until he gave her something. It's what she would do with a witness.

"Don't tell me you don't know. The chick with the wet stringy hair in her face that looks like a grown-up version of the girl who climbs out of televisions. She can't get out of there can she?" Barry asked. He tried to smile, but he wasn't joking. He could deal with a real-life monster in her life. It was the specters he couldn't fight. Olivia was on her own for those.

"Out of where?" Location was important.

"The mirror," Barry said.

"Only in the mirror? Nowhere else. You're sure?"

"Of course, I'm sure. I don't see something like that every day."

Olivia was satisfied it was the same as Silas but different than with Jon and Ross. It had to mean something. "No. She can't get out." *Not without help.* The house was blessed. She would have to add those questions to what she already planned to ask Father Dominic. Olivia chided herself for not scrubbing down the mirror as planned. Maybe the lapse was the loss of more brain cells in favor of the flourishing life inside of her. It took a lot to grow a human.

"I'm not embarrassed to say it scared the shit out of me but considering it's your house." Barry managed to pull off a smile this time. He would rather talk about the dead than anything else she might want to say to him.

Olivia sighed, already starting to formulate a plan. "It's nothing I can't handle. It's a haunting. Probably one of my ancestors. Lily's house belonged to my great grandmother."

"That's one fucked up family reunion, if you ask me," Barry said, feeling happier than he should have been when he saw her smile. "Normal people can't handle this kind of stuff. Remind me how you do this again."

Olivia had long accepted the fact she was born to this. Whatever this was. "Natural selection. Genetics, maybe."

Gran tried to tell her. So did the demon *Alleracsap*. The monsters would never stop, so Olivia stopped running and embraced her destiny. The night in the barn was just the beginning.

Depending on how long one went back in history, maybe it was a lost talent. Like dealing with demons, Barry knew better than to suggest it. "I guess a haunting, even a scary looking one doesn't compare to the other thing."

The *other thing* was code for *demon*. The one who appeared in her living room. The one who killed Mark. The one who whispered in her ear tonight. "Not even close." At least the haunting was a door she could close.

"Did Lily use the downstairs bathroom?" Olivia asked. "Did she see it?"

227

"She did, but lucky for her she didn't see what I saw." Barry considered the night's events. "She must have seen something like it though. It could be why she shot up her bathroom and why she asked for some drugs to sleep."

"Did she tell anyone what she saw?" Olivia asked. Lily had been too frightened when Olivia arrived to tell her anything.

"According to the officer, she heard a noise and thought she saw something in the dark. She mentioned her husband had a similar incident last week. She said she was scared and just started shooting." Except no one was there. After meeting Olivia, Barry knew it didn't have to be a person she saw, but if Lily didn't see the girl in the mirror, what did she see? "I'm betting it wasn't what I saw. It would be hard *not* to talk about it. Whatever it was, she couldn't describe it. Maybe she's better off."

If Lily couldn't put it into words, then it wasn't the girl. It was something else. "Agent Sharpe saw the girl in Lily's bathroom," Olivia admitted. "Silas saw her too. In our downstairs bathroom, just like you," Olivia mused. She was developing a theory.

"But not you. You haven't seen her?" Barry asked.

"No."

"I'd think you would be the first one she'd want to see."

Silas said the same thing. "She may not realize she needs my help. She might not know she's dead." Not if her family placed the blessing right after the death. Because they knew something. *Or feared something.*

"Then why are us guys the lucky ones?"

"Maybe it was a man that caused her demise."

Barry took a long sip of his water. It was a baited statement. "So, you're saying men are the problem?"

"The world was different a century ago. And let's face it, it's different for the women in my family. Olivia had read enough history to know what happened to women who possessed gifts like hers. She would have met her end on a fiery stake or tied to a rock and thrown into a river.

"What did you tell Lily when she asked who you were?" Olivia asked, changing the subject.

Barry shifted in his chair, feeling uncomfortable as they wandered back to more personal topics. "I told her we worked together. That we were friends." Barry looked at her, and she looked back, never wavering. "You saved my life. That makes us friends, right?"

"I'd like to think we are."

We're more.

Those were Barry's words inside her head. Olivia shut them out before she heard more.

"Amanda is trying to be my friend."

"Lily would be a better choice," Barry quipped, his eyes darting away from her now.

Olivia ignored him. "Amanda says she loves you." Her words were gentle, trying to lead him somewhere he didn't want to go.

She expected him to keep talking, but he couldn't. If he did, he might end up saying things he shouldn't.

"I don't think either of those things are true." This time he did look at her. "Amanda doesn't want to be your friend. At least not for the right reasons. And she doesn't love me. She only thinks she does."

Olivia stood firm. "When I said you need to let go, I wasn't talking just about Mark."

"You also said everyone was where they should be, but not me. Where am I supposed to be?" Barry dared ask.

Tears pooled in her eyes. "Not with Amanda."

At least they agreed on something.

Barry reached out, wanting to touch her, but didn't. He used his words instead. "Don't cry, please don't cry."

Olivia didn't move. "Try." She blinked against the tears and fought back the anger struggling to get free.

"I can't give her what she wants."

"I know. Try for you. Not for her." Her words were a sob.

Barry's jaw clenched as the emotions welled inside of him, resentment, loss, all of it. She wasn't talking about Amanda. He should never have turned her away the day she came to him after Mark's funeral. She hadn't committed herself to Silas, at least not physically. Barry knew it without being told. If she had, she never would have shown up at his condo. If he had accepted her offering and shared his grief with her, they wouldn't be here, not like this. They would be inside. Together. But things wouldn't be right. There would be something missing.

"I want you to do it for you. You have so much to give. Don't let it go to waste," Olivia pleaded.

His eyes said what he couldn't. The words filled her head and the tears leaked from her eyes until she had to look away.

"I'm happy for you, Olivia. Especially now." Her admission of pregnancy had cut him to the bone, but it also set something free. This time he did reach out and touch her, just for a moment.

Barry placed his hand gently on her midsection, conveying his allegiance there as well. "Silas gave you something I'm incapable of giving. To anyone. Even you." He had never been surer of his role in her life than right now. There was a reason he was her protector and not her lover.

"It's why the second marriage was so short. I couldn't give her what she wanted most, and I wasn't enough."

Olivia took a moment to consider his confession and what it had taken to say those words. She thought of the promises she and Silas had uttered to one another when faced with the same dilemma.

Barry stood. He couldn't be there anymore.

"This isn't about me," Olivia said softly.

"You don't want it to be. I don't want it to be. But it is," Barry confessed. Frustrated, he headed for the steps.

Olivia followed him. "It's more than that. You have to go to Amanda and say what you need to say. She's poison."

Barry turned back, forcing his hands into his pockets. His fists clutched the folds of fabric as he struggled not to touch her. "I will," he said, resigning himself to his fate. "For you."

I would do anything for you.

Olivia hugged herself and the life inside of her.

I need you in my life, we all do.

They were Olivia's words. Inside his head this time.

Chapter Twenty-Five

Olivia gave Silas the full version of what happened at Lily's house before falling asleep while still on the phone. She woke up missing him. His text mirroring her thoughts helped. The timestamp told her he sent it just after she stopped talking. She read his words to start her day.

Downstairs, Lily hobbled around enough to make herself a cup of coffee. She was reclining on the couch, her feet up, watching TV, when Olivia came downstairs to let the dogs out. Lily muted the discussion on the perks of shiplap and waited for her.

"Please tell me I didn't wake you," Lily greeted her. "I slept so well, thanks to the drugs, but when they finally wore off, I was wide awake."

Olivia smiled as she returned with her own cup, filled with more creamer than usual. Coffee actually sounded better than her favorite water. She needed a little jump-start to her morning. The life inside of her was taking what it needed, leaving her to fend for herself. "You're fine," Olivia assured her and sank down in Silas's chair, catching a whiff of his woodsy scent. Olivia leaned back and basked in hints of him left behind.

"I can't tell you how much I appreciate you letting me stay here last night. I don't know what I would have done if you weren't home. I couldn't stay there." Lily lifted up one of her feet. "And I don't think I could have gotten very far."

"Don't worry about a thing," Olivia said. "I'm sorry I didn't get a chance to say goodnight."

Lily waved her off. "You left me in good hands." She smiled and winked. "That Lieutenant Bartholomew is such a gentleman and very handsome." She was beaming now. "He said the two of you worked together and that you were friends. Why haven't I seen him around?"

The next time she talked to Barry, Olivia would have to tell him he had a fan. "He works a lot," Olivia said, hoping to halt any more small talk about him.

Lily rolled her eyes. "Of course, he does," Lily said with a smile and sipped her coffee.

"The EMT told me Ross won't be home until late tomorrow. Please stay with me tonight," Olivia suggested.

"I can't put you out," Lily protested, but her eyes showed gratefulness. The woman was frightened to be in her own home.

"It's no bother, and I would really like the company. Silas is gone, and I'm feeling kind of lonely." After all the years Olivia spent alone it was an unexpected confession. "I can make dinner, and we can have a nice quiet girl's night. What do you say?"

"I'd like that," Lily said.

For a second, Olivia thought she was going to cry.

"I know last night was scary."

"I was probably just overreacting," Lily looked away.

"No, Lily, you weren't." The tone of her voice reclaimed Lily's attention. "I was in your house. I don't know what you saw, but trust me, you were not overreacting." Olivia hoped if she opened the door, Lily would feel comfortable enough to step through it.

"That's just it. I didn't really see anything. Except the darkness, but I was so scared. It felt like my skin was moving." Lily's hand trembled as she said it.

"You weren't imagining things," Olivia assured her. "I felt it, too."

"Really?" Lily's pupils expanded, making Olivia wonder if her admission made it better or worse. She decided to keep talking. Making a plan to move forward was better than staying in place.

"I'm going to see a priest friend of mine today. It's our Sunday to take the dogs to the Alzheimer's Unit. I was going to discuss your situation with him if that's alright with you."

Lily nodded her head in agreement, eager for help.

"I know he'll agree we should bless the house and put the medals back. You don't have to be there, but it should need to be done sooner rather than later. I'm going to ask if he can do it tonight."

"It's that bad?" Lily asked, her voice barely above a whisper.

"With a disturbance such as yours, it opens a door. Blessing the house will seal it shut. I want you to feel safe about going back."

"A door to where?"

Olivia hesitated, searching for the right words, the simple ones. "Different planes of existence. Souls caught in the in-between weaken the thin fabric between the planes. What I felt, and what scared you, doesn't belong in your house. Father Dominic can help make things right."

"I don't know what to say, Olivia. Thank you doesn't hardly seem enough."

Olivia smiled. "You can do something for me in return if it makes you feel better."

"Anything."

"I found some old family books I spoke about the other day. The ones kept by my grandmother and by her mother before her. They might be good reading material this afternoon while I'm gone since I never got around to doing it myself." Olivia had decided that hearing her family history in the third person sounded like a much better plan anyway. "Knowing the history of your house is our best way to find out who this woman is who keeps showing up in your bathroom." *And mine.*

****

"You're not yourself today," Father Dominic said as he and Olivia strolled the peaceful grounds outside the Alzheimer's Unit. They visited at least once a month to spend time with the clients. The dogs were a special treat. Pet therapy was good for patients in long-term care. While taking a sabbatical from the priesthood, Dominic spent time working as a social worker. This was one of the facilities he once serviced. He requested Olivia's companionship as part of a project for the local diocese to give back to the residents and their families. Dominic missed having a flock of his own, and Olivia missed caring for patients. Coming to a place like this, and doing this kind of work, satisfied both their needs to give back to the professions that cast them on the paths they traveled now.

"I am not myself," Olivia agreed. She took a seat

on the closest bench and lengthened the tether of Daisy's leash. As a natural runner, the greyhound needed an anchor while Alvin followed Olivia freely. She sighed with weary, pregnancy-induced fatigue. She could already tell the difference. The life inside her was growing and already taking from her what it needed without regard. She was agreeable but recognized the need to refuel.

"You're not ill, are you?" Dominic hedged. There was something different about her.

"No, I'm not ill," Olivia assured him. "Just in transition," she said and left it at that. Her pregnancy wasn't what she had come here to discuss. Besides, he would know soon enough. "I have a request."

Dominic gave her a look of submission. He would do anything she asked.

"I'm in need of a house blessing," Olivia told him.

Dominic's brows rose and fell quickly, getting lost in the blackened leather of his smooth skin.

"Not my house," Olivia rushed to assure him. "One once inhabited by my ancestors. It was blessed at least a century ago, but the new owners are renovating, and the St. Benedict medals buried there were inadvertently removed." She paused a moment as she pushed through an unexpected surge of nausea.

"Has it released something?"

"Yes," Olivia said. She closed her eyes and swallowed, waiting for her stomach to right itself again. "It began as a haunting, but now I think there is an opening."

"And others are gathering?"

"Yes. I walked the house myself last night, and from what I encountered I believe a blessing should come sooner rather than later."

"Or more will follow," Dominic said for her. He trusted her judgment. He met his first demon working with her. It was ironic how a few short years later, the Church welcomed him back into the fold only to train him as an exorcist. "They came in search of you."

Olivia resisted the urge to look at him. Instead, she kept her eyes straight ahead. Now would probably not be a good time to tell him her own personal demon spoke to her last night. She and the archbishop had discussed her demon affairs, but only so far as her family history. Her lineage was long and complicated. The archbishop never said it, but she knew he believed the demon would have departed with Jamie. He also knew enough not to push her because she would seek his counsel in her own time. Eventually, Olivia knew she was going to have to break down and confess. But now was not that time.

"I can do it tonight, after mass," Dominic said when she didn't respond. "I will need to speak with you first however, so I'm fully aware of what I'm dealing with."

Olivia nodded. "I'll know more when I get home, so come to my house first.

****

Sunday afternoon stretched long and empty without Olivia. Silas had taken the day away from the investigation. Without Olivia to soothe his wandering thoughts, Silas found himself on the dirt road where Ava and Dorcas met their end. He parked where their bodies were found and walked to the crocodile pond. The caution tape from the day before was still in place. The water stirred, and he saw a pair of eyes float to the surface. They were cold and flat as they stared back at him. They were ancient eyes, absent of emotion. This predator was almost unchanged since its creation.

Man and beast stared at one another. Both alpha males, both sitting at the top of their own food chain. The crocodile blinked first and dipped back below the surface of the cesspool. Silas stood there for a long time, waiting, but it never resurfaced.

Back in the car, Silas continued his drive and ended up at the abandoned McCleary house. He brushed aside the crime scene tape and entered through the front door. From the looks of the place, it had been thoroughly processed. Stepping into the girls' room caused the flesh to rise along the back of his neck. The sensation was similar to the one his wife could awaken with a brush of her nails. Only this time, it settled in the pit of his stomach and not beyond.

Silas studied the bed belonging to Ava. He wondered about the necklace hidden under the pillow and the pet collar tucked beneath the mattress. The little band of leather belonged to the bunny that used to live in the cage outside in the backyard. Were they keepsakes, a homage to the passing of something loved? Or were they trophies?

Silas turned to go and caught sight of the still-covered mirror. He stared at it for a long time, thinking about the watering hole down the road. He was reaching for the cloth even before he realized it. When the sheet slipped, revealing the glass, Silas swore it was the woman from the shower in his own home staring back at him.

Chapter Twenty-Six

By the time she headed home with the dogs, Olivia's momentum was gone. She scrapped the idea of a home-cooked meal. With Lily in agreement, she defaulted to Thai take-out instead. Olivia enjoyed their time together. They never spent time alone with just the two of them. It had always been a couples' event. It was a stark contrast to the forced time she spent with Amanda.

Father Dominic arrived after mass, just as promised. Olivia made the introductions and asked Lily to tell them what she learned from her history reading. They had put off any discussions until after dinner. Olivia didn't want to hear about her family until the priest arrived. Once was enough.

"I have to say you have a fascinating family. I hope you let me read more."

Ever since her experience in the barn, Olivia felt an internal push to learn more about her past. Now that she was adding to her family tree, she had to do it. Olivia could no longer hide her head in the sand. Lily, serving as an intermediary, could provide her with a solution.

"From what I've read so far, I think I already have a pretty good idea who the girl is that Ross saw in our bathroom."

"Start at the beginning and pretend I know nothing." It wasn't a lie.

"The house where Ross and I live was originally the home of your great-great grandparents, Jonah, and Abitha. Apparently, they had quite the love affair. He built the house as gift to her on his family land. He was a successful farmer in the area while Abitha was known to be a skillful Apothecary. People would travel from miles around just for her herbal teas and her healing salves."

Olivia couldn't help but wonder if those treatments had anything to do with witchcraft or if they were strictly for medicinal purposes. If she had to guess, she would say a little of both. Probably they were the roots of Gran's kitchen magic. She just failed to carry on the family tradition.

"Back then, a large family was needed to work the land, but for most women in your family, one child at the most was all they could conceive. And always a girl. However, Abitha was lucky. They had no boys, which could be why the farm ended, but Abitha and Jonah had two children. A set of twin girls, Esme and Ella. With twins, there is usually a weaker of the two. In this case, it was Ella. She was described as small with wispy blonde hair. Esme was the stronger one. She was said to be as vibrant in personality as her red hair and enchanting emerald eyes." Lily stopped and stared at Olivia. "Probably a lot like yours, I would imagine."

Silas often commented on her eyes. He said they glowed. Mainly when she was excited.

"Esme, as the oldest, was your grandfather's favorite. She was expected to be the one to carry on the family. From the time Esme was six years old her constant companion was Lenore. Her family worked on your grandfather's farm. By the time the girls were

240

fifteen the relationship had grown into something else."

Olivia feared the worst, imagining late-night rituals performed in blood under the full moon. "What do you mean *something else*?"

"The words aren't the same from that time period, but from reading the entries I'm pretty sure they were lovers. I believe that was your grandfather's suspicion as well. He quickly found a suiter for Esme and a quick engagement ensued. This caused a great deal of conflict within the family. I think Esme truly loved Lenore. But your grandfather was not a man to be crossed. He sent Esme and her new husband Jonathan away. Then he banished Lenore and her family from his lands. Days after they left, a terrible rainstorm came. It rained for three days straight. On the first night, the family saw Lenore through the lightning strikes that lit up the sky. She was hanging from a tree outside the house. Apparently, she was so overcome with grief over losing Esme, she hung herself. On the third and final night of the terrible storm your grandfather also died. He drowned in his own bathtub."

****

"Did that give you enough information?" Olivia asked. She and Father Dominic had moved out to the front porch, leaving Lily behind inside.

"We have to consider maleficence was involved," Dominic said, stepping off the porch on his way to next door. He stopped when he realized Olivia wasn't following. He turned to find her still lingering at the edge of the porch.

"Lenore's been seen in the mirror of my downstairs bathroom. But only in the mirror. Will blessing Lily's house break the connection as well?"

Dominic retraced his steps to the bottom of the porch and considered the implications. "The fact she only appears in the mirror here might indicate she is trapped. If the blessing doesn't rid her from this place, she may need help crossing to the other side. This land was owned by your grandfather as well. Blessing the dwelling might not be enough."

"But she can't enter here, not as a malevolent spirit, not after the blessing the archbishop provided after…." Olivia looked over at him. She didn't have to remind Dominic what they faced together in this house. The force of the demon sent the priest to the hospital.

"True," Dominic agreed. "Your house is secure."

"Then what's in my bathroom isn't a haunting. It's a plea for help."

"If that's the case, then she's looking to you." He said it simply, even though the ramifications were anything but.

"If Lenore killed herself, willingly, then she wouldn't need assistance. She wouldn't need fare to cross the River into Hell. She would be welcomed with open arms," Olivia explained her theory.

"Then why was the house blessed?"

"You used the term *maleficence*," Olivia pointed out. "We are speaking of my family, and that is where your thoughts took you. I don't doubt you. I think this involved murder, possibly two."

"Lenore and your grandfather."

"I just don't know if there was one perpetrator or two. I'm guessing two, both my grandparents."

"You think your grandfather killed Lenore?" Dominic asked.

"He had means and motive. Lenore was a young

girl easy to overpower. Given her feelings for Esme, making it look like suicide was clever," Olivia proposed, distancing herself from the fact she was talking about her own family. "With her apothecary skills my grandmother would have known how to make her husband's death look like an accident. Jonah's death certainly had a poetic sense of justice to it, don't you think? Since Abitha was left the head of the family, she would have been the one who asked for the medals. Because she knew the truth."

"Atonement for her sins?" Dominic suggested.

"Or protection from them. She would have wanted to protect the rest of her family from what she did. Evil senses evil."

Dominic couldn't help but agree. The suggestion was sinister but truthful. "There is darkness in your family. The women are powerful, and they can go either way. Into the light or into the dark."

It seemed the theme didn't change. It only skipped generations. "The dark is easier. It beckons."

"You are correct. Either would be a reason to have the house blessed."

Olivia reached for his hand. "Then peace be with you. This is the key to the Forester's house. I cannot join you on this one."

Her words stopped him. The priest had watched her face down more than one demon. Her reluctance now sent a chill down his back. "Is there something else in the house you're not telling me? Should I have called the archbishop?"

Olivia dismissed his concerns with a shake of her head. "No. This is about me. I have responsibilities. Just as Esme did."

Dominic looked down to see she had slid her arm protectively across her midsection. He didn't ask what she wasn't willing to tell. He didn't have to.

With Dominic gone, Olivia peeked in on Lily. She was stretched out on the couch with her eyes closed. She had taken a pain pill after her storytelling. Olivia decided to remain outside until Dominic returned. A cup of chamomile tea was waiting for him. It calmed the spirits. She already had one. She needed it to stop the raging thoughts inside her head. Gran had done well not to share family stories with her.

"Was it a haunting?" Olivia asked when the priest finally rejoined her.

Dominic sank into the chair next to her, grateful for the tea. He didn't speak for a long time. She wanted to hear, but he wasn't sure he wanted to tell.

"Yes. You were also correct to close the door quickly. There was something else in the house," Dominic confessed. "Your demon greeted me." The hiss had come in his ear at the first sprinkle of holy water in the bathroom. The odor of sulphur flooded his nostrils until he gagged.

"*My demon.* Why do you say that?"

"*It* spoke the words, 'S*he is mine'. It* knows you're with child. He told me so." Dominic's mouth was dry as he said it. He would have to report this to Archbishop Mendoza. "It was the Church's belief the demon departed with the boy."

Olivia had tried to tell the archbishop. Now he was going to hear the news from a priest.

"You could have mentioned this when we spoke earlier." Dominic meant it to be a rebuke, but his words carried no conviction. He was more worried by the fact she showed no surprise at the news.

"I didn't know he would speak to you. Besides, he's wrong." It was a theory she had been working on since the night in the barn. Her discussion with Silas the other night helped solidify it. *Alleracsap* was eager to accept the souls she offered. She settled the debt and gained Jamie's freedom at the same time. The demon's reappearance meant he was seeking something else. Not a possession, but an allegiance. "What if he is mine?"

Dominic's hand trembled as he reached for his tea.

"You said my ancestors can go either way, to light or the dark," Olivia recalled.

"Did *It* tell you that?"

"In not so many words. Just as you did," Olivia reminded him.

"He's drawn to your light which means he will try and take it." Her silence was his answer. "Demons trick and taunt and twist the truth to fit their needs. Never forget that," the priest cautioned.

"My light is too bright," Olivia told him.

Ana Lutz and Andre Roche conjured dark magic. Olivia harnessed the energy from their magic and bent it to her will. It was a power she did not understand. The forces Olivia felt coursing through her that night were seductive, intoxicating even. Only by faith alone had she not taken that path again. But it was always there, the lure of its power lurking just within her grasp.

"Do you believe my ancestor Sarah Osborne made a deal with a demon?" she suddenly asked.

"It is possible," he finally said.

"Because she was a poor, uneducated woman who came up with a brilliant defense?" Olivia theorized.

Dominic could offer no defense against her logic.

"It does beg the question."

"Do you think she made a deal with him, to escape death by hanging. Or perhaps even public knowledge of what she was?"

Dominic, her friend, was taking too long to answer. He was having to craft his answers. As a profiler, she knew someone who was being honest, either with her or themselves, didn't have to do that.

"Again, it is possible. Demons make deals," Dom acknowledged.

"So do witches." Olivia added.

"It could explain why your family followed the dark path," the priest offered.

To Olivia, his answer sounded like an offering. *Or a diversion.*

"Until it stopped with my gran."

Dominic concentrated on his teacup. It was empty by now but gave him time to think about asking things he didn't want to know. In the end, he did as he must. "What are you getting at Olivia?"

"That the demon can't take from me what isn't his."

The conviction in her voice frightened him as much as the burning glow of her eyes.

****

Lily was still on the couch when Olivia came back inside, but she was awake this time. "Do you want to be alone?" Lily asked.

"No. I'm not sure alone is exactly what I need right now." Olivia sank down in Silas's chair. A wave of disappointment washed over her when she realized his scent was gone.

"Can I ask you something? Do you attend mass?"

It was something Lily had wondered about. She knew Olivia was devout, but Olivia hadn't been to church all weekend. She could have gone with the priest, but she didn't.

"I do not." She saw the surprise cross Lily's face. "My grandmother did enough of that for both of us," Olivia smiled. "For as long as I can remember my gran went to mass every morning. I, however, don't believe you have to worship publicly to be steadfast in your faith."

Saying it reminded Olivia, she was crafting her own answers. What she told Lily wasn't the whole story. As she grew older, being in the church came with physical manifestations. Her skin prickled and itched. Gran said it was the turmoil of emotions beating down on her and granted her a reprieve. As a vessel, Olivia was a repository for the feelings of others. Churches were full of emotions, both happy and sad. The same could be said of hospitals, yet that was where she chose to work, and her reactions were not the same. She wondered if Gran ever realized the same thing.

"How about you tell me what happened to Esme over a nightcap?" Olivia suggested. She fetched wine for Lily and more tea for herself. Olivia considered adding something a little different this time, something for sleep. It was something her gran used to make. Now she wondered who created the concoction. Considering it could have been Abitha, Olivia decided against it. She wasn't ready to trust her just yet. She had the baby to think about.

"Esme returned home, but only long enough for her father's funeral. There was no funeral for Lenore unless the family did it privately. Because it was believed she committed suicide, the local parish wouldn't bury her. There's no mention of her family again. My guess is they slipped away and never returned. So sad one event broke apart two families."

"What happened to Abitha?" Olivia asked. Despite her lack of trust at the moment, she couldn't help but feel sympathy for her great-great-grandmother. Abitha had been forced to choose between the man she loved and her own child.

"Your family continued. Abitha was a strong woman. She lived a long life. I also think you should know she isn't the only one of your ancestors to be blessed with twins. I found several instances of twinning in your family. All girls, but they looked nothing alike, like Ella and Esme. It means the twins are fraternal—two eggs, two sperm, which also means it's a genetic trait passed down through the females."

Lily caught the look Olivia was giving her. "You look surprised. I wasn't always married. Ross and I met in college in chemistry class. He was originally pre-med before he found out he was better with numbers. I graduated, like you, with a bachelor's degree in nursing."

"I had no idea."

Lily smiled. To Olivia, it looked sad.

"I didn't work much after I got married. I got pregnant pretty quickly, and Ross wanted me home."

Olivia wanted to ask something else, but Lily cut her off. It made Olivia wonder if Lily was avoiding her past as much as she was.

"Esme mourned Lenore. Esme wrote a letter to her mother, which Abitha kept, saying she believed the rain to be the tears Lenore shed for the life they would never share. It tells me, Abitha knew her daughter's secret. Despite all of that, Esme remained true to her family expectations and stayed with her husband."

Given the times, Olivia knew Esme really had no other choice.

"She never returned home to the family land."

"Did Esme have children?" Olivia asked. Continuing the family line had been what her father wanted. The need for procreation, in part, was what kept her from her love.

"She did actually."

Olivia saw on her face, what should have been a happy event hadn't ended well.

"She died in childbirth. But not before successfully delivering twins—more girls. Out of curiosity I searched the three books you gave me and nowhere in there is mention of a male child."

Olivia recalled Dominic said something similar when they discussed her gifts. Her family had gone centuries without the birth of a male. It was more evidence Gran was right when she said their family was reaching the end of the line. Genetics was wiping away their gifts.

"A hundred years ago it wasn't uncommon for twins not to survive. The fact the twins in your family did, shows the strength of the women in your family. They have strong genes. They might not have a lot of babies, but when they do, they're good at it. I looked up the names of Esme's children. She named them Philopena, which means 'unfinished' and Lenore. It sounds like a tragic love story. She and Lenore never got to be together—not really."

Olivia let out a sigh, stopping the flow of her own

memories. How often did Esme wonder what her life would have been like with Lenore? Did those feelings ever go away, or did they evolve? So much sadness. So much loss. Olivia truly hoped Esme found happiness somewhere along the way. What of Lenore? Was she waiting for Esme on the other side?

Olivia pulled herself free of her thoughts. She knew where they would lead. Jason.

"What happened to Ella, Esme's twin?"

"You really don't know your family history, do you?"

"That's why you're reading these tales of tragedy," Olivia smiled. Twins would have been a valuable piece of history. Especially since Gran stressed how important it was to have a family. Olivia wondered how to tell Silas about the possibility of more than one baby.

"Abitha built this house as a wedding gift for Ella and her husband as a way to keep the family together since Esme never returned. Ella didn't have twins, but she did have your Gran, Genevieve. It's a beautiful name. It's biblical. Genevieve was the name of the patron saint of France. She proclaimed she lived only for God."

Olivia smiled. *Genevieve*—it was the girl's name she and Silas had picked. In true Silas style, he had already shortened it to Evie. Considering what Lily had just told her, they might need to find another one just to be safe.

"You know what this means," Lily called to her, sounding giddy. "It means you could have twins," she said with a gleam in her eye.

Instinctively Olivia's arm slid across her midsection.

"Don't try to look like you don't know what I'm talking about. A woman, especially a mother can tell. I noticed you haven't had a drop of wine all weekend. Don't worry. Your secret is safe with me. Not that you're going to be able to hide it much longer."

Chapter Twenty-Seven

The text was waiting when she woke up.

—I need you back. I booked you on the noon flight out of San Antonio.—

****

Silas watched the firemen patrol the area like ants on a mound, looking for hot spots.

Tunney passed him a large cup of coffee. Black. No cream. No sugar. "Any word on what could have done this?"

"None."

"Glad we processed when we did," Tunney muttered, sneaking a glance at the senior agent. He looked tired. He had been up since four when the call came. Maybe before that. Tunney guessed he hadn't slept much since Olivia left.

"Not a damn thing in there for this to happen," Silas told him. Except maybe the mirror he uncovered. Or did he? He was a little fuzzy on the details. The time he spent here yesterday was a blur. Silas told himself it was the heat or maybe the bourbon. All he knew was everything would be back in its place before the end of the day.

Tunney had to agree. The little shack of a house sat empty for over a year. Why now? "There's been a lot of media attention," Tunney suggested. "Maybe someone was tired of looking at it."

"Maybe someone needed this to be over." The sentiment was his, but Silas knew he wasn't the only one who felt that way. Two suspects bubbled to the surface. The owner who had been unable to rent the place and Sherrie Knowles' sister.

"Did you read that *Monster of Eden* story?" Silas asked.

"Yea. You won't like it. The wildlife agent was right, these crocs have been around for decades. The story goes some carnival people brought them here in the thirties. There were some pretty strange stories about what went on back here, some of them involved rituals and worship."

Silas decided to toss his coffee. "Sacrifice?"

"The usual suspects," Tunney affirmed.

"Then I guess it's a good thing Dr. Osborne is returning early."

Tunney was glad to hear it. The big guy seemed to have wilted in her absence. "Since I already know everyone, I'll start canvasing the neighborhood. Again."

"Thanks," Silas said. "I'm heading to Tampa in a few hours. We meet with Pittman tomorrow. Afterward, the plan is to track down Melanie McCleary. You and I will meet with Dr. Osborne when we get back late Tuesday. Hopefully, we'll have forensic evidence to review from the house."

Before the fire destroyed whatever was left.

"Make sure we know where Sherrie Knowles' sister was last night and Phil Sanderson. He owns the place." So far, they were his only two suspects.

****

Olivia watched as the phlebotomist filled multiple

tubes of blood. She wondered if they were going to drain her dry. Once the last one was filled and the sticky material applied to the crook of her arm, the technician escorted her down the back hall to her physician's office.

"I heard you were in the office," Tammy Murdoch greeted her. "Congrats! I'm so excited for you." Dr. Murdoch was an engineer before going to medical school. Olivia chose her for her logical approach, but she was also passionate about her job. Being a nurse, Olivia was pleased she could find someone who could do both.

"I was wondering what you were going to decide when you came to see me next month." The doctor knew how hard Olivia had been trying. She and her patient were almost the same age. Tammy Murdoch felt a kinship with Olivia. She knew the perils of starting a family in her forties. She had done the same.

Olivia smiled. She liked the frankness. Her clinical background gave Tammy the encouragement she needed to speak freely, a trait Olivia highly appreciated. "The news came just in time. I think we were about done."

Tammy nodded. She had seen her share of couples struggle to conceive, but Silas and Olivia Branch weren't the average couple. Despite their desire for a child, their commitment to each other was strong. It wouldn't have surprised her if they decided to stop trying in favor of preserving the relationship. She was glad it didn't come to that.

"I'm a firm believer everything happens in its own time." Dr. Murdoch reached for a small plastic bag and handed it to Olivia. "This is a variety of prenatal vitamins. See which one works best for you. Let me know, and I can call in a prescription. If nausea is a problem, you might want to wait to take it at lunch rather than first thing in the morning. If nausea is interfering too much with your daily life, let me know. I can give you something for that as well. Are you experiencing any symptoms?"

"Nausea and I are getting acquainted," Olivia confessed. "So far, it's nothing I can't handle. It comes out of nowhere, yet I'm hungry all the time. I can't stop thinking about key lime pie and melted cheese. I'm exhausted, but I can't always sleep. I think my waistline is disappearing already. And my boobs hurt, but on a positive note, they look fabulous."

Tammy resisted the urge to laugh. "Sounds like you're right on track." She clicked open the tablet she carried and referred to the notes the technician had already entered. "From the dates you gave, it looks like you could already be eight to ten weeks along." A little farther than she would have expected. Most women in Olivia's situation tested obsessively. They ended up finding out as early as three or four weeks. It made for a very long pregnancy.

"I waited," Olivia explained.

It was more evidence her patient had been nearing the end of her journey. "I will request a quantitative test, just to see where you are." Someone in Olivia's situation would want to know the exact dates. Maybe she'd given up counting those as well. This baby had snuck in there just when Mom and Dad were ready to give up. "We'll also check for anemia. We should have most of the results later today. If anything comes up, I'll call you."

Tammy punched in some information and studied the results. "Based on these dates, it looks like you're due sometime in late January."

Olivia took a deep breath. *Wow. Someday* had just gotten a whole lot closer. This was really happening.

"Considering how far along you are we could have done a gender determination test today," Tammy said with a smile. "We still could. It would be one more poke if you want."

The thought stopped Olivia short. When she went to nursing school almost twenty years ago, there was no such thing. She hadn't even thought about it.

"I'm overwhelming you, aren't I?" Tammy said, reaching over to pat her arm. "I'm sorry. It's just women our age, make me really happy. Most of us thought we might have waited too late. I know I did."

Olivia looked across Dr. Murdoch's desk and saw the little cherub face of a baby girl with dark hair and luminous blue eyes. She and Silas could have a child that looked like her. *If* she took after Silas. "Silas isn't here. I'm catching a plane in a couple of hours to join him. I'll let you know when we get back."

"No rush," Tammy assured her. She had wondered where he was. She had already pegged him as one of those husbands who would attend every visit. She liked those couples. She wished she had more of them. "I'll want to see you for a sonogram in a week or so. So, make an appointment on your way out. We can do the gender determination then, or you don't have to do it at all. This is your time, Olivia."

****

"I talked to Martin and he's going to send some guys out today to clean up the bathroom. Then we'll talk about options for a replacement," Lily explained once Olivia returned from her early morning errand. "You're sure you don't mind if I stay?"

"Of course not," Olivia told her between alternate bites of fruit and croissant. She had stopped on her way home for a variety of breakfast options. So far, she was indulging in all of them. "It's not like we're going to be here." Lily was rescuing her from a problem she didn't want to deal with. With a projected due date in mind, her head was swimming with all things baby, and there was no room for thoughts of Amanda. Besides, if Barry was going to cut ties, she needed to do the same. "You're doing me a tremendous favor by looking after the dogs." Lily's need for a place to stay saved her.

"You can stay as long as you like," Olivia assured her. "When will Ross be back?" She realized her neighbor hadn't mentioned her husband all weekend.

Lily nodded, grateful for the woman she hoped was going to be her new best friend. She was going to need one. "Not sure."

Olivia caught the change in Lily's tone. She didn't even have to ask.

"Ross is having an affair."

She has red hair. Olivia saw the flash of red the morning they came for breakfast.

"I told him not to come back until he knew what he wanted."

****

Silas was waiting for her just outside baggage claim. His kiss was brief but full of a need that matched her own. "I don't know about you, but I really hope you're taking me somewhere we can be alone and not to another crime scene," Olivia told him. "Snacks would be good, too."

"Way ahead of you," Silas assured her.

****

Silas propped himself up on his elbow and gazed down at his wife. She was indulging in the fruit cups she adored. He had stopped at her favorite bistro chain and gotten her some, along with plenty of sparkling water. With their heads clear, now they could talk. He rested his other hand on her stomach, liking the rhythmical rise and fall of her bare skin. "I wanted us to revisit the sushi place but thought raw fish might not be such a good idea," Silas told her. He had even booked them in the same hotel where they stayed when they were here before. Only then they didn't share a room.

"Good call," Olivia told him and offered her spoon, sharing some of her fruit. Seeing how much she was enjoying it Silas couldn't help but smile. "Don't get used to it," Olivia told him. "If my appetite keeps up like this, I'm not going to be much in the sharing mood."

"Feeding me is what got us here." The night the case ended, he and Olivia were the only two agents left in town. Dinner was Silas' idea. A few sake bombs later, Olivia was feeding him sushi. Having her fingers on his lips and in his mouth was all the encouragement Silas needed to make the first move and kiss her. Olivia's response caught him off guard, signaling he wasn't the only one interested in where this might lead. Nothing happened that night, but it was a beginning.

"Room service is an option," Silas suggested.

"Even better. I won't have to get dressed."

"You'll hear no complaint from me." Silas smiled as he handed her the menu. "Indulge," he said, stroking the small bruise in the crook of her arm, a souvenir from the morning blood draw. "Are you ready for this?"

"With you." Silas brought her arm to his lips, kissing the bruise. "Don't send me away again," Olivia whispered.

The force of her plea was strong, with tears forming in her eyes as she said it. Maybe it was the pregnancy hormones he read about.

"At least not until this is over. The baby, I mean."

He bent down and kissed her forehead. "Not again. I promise."

The rest of their evening revolved around everything baby. Olivia felt officially bitten by the baby bug. Silas surprised her by suggesting they paint the nursery themselves. He wanted to make the room their own. More importantly, they mutually agreed to take the test to learn the sex of their offspring. Whether or not they would share their findings was still up for discussion, but they wanted to know whether they would be sharing their home with a Genevieve, named after her grandmother or an Ellis, a nod to Silas' dad.

Maybe it was all the happy thoughts that made the nightmare even more terrifying.

****

"So, how are things at home?" Silas asked once they were on the road the next morning.

"We're on our way to see a confessed killer and you're going to lead with that?"

"We have a three-hour drive ahead of us," Silas reminded her. "We have plenty of time." He was glad to see her in a chipper mood. She woke briefly in the night with tears on her face. Something she never did, despite the nasty things she had to dream about. She nestled into him, seeking refuge instead of talking about it. She hadn't mentioned the incident, so maybe it got lost somewhere in her sleep.

"I'm curious what I missed," Silas prompted her.

There were many choices, but Olivia decided to start with the Foresters first. If she didn't, they would never get past the topic she had promised to tell him about two days ago. Instead, Olivia began with what happened Saturday night after the party. She gave him the edited version of what Lily did to the shower and summed it up with Father Dominic blessing the house. Olivia specifically left out the part about *Alleracsap*. She didn't want to give the demon any more attention.

"Does that mean I can safely use our downstairs bathroom?" Silas wanted to know.

"Not entirely sure. You'll have to tell me. Apparently, the apparitions are gender specific."

"Interesting. I'm sure there's a story behind it."

"There is. But that one's definitely for another time," Olivia assured him. With the baby on board, Olivia started doing some family reading of her own. The women in her family had interesting pregnancies. Olivia hoped that was the reason for her nightmare. At least that's what she told herself.

"Anything else?" Silas wanted to know.

"Ross is having an affair, and I think there's something wrong with Amanda."

"And I thought we were going to have a normal couple conversation" Silas grinned.

"Is that possible?"

"Tell me about Amanda first."

"It's not going to work," Olivia said, her eyes focused on the road in front of her.

"Of course not. Amanda only pretended to want to be your friend. She's jealous and that's why it's not going to work between her and Barry either." Now that Olivia knew Amanda's true intentions, Silas told her his.

Silas never called the lieutenant by name unless it was personal. "There's no reason for her to be jealous of me," Olivia protested. Discussing a killer would have been easier.

"Maybe not to you. Jealousy is tricky. Isn't it one of the seven deadly sins?" Olivia had many gifts, but understanding personal relationships involving her wasn't one of them. Barry Bartholomew wasn't in love with Amanda. Silas knew why. *Did Olivia?*

"Envy is one of the seven. Covet is on the top ten, so conventionally speaking I'd say it makes both lists." Olivia decided she didn't want to explore the motivations of Dr. Amanda Greene any longer. "Ross is having an affair."

"I suspected that," Silas said.

"You knew?"

"He didn't say. He didn't have to. His sudden motivation to get in shape, gave it away," Silas told her.

"We should stick with killers and interlopers," Olivia suggested. "Since you knew everything else, do you happen to know a Samael Knight?"

Silas ran the name through the contact list in his head. "No. Should I?"

"I found one of his business cards in our house when I got home. Someone put it through the old mail slot."

"Disguising the sender's location," Silas said. "It sounds like I need to know him. What did he want?"

"Don't know. I'm sure he'll keep until we get home." A quick internet search for *Knight Industries* only led her down rabbit holes with no resolution. "Now, your turn. Why did you really want me to come back early?"

Chapter Twenty-Eight

"The fire marshal's report says 'it looks like' the wiring wasn't up to code. Still, there's been no utility service in at least a year." Silas said what Olivia was already thinking.

"The fire originated inside the house." The findings might have been inconclusive, but Silas had worked with Olivia long enough to know there were always other reasons. Standing among the ruins of the McCleary house is what prompted him to speed up her return. That and he missed her.

"So, no electrical storm?" Olivia asked, playing along. Silas had printed the fire marshal's report for her review, but the more she read in the car, the more she feared she would lose her breakfast. She had only hit the highlights.

"Are you suggesting a force of nature?" Silas asked.

"Not the kind the fire marshal would look for. Nature is a powerful force. It has magical properties, if you know how to use them. From what I heard in those trees, I think we're dealing with something very old," Olivia speculated.

The back of Silas' neck tickled with her words.

"Just throwing it out there." Olivia tried to lessen his discomfort with a smile. "Moving on, from the looks of things it seems the flashpoint was the girls' room," she surmised. "Do you think someone had something to hide?"

"If so, they were a couple of days too late. Forensics cleaned that room out." *All except the mirror on the wall.*

"Someone could have panicked," she suggested.

"*Someone* could have." Silas knew what she was doing. Playing detective. Test driving a theory the DA would float once they all convened again. "In my opinion, the only person who might have wanted to torch the house and that's a pretty big might, couldn't have."

Larry Wayne Pittman was sitting in a prison cell waiting to see them.

They tabled the discussion for now and Olivia moved on. "It wasn't all drama for me this weekend. I did find a little time for some research. The tic-tac-toe designs we found on all the burial sites have bothered me from the beginning."

"Juvenile," Silas said for her.

"That is the word I used, but tic-tac-toe didn't start out as a kid's game."

Why was Silas not surprised? "Of course, it didn't."

"The origin of the game comes from medieval pagan rituals. The nine-squared grid was thought to hold magical properties. In the Middle Ages it was called the *Magic Square*. Drawings have been found chiseled across Rome, but some historians believe the magic square originated in Egypt."

"Remind me that we will never teach our child this game."

"Such fundamental games are important to social

and cultural aspects of life, Silas. Like military strategy." Olivia smiled, liking the thought of him as a father. "But I hear what you're saying." He was going to be surprised to learn some of the things she did want to teach their child. But that was a discussion for another time.

"Where are you going with this?" Silas wanted to know.

"Didn't you say the wildlife guys suggested someone was feeding the crocs? I was thinking pets might make nice appetizers."

If he didn't know her, Silas would be seriously worried about the suggestion. Still, it was a disturbing thought. "Guess I'm glad we can't drag the pond," he said instead. "Tunney read the magazine article about the monster of Eden. It referenced crocodile worship and strange rituals going on back before that trail of houses was built."

"That could explain the lingering magic I felt out there. It clinging to the trees, like the energy I feel at death scenes." Maybe the whispers she heard were ancient as well as foreign. Egyptians worshiped crocodiles. For the briefest of seconds, Olivia wondered how it would feel to tap the energy in those trees. She shook herself free of the temptation before it could take hold. "Back to the game. There are nine squares in the tic-tac-toe board. There were nine graves,"

"Ten if you count Ashley Knowles," Silas reminded her.

"Three in a row wins the game. There were three murders. Ashley's burial was incidental," Olivia countered.

"If you don't count Ava and Dorcas."

"Their death wasn't part of the plan. At least not that one. I don't need to point out that the killings stopped with their murders. That's the part no one wants to see."

Silas knew where she was going. It was time to tell her what they found in the room. She had a copy of the evidence list in her lap, but she couldn't read it any more than she could the fire report.

"A candy wrapper and soda can were found in the girls' room. From your interview notes with Sherrie Knowles, it was the same kind she gave Ashley the last time she saw her. I'm guessing you're going to tell me it's too much to hope all three of these girls liked the same things or maybe they were just messy."

Olivia made no comment.

"Tunney also found Ashley's necklace."

Olivia didn't seem surprised.

"Under Ava's pillow."

"Have you pulled the clothes Ava and Dorcas were wearing? The ones from the last day anyone saw Ashley." Olivia asked.

Silas swallowed. She was heading to the place he had dreaded all along.

"Ashley had a massive nosebleed. There would have been blood spatter. Hobbs can explain away a lot of things, even the necklace, but not the DNA."

"You don't want to say it, do you?" Silas finally asked.

"The truth isn't always visible, not to everyone," Olivia reminded him. "I'm not saying anything until I talk to Larry Wayne Pittman, and he tells me something more than he just needed to make sure they were dead." Olivia stared at her husband, letting the implication of her words take hold. "Do you think the FBI or anyone else wants to hear the truth?" It was the story of her career with the Bureau. They handed her the dirty work no one else could solve but didn't want to believe her findings. It was a dysfunctional relationship.

Silas spotted a parking lot and turned in. They were only three miles from the prison, but what he had to say couldn't wait. Sometimes there were no more second chances. Silas put the car in park and turned to face her. "Do you remember what I said just before you left the other day?"

"*This changes everything,*" Olivia repeated. The breath caught in her throat as a somber realization settled in the pit of her stomach. Olivia knew this was coming. *Another due date.* Her days with the FBI were coming to an end. Her two worlds could no longer coexist.

"Listen to me, Livie." Silas reached for her hands, taking them in his just like he did the day they said *I do.* "I don't want you doing this anymore. I haven't wanted it for a long time. Not since you lured Jamie to your house and then the thing with Roche. I can't stand you being in danger. You're my wife and now you're the mother of my child. I can't let anything happen to you."

"Silas, you can't protect me," she said. *Or our baby.*

"I have to try. I have to protect you from what I can." Silas was talking about the two-legged monsters they hunted. The things beyond his control drove him mad. It's why they talked around them and not about them. For anything more, she had Dominic and Archbishop Mendoza. It was their silent agreement.

"You can't stop me from being me."

Olivia squeezed his hands, and Silas sensed there was more.

"Last night I saw your death."

Silas reached over and swept her tears away. "How can you possibly know that?" He was ready to argue to make it all go away. "It was just a bad dream. Pregnancy hormones or something."

"I don't think we're going to find anything about what I'm experiencing in any of those pamphlets the doctor gave me. We're on our own with this one."

"Gran?" Silas asked hopefully.

Olivia shook her head. "Gran might have stressed the importance of procreation, but she never went into detail. I've been reading about the women in my family. Most of them only have one pregnancy. Maybe it's because of the visions. It's been less than a week and already, they're getting to me. I can't shut them out."

"Tell me about them."

"Before last night, there was the one about Tunney's past, and the one about Ashley's grandmother. I had another the night of Amanda's party. I could have sworn it was Mark and a woman walking and holding the hands of a child between them, a boy."

Given Olivia's gifts, pregnancy was bound to affect her differently. She was right. They weren't going to find an answer in *Exceptional Expectations: The New Mom's Guide to Pregnancy*. "You think it's the pregnancy?"

"It has to be the baby. She's bound to get some of my abilities, but there are other kinds. Gran told me there were stories of those who can see things other than the dead."

"Like being clairvoyant?" Silas asked. It could explain her seeing his future death.

It wasn't a question the Silas Branch she met would have ever asked. He had educated himself since. "Yes, but it isn't just about being precognitive or seeing the future. The word clairvoyance is the combination of two ancient words, *clear* and *vision*. It can also mean retrocognition, meaning the ability to see the past. I've experienced both. Based on that, I'd say our baby is becoming one of them. She's sharing my body. There has to be a transference of some kind."

Silas replayed her words in his head. "You said *she*. I thought you said you didn't take a test."

Olivia hadn't realized. "I'm playing the odds. There hasn't been a male child born in my family in over a century." She wondered how Silas would take the news. She felt the pin-pricks of tears when she saw his huge smile.

"*My girls*," he said. "I like the way that sounds."

Olivia swallowed the sob that had formed in her throat.

Silas saw the tears in her eyes and took her hands back. "Think about it, Livie. Only one of your visions came true. One can't happen and the other is the past." He squeezed her hands for reassurance. "Maybe we do have a visionary on our hands, but the reality is, I will die, Livie. One day. So, will you. The future isn't set in stone. Maybe it won't happen the way you saw it or even when."

Olivia looked into his eyes and wanted to believe. She shook her head in agreement. "Maybe you're right." *He had to be*. "But it doesn't change the fact of who and what she is. And it won't stop the monsters from coming."

****

They were almost to the prison when Olivia's phone buzzed. Only because the incoming call was from Tammy Murdock's office did she answer.

"I hope I'm not catching you at a bad time. Do you have a minute?" It was the doctor herself.

"Is something wrong?" The tightness in Olivia's voice caught Silas's attention.

"Nothing other than my own curiosity. I'm just trying to sure up your due date. I wanted to verify the date of your last menstrual period again."

"My dates are correct," Olivia said. "I've been plotting them for a year." Menstruation, ovulation, copulation. Her heart was thudding in her chest, fearing the worst. She dared not look at Silas, or the tears would start again.

"I just needed to hear it from you. I got your blood work back and your hormone levels are pretty high for this stage of pregnancy."

Dr. Murdoch's words hung, suspended in time.

"What does that even mean?" Olivia asked.

"One of the blood tests measures the amount of pregnancy hormone in your system. It's used to gage how far along you are. Your numbers are higher than I expected for the dates you gave me. The easiest explanation would be that your dates were off and you're actually farther along than we thought."

"I'm as regular as clockwork. That's why the rhythm method works for me. Since I can assure you, my dates are correct, what is the alternative explanation?"

"More than one baby on board. It would explain the high level of hormones. I don't see a lot of family history in your file. Did anyone in your family have twins?"

****

"So, there could be more than one baby?"

Silas rarely lost his cool, but he was losing it now. Olivia couldn't help but smile. Focusing on him made it easier to ignore her own mounting anxiety.

"Maybe."

"How did this happen?"

"There are twins in my family. Another thing I learned this weekend."

"First we can't get pregnant and now we could be having two?"

"I blame you," Olivia said, still smiling. The statement only seemed to confuse him more. "If I dropped more than one egg, don't you think your sperm would more than do their job and impregnate everything they came across?" She smiled.

It took a moment for her words to sink in. She was making a joke. Silas finally let out the breath he'd been holding. "Well, when you put it that way." A lazy smile played across his face.

Olivia beamed at him. "There's the Silas Branch I know. Now let's go." She would never admit it, but at the moment she would rather talk to a killer than contemplate the next seven months of her life.

****

Barry managed to dodge Amanda's calls since the party. Fortunately, Norma was there to give him the head's up when his luck finally ran out. He entered his office without greeting, shutting the door behind him.

Barry stared her down, forcing Amanda to go first with a desperate hope it would all end here.

The lack of emotion on his face sent a wave of cold through her. "I don't like coming here like this."

"Then why did you?"

"I didn't know how else to get you to talk to me. You're not answering my calls." There was a hitch in her voice. Tears wouldn't be far behind.

Barry knew it was a shitty thing to do, but he was doing his best to avoid conflict. Especially when it involved Amanda. When pushed, he did what he did best in personal relationships—nothing.

It was anger she felt, but Amanda let the tears pool in her eyes. "You couldn't answer me? *Something*? Some acknowledgement I even exist for you?"

"No answer is an answer." Another dirty deed on his part. If he pushed enough, maybe she would just go away.

Amanda shook her head, flipping the switch from tearful to volatile. "You're not going to get off that easy."

Maybe that's what scared Barry—her unpredictability. She had flown right under his radar from the start. Barry considered his words carefully. "I can't give you what you want. I think you know that. Why make this any harder than it has to be?"

"Because I'm not the one?" Amanda couldn't keep the words to herself anymore.

Barry felt the first stirs of anger. "Let's not go there."

"I know where you went. You just couldn't stay away from her, could you?" Amanda could no longer control her anger.

Barry wouldn't give in. He couldn't let her turn on Olivia. "Don't make this about something it's not."

"Is that your way of telling me it's you, not me? How cliché."

"I can't give you what you want" Barry said again. "You should think about that."

"I know your secret."

His breath caught in his throat. He had many—not all of them his.

"You left me to be with her. How do you think her husband will feel when he finds out?"

Amanda was threatening him, which meant she was threatening Olivia. Volatile had just turned vindictive. In his mind, Barry saw himself crossing the room and putting his hands on her, but that wasn't him. It was his father, a demon he forgot he had.

"How do you know I didn't come back?"

Amanda was confused.

"How do you know I didn't come back?" Barry repeated.

The guilt passed through her eyes like clouds across the moon. Barry had seen the look before. Amanda wasn't the first woman he had driven away, but with her, he felt relief, not betrayal. This time it wasn't just about him. He had another to protect.

"We all have secrets, Amanda."

Chapter Twenty-Nine

Pittman's attorney was waiting for them. Rayland Murphey began his career as a public defender. He had been out of the courthouse basement less than six months when Pittman called him after seeing his face on a bus stop bench. None of it would have happened if Murphey's grandmother hadn't died and left him enough money to open his own practice. The way he figured it, he had at least a year before he either starved to death or went crawling back to the public defender's office. His former employer's expectations weren't high. They would have taken him back. Luckily neither of those things happened because he was the only attorney who would take Pittman's case.

"Just so you know, Mr. Pittman is speaking to you against my expressed wishes." The shuffle from one foot to the other erased any sort of confidence the attorney hoped to convey. He was a nervous man in general, but the FBI intimidated him more than any of the thugs he represented.

"I would expect nothing less," Silas said. The three of them were sequestered together, waiting for the guards to transfer Pittman to a room where they could talk.

Murphey snuck a glance at Olivia. If they had to meet with the FBI, why couldn't it just be her? She was the only reason his client had agreed to the meeting.

Murphey guessed the big guy was along for the show. Or he didn't feel comfortable allowing the doctor to come alone. "Despite my client's confession, I'm continuing to appeal."

Olivia focused on his words. She also couldn't be idle. They had that much in common, although for different reasons. She was fighting the onslaught of pings on her psyche. Prisons, like hospitals and churches, were smoldering cesspools of emotion. Olivia tried to prepare herself, but her center was off. Just like the visions, the life inside of her was emerging, her fierce protectiveness fighting to suppress its curiosity.

"How successful do you think you're going to be?" Olivia asked.

"I have no illusions my client will never set foot outside these walls again. I'm seeking life without possibility of parole. I want the lethal injection off the table." It was the first time Murphy showed any confidence. It meant he believed what he was doing. Olivia admired him for that, no matter how misguided.

"You think I can help you with that." Olivia said.

Silas started to say something, but Olivia calmly placed her hand on his arm.

"You're the only one he agreed to see, besides me. He says you'll understand. That you're not like the others." It was a sentiment his client repeated over and over, like a mantra. "Given your background I don't believe you want him to die," Murphy had done his homework.

Before the FBI retained her consulting services, Dr. Osborne had testified in defense of people just like Larry Wayne Pittman. Those who carried something dark inside of them. The ones she helped defend didn't walk away. They just didn't end up in a place like this. Murphey believed she could do the same for Pittman. Asking to see her was a brilliant strategy on his client's part, but only if he told her about the others. The case of Ava and Dorcus was over. Pittman ended it with his confession.

"Does your client want to live?" Olivia asked. In her experience, it was a killer Murphy had to convince, not a judge.

The question stopped him short.

Olivia had seen the look before, back in her nursing days when she worked with the old and dying. Family members got so wrapped up in their own needs they never stopped to consider if their loved one wanted to be saved.

Olivia repeated the question. "Have you asked your client what he wants?"

Murphy looked shocked at the suggestion. "Why wouldn't he want to live?"

"He doesn't measure life the same way you or I do. In here, time is different."

"Isn't all life precious?" Murphey countered.

"Life is precious, Mr. Murphey, but it's not for us to choose for your client. He still has choices. Choosing death is a choice," Olivia reminded him.

The look on Murphey's face said he was just trying to save a life. Olivia almost felt sorry for him, but Pittman had sealed his own fate before he ever met Ryland Murphy. Pittman was the one who called police officers to his apartment. The confession was out of his mouth as soon as they Mirandized him. Saving his client's life was all Murphey had left.

"Doesn't wanting to die sound like he's crazy to

you?" Murphey insisted.

"Not according to his psych eval."

The clank of leg irons told them Pittman had arrived.

****

Pittman took one look at his attorney and asked him to leave. Silas was next. "I remember you from last time," Pittman said, eyeing him up and down. "I didn't like you then either. You can go with him," he said with a nod toward Murphey.

Olivia gave Silas a look that told him she was fine on her own.

"You always do what she wants. Don't stop now," Pittman encouraged him. "You'll get her back. I promise."

With her escorts gone, the guard moved closer. Olivia stopped him with a shake of her head. The roar of psychic static had faded like background noise, and she was finally comfortable. Either she had adjusted to her environment, or Pittman came with his own set of armor. She didn't want another being disrupting the calm center she found.

"I had to get rid of them," Pittman told her. "This is just between us."

"I'm listening." Olivia needed Pittman to know he could trust her.

"This isn't about Ava and Dorcus."

Olivia hesitated. She thought she had found clarity, but now she was unsure. She never believed he was involved with the other murders. Could she have been wrong all along?

Pittman sensed her hesitation. His eyes turned flat and cold. "I didn't do the others. You know that. I may be a lot of things, but I'm no liar."

Something was different. Pittman wasn't like this before. He had been clear and focused. Today he was wandering. "This is about you?" Olivia hated that her words came out sounding like a question.

"Me. The others. *You.* I know what you are. You see them, too."

****

Silas was never good at waiting. Especially not with Olivia in a room with a murderer. He needed to find something to do. He went to the window and flashed his FBI credentials. "I need to see the visitor's log for Larry Wayne Pittman." He was tired of listening to Murphey's running commentary on what may or may not be happening.

"I told you he doesn't see anyone but me," the attorney objected.

"The page we signed in on was new, so I only have your word on that."

"Are you saying you don't believe me?"

"Maybe I'm just naturally curious," Silas told him. "More likely, I don't trust you. You're his attorney. It's your job to protect him. Besides, you have no idea what your client does when you're not around." Silas never moved from the window. He knew from past experience the longer he hovered the less time it would take the person on the other side to fulfill his request.

"Why do you need to see the visitor log?" Murphey sounded frantic.

"Because I can," Silas growled. He didn't care if he was being an asshole. Something wasn't right. He turned from the window and stared down the little man. "For someone who was protesting about us being here, you sure left without a fuss." Pittman had been in a hurry to get Olivia alone. Was it because he had been asking to see her for months? What couldn't wait? For a man in his position, time was all he had.

"Larry is a lonely guy. Dr. Osborne is a beautiful woman. I don't think he's even seen a real woman since he's been here," Murphy said the first thing that came to mind.

"Not a good place to go with me," Silas snapped. He pivoted toward Murphey, prompting the attorney to vacate his seat and wedge himself in the nearest corner.

"Larry said he didn't want us there. I need my client to know I'm on his side," Murphey amended.

Lucky for Murphey the clerk reappeared at the window. "Logs for the last eight months. Anything farther back, I'll have to look somewhere else."

Silas murmured his thanks. The most recent dates were at the bottom, so Silas started there, his finger trailing upwards. There was an uptick in visitor traffic last week, after the discovery of Ashley Knowles' body with both Melanie McCleary and Dorcas' mother coming to see Pittman. It looked like they came together. Silas wondered what the mothers of Pittman's murder victims had to say to him. Whatever it was, Melanie McCleary asked for more. She was the last one on the visitor long, alone this time.

Other than that, Pittman's main visitor was Murphey. There was a recent pick-up in visits between the attorney and client beginning a few months back. It must have been when Murphey hatched his plan for an appeal. Near the top of the page, Silas saw Terry McCleary's name. He came only days before committing suicide. Silas wondered if something

Pittman said pushed his cousin over the edge.

Silas was approaching the eight-month mark the clerk mentioned when Silas noted a second page. He almost disregarded it until he realized the time frame was right for when Pittman started asking to see Olivia.

That's when he saw what shouldn't have been there.

"Guard! I need a guard!"

****

Finding the bad guys was the one constant in Barry's life. He stared at the computer screen, comparing photos taken by the processing team after the break-in at Smythe's to the ones taken the first time the place was processed. He sifted through the boy's life, looking for anything he might have missed. The boy went back home when he had no place left to go. Now, even with cash in hand, where else could Smythe go?

"I think I have something you've been looking for," Will said. Without waiting for an invitation, he came inside and closed the door behind him. Classes had resumed at the Academy, but with Silas still gone, Agent Sharpe dismissed them early.

"Frank Tobias asked me to bring you this." Will offered Barry the paper in his hand. "He's emailing you the more tedious results. It's him. It's Smythe," Will told him. "Hair from the cloth materials and DNA from the soda cans found at the state hospital confirm it."

The fact they found hair matched the witness reports from the surrounding neighborhoods. It had been a year since Smythe's escape, plenty of time to grow his hair out of his *buzz cut* appearance.

"The prints in the closets belong to Smythe as well,

on the underside of the floor boards. Exactly where you would find them if you were the one removing them." Will smiled.

Barry sat up straight, the kaleidoscope of information falling into place. He took the paper and stared at it as if making sure it was real. He had been right about Smythe's whereabouts all along. Barry sank back in his chair as the realization washed over him. Smythe was here to stay.

"You and your crazy map. You were right all along," Will told him. "Smythe got flushed out of his hospital hideaway, and he headed straight home. He had no place else to go."

"Because there was something in there he needed."

"Cash?" Will asked.

A slight nod from Barry confirmed it. He glanced at his cell phone. Time to call Brennon Kaine. The fancy, gun-for-hire Long Island attorney wouldn't be happy about the call, but he would take it given this was for Olivia. Barry and Kaine wanted the same thing. To keep Olivia safe. Even if that meant denying Smythe his freedom.

"You're sticking with your theory this guy isn't going anywhere?" Will asked. "Even with cash in hand, you're sure he'll come for Dr. Osborne?"

"It's not a matter of if, but when," Barry said with conviction.

****

"I was thirteen when it happened the first time. Even before then I just knew. Kind of like how you know stuff. The guy down the street who liked peaking in windows. The school bully who stole the weaker kid's lunch money. The guy who had a thing for little blonde girls."

Pittman was describing the same incidents she read about in the file provided by the Department of Justice. The DOJ collected them as a way to document a history of criminal behavior. What was Pittman's reasoning? What was this history supposed to mean to her?

"My nan knew what I was. She's the one who schooled me."

Olivia couldn't help but think of Gran. "What did your nan tell you?"

"We're born with it, and there's no getting away from it. She taught me what it meant and how to protect myself for as long as I could. She always knew I'd end up in a place like this. It never goes away. You know that."

"How did she know?" Olivia pressed.

"It's a family trait. My nan was a *Seer*. She made her living telling fortunes in carnivals. It was hard. Most of what she saw wasn't good and people don't want to pay for bad news."

Olivia thought of her vision of Silas. "Did her visions come true?"

"Nan said the visions were a peek into the future, only visible at that moment in time, like a magic ball. Look again and they could change. Dorcus' mama could see things. It's why she turned to drugs. Drugs help you forget what you see and what you are."

Her own mother had turned to drugs and skipped town when Olivia told her about the dead woman in the bathroom. She was four. How could Pittman possibly know that?

Pittman leaned closer. "Not all people can handle what they've been given. This place is full of them. But you know that, too."

The suspects that sat across from her were different than most. By the time they got to her, they were no longer trying to escape—at least not physically. What they were seeking wasn't freedom but understanding.

"It's how Terry knew to call me. He needed my help. Family first. I'm sure you've heard that somewhere."

Pittman's talk of family was a theme.

"Terry was the one who put it together. Dorcas was different. He and Melanie weren't the first people to try and take Dorcus in. When the pets went missing in the neighborhood, Terry realized it was pets of girls Dorcus didn't like. But by then it was already too late. Dorcas had moved on to something more than pets. The first missing girl, Brittany, was Ava's friend."

The teacher, Ms. Snively, had suspected Dorcus was the cause. But no one wanted to hear what she had to say.

"No one wants to hear a little girl is evil," Pittman said as if reading Olivia's thoughts. "Terry asked me to come and take a look. He said he thought the sheriff suspected something, but there was no proof. You don't make an accusation like that without something to back it up. Otherwise, you end up sounding just as crazy as me." Pittman held Olivia's gaze while he said it. "Or you."

The realization sent a tickle along her hairline.

Not all gifts are created equal. The words weren't Pittman's. They came from *Alleracsap.*

Pittman pinched his brows together with his fingers, taking a moment. Making Olivia wonder if he heard them, too.

"Anyway, it took me awhile to get out there. I was laid up with back surgery."

"What did you find?" Olivia wanted to know.

"The first time I saw Dorcas I knew there was something dark inside of her. She would suck you in with her eyes. Big, luminous things. If you looked too long, you'd get lost. They were flat, bottomless pools of black. I knew then I was too late. She had already infected Ava. Terry could see it. By the end he was afraid of his own daughter. He thought he was crazy."

"Was he?"

"It can make you crazy knowing this kind of stuff. Having to live with it," Pittman suggested.

Pittman's diagnostic work-up was negative for schizophrenia, bipolar disorder, and all the usual suspects. He was sane. As sane as she was.

"Ava loved Dorcas. She always wanted a sister. Terry's mistake was waiting on Deb. He wanted her to take Dorcas back. I told him it didn't matter. The damage was done."

"So, what was the plan?" Olivia knew what Pittman had done. She wanted to know why.

"To put her down. She was too far gone."

Chapter Thirty

Pittman sounded like he was talking about an animal.

"My mistake was listening to Terry. I'd always done things my own way." Pittman shook his head, looking regretful. "Deb skipped after she got out of rehab. It was on purpose. She didn't want Dorcas back. She knew what she was."

There was a break in the killings during the holidays. Now Olivia knew why.

"So, it was on you. You had to step up," Olivia said, filling in the blanks.

Pittman nodded. "Had to. That thing inside of Dorcas was growing. She was close to her time."

"You mean puberty?"

"My Nan said when a girl changed into a woman, her power was only just beginning."

Her gran said the same thing.

"As soon as the new year came, they started feeding the croc again. Putting Dorcas and the croc together was like two bad things found each another. Every time they fed it, her power grew. It's what they call a symbiotic relationship."

The description wasn't Pittman's. Olivia had read his file. He barely made it to high school after failing the third and sixth grades. He didn't improve until he found vocational classes. The man could repair anything. But she would get to that later. Right now, she needed him talking.

"What kind of power?" Olivia asked.

"To infect, to manipulate. She had to be stopped. There was nothing else to do."

"So, why that day? Did you know about Ashley Knowles?"

Pittman sighed, remorseful. "I didn't know until that day. I still feel bad about her. If Terry had just let me do it sooner, I could have saved that little girl. Maybe I could have saved Ava, too."

"What happened?"

"Ava told Terry what they did. Just before he left for work that Saturday morning."

"What did Ava and Dorcus do?"

"They bashed Ashley's head in with a rock."

Pittman was telling the truth. He always had. No one outside the task force knew how Ashley died.

Silas told her they found Ashley's necklace in Ava's bed. *Was it a keepsake or a trophy?* "Did Ava feel bad about it?"

Pittman shook his head. "Nah. She was bragging."

Trophy. A wave of nausea swirled through her.

"Terry called me and gave the word. I did it before I went to work."

"Why two guns?" Olivia wanted to know.

"I had no choice, not once I knew what they were. I told you, I had to make sure they were dead. I'm not that good a shot, and I wasn't about to get out of the car. Guns are messy and traceable, but I couldn't do it any other way."

It was then she knew he had killed before. Olivia closed her eyes, trying to stop the stream of images coming from Pittman. There were so many. But they all deserved it in their own way. When she opened her eyes, he was watching her.

You didn't let me in last time. It's the curiosity inside of you that's letting me now.

Olivia cleared her throat and her mind, chasing him away. "Terry wasn't there with you that morning?" It made no difference to the investigation, but Terry's suicide played on her mind. What was the trigger? The death of his daughter or something else?

"I told him he couldn't go, even though by the end he could see what I could see."

"And what was that?" Olivia needed Pittman to say the words.

"The chaos. Terry was what my Nan would call a late bloomer. For some it doesn't always come out—not unless you cross paths with one of those things."

"What are *those things*?" Olivia pressed. It sounded like he was talking about possession but she didn't want to put words in his mouth. That would be too easy.

"Not demons, if that's what you think," Pittman said what she wouldn't. "I can sense them, but I can't do anything about them. This thing was human, once. But by the time it found Dorcas it was neither dead or alive, stuck in the in between. My Nan called them *wanderers*. Tortured spirits that take refuge in unsuspecting hosts, creating havoc wherever they go. He gave it a fancy name. He said it was a *dybbuk*."

The other world is so old it has seen more religions come and go than we will ever know.

It sounded like something *Alleracsap* would say, but the demon was strangely quiet. It was Pittman or part of him. Someone else had joined their conversation. Or maybe they had been there all along.

He who?

Dybbuk was a Jewish term. Again, not something Pittman would know.

Pittman didn't give her time to ask. He just kept talking, rushing to get to the end.

"After seeing what was in his own daughter, Terry couldn't stop. That's what he told me on his last visit. It's also why he blew his brains out. It's an awakening. Once it happens there is no going back. Those who are gifted are part of a collective as ancient as creation."

Gifted. It was the description Olivia embraced after saving Barry in the barn. This wasn't Pittman's story.

"I know you've heard the names, *Seer, Teller*."

Pittman paused, waiting for her to talk, but Olivia baited him with her silence.

"The old people you used to look after make easy targets. The demons are free to come and go, like a revolving door. You would have crossed paths with a *Hunter* in one of those places. Since you don't know what I'm talking about, then they never saw you coming, either. Good thing for you."

"What are you?"

"I see the chaos and rub it out. Like with Dorcus. That makes me just a *Cleaner*."

No matter how ancient, there was still a hierarchy.

"I don't seek the evil ones. Haven't you ever wondered why they seek you?"

Olivia had heard enough. "You sound like a tool to me. Today I think you're nothing more than a messenger," she said, using his own words against him. Olivia leaned in, her green eyes blazing. "Who's at the head of this serpent?"

Clever girl...

A hot wind hit her face followed by the feel of sand against her cheeks. Olivia squinted and saw a giant orange sun kiss the open landscape before her. Shadows of black danced in the distance chanting a language that reminded her of the trees by the crocodile pond. A lazy river rippled in front of her. Before she could see the monsters beneath, she was back with Pittman.

"He told me you would come. All I had to do was ask. You always take the side of the broken ones. Because you're broken, too. You're much more than a *Reader*. You're in the middle of two worlds. It's how you can see the demons. How they can see you. You walk where they walk. It vexes them they're not free to do the same."

Vexed. Another word that didn't belong in Pittman's mouth.

"The *Collector* thought it was time you know the truth." Pittman reached for her hands, but she was too fast, and his chains were too short. All he got was the brush of her fingertips, but that was enough.

Pittman gazed at her in awe. It was just him this time. Whatever had been inside of him had slithered away. "There's not a lot of us left. You're having visions, aren't you? It's because you have a *Seer* and a *Teller*. It's their curiosity I feel. Tell me, have you found your *Watcher*?"

Watcher was a word Olivia had heard, but not from Gran. She read it in a transcript detailing the events of her night in the barn. It's what Ana Lutz called Barry. "Why? Are they gifted, too?"

"Not until they cross paths with someone like you.

Some say the devotion is stronger than love. Your Watcher would die protecting you," Pittman said with assurance.

Finding the life inside of her made Pittman change course. She needed him to tell her something she didn't know. "Tell me about the Collector."

"He's already found you. You need your Watcher. So does Mr. FBI."

Olivia saw movement outside the room. Silas was pounding on the window with two guards on either side of him. His voice was muffled, but his words were clear.

"Don't say a word. Don't say another fucking word to her!" Silas yelled.

With the guard occupied, Pittman made his move. His whispers were frantic.

Olivia swayed at his words; the shouts to stop brought her back. Silas had broken away, but the guards were gaining on him. Silas was heading straight for her, ignoring their orders to stop, moving as if she was in danger, but so was he. The one she had dismissed was between Silas and his goal.

Instead of letting him through, the guard stepped up to block Silas' path. The guard reached for his baton and yanked it from his holster. With heightened senses Olivia watched thick fingers clutch the weapon and the muscles beneath the guard's shirt ripple. As he prepared for impact Olivia sensed no fear. Only sport. It wouldn't be a fair fight.

One of the guards Silas had shaken loose, caught up to him and struck him from behind. Silas swayed. He remained on his feet, but just barely. Momentum and desire to get to her propelled him forward. The guard in front of her raised his club and charged. Silas' arm came up.

Her fight-or-flight instincts kicked in as she tugged herself free of Pittman. Olivia slid out of her chair with a skill she knew she'd soon lose. Prisons were cesspools of emotion. The power they generated pooled around her. The hair on her arms rose as the energy seeped into her.

The word slipped passed her lips as a whisper but transformed itself into a bellow.

"*Prohibere!*" The ancient word echoed off the walls forcing the men to stop.

Olivia's breaths came fast. She didn't realize her own strength. What she had taken she couldn't hold long. With a never-ending source, there was too much of it.

"Thank you," Pittman sighed from behind. His mind was quiet for the first time he could remember. She had sucked out all the bad.

"Do you trust him?"

Pittman was lost, staring into space.

Olivia slipped into the quiet vacuum of his newfound peace. Her thoughts collided with Pittman's. *The Collector! Do you trust him?*

No.

Then get out—while you can.

A wave of vertigo filled her, pulling her from the calm, and thrusting her back into the storm she conjured.

I'll be back, Olivia promised.

The look on Pittman's face told her he was already gone.

Olivia teetered on the edge before letting it all go.

The ball of energy she had gathered slipped through her fingers like water. For a moment, the silence was deafening. It shattered a second later as the guard's baton clattered to the floor and rolled across the room. The guard stared at his hand like it wasn't his own. Silas caught his breath and rotated the shoulder where he had been struck from behind. Guards rushed him from all sides. They were about to grab him until she stopped them again. This time just with her voice.

"Touch him again, and you'll have me to deal with."

****

The entire prison was silent as the guards escorted them down the hall to another room. They shut them inside and left. Olivia heard the lock click behind them.

Silas turned on her as soon as they were alone, his words coming in rapid fire. "What the hell just happened? What did you say?"

"I told them to stop." Now that they were out of the room and away from Pittman, she felt weak and shaky.

"Not in English."

There were other words to choose from, but she didn't understand them. Only one language was familiar. "Must have been Latin," she muttered.

Silas reached out and ran his hands up and down her arms as if making sure she was real.

"The baton would have snapped your wrist and struck you in the face fracturing your cheekbone, maybe giving you a concussion. From there, I couldn't tell you what would have happened." She was meant to defend him.

"Tell me what Pittman said."

Olivia didn't hear him. She was in a damp place.

One that smelled of human waste. It was cold even though outside those walls it was springtime in Massachusetts. The figure in the corner was dressed in rags as she drew her last breath. *Vows are important.*

"You are the father of my children. You have given me the greatest gift I could ever ask for. Family." Preserving it was all that mattered.

"You're scaring me." Silas whispered.

Olivia tried her best to reassure him, but her words were flat. "I'm fine." She moved beyond his grasp, looking for escape. She tried the door. Still locked. They were trapped. "We, *I* need to get out of here." She wasn't the only one with access to the energy of this place. It had to be the Collector. Leaving here would sever the connection.

"Samael Knight, the guy with the business card, used Pittman to make contact with you. I saw his name on Pittman's visitor log. I made some calls. His name is on file with Interpol," Silas told her.

Olivia rubbed her head to stave off the headache starting to form.

"He's a procurer of ancient artifacts. Probably more."

Procurement. The word swam in Olivia's head. Lazy at first and then a deep dive.

Samael Knight was the Collector.

Chapter Thirty-One

Zavalla hosted the meeting with the FBI in his office. It was a tight squeeze.

"Why is he not answering?" Barry asked.

"They're in Gainesville. They must still be meeting with Larry Wayne Pittman," Jon Sharpe told him. When Silas didn't answer, Barry passed the call on to Sharpe. Even he couldn't reach Silas. "They take your cell phone in prison. Federal agent or not," Sharpe told him.

"He took Olivia?" It sounded like an accusation.

Will shifted in his chair. He knew the tone.

"Yes, Dr. Osborne, is with him," Sharpe confirmed. "She is the one interviewing Pittman. Talking to killers is what she does," Sharpe reminded Barry.

"The mayor's going to want an action plan," Zavalla said even though no one was listening. All eyes were on the lieutenant.

"You suspected it was Smythe all along. It's why you wanted to talk to her alone. That was reckless," Sharpe said.

The accusation caught Zavalla's attention. "Is that true?" The last thing Zavalla wanted was a run-in with Silas Branch.

"Dr. Osborne is the one who suggested I investigate the neighborhood surrounding the hospital,"

Barry explained, noting Sharpe's not-so-subtle reminder. "Her request had nothing to do with Smythe. It was only later that I realized the area coincided with Smythe sightings," Barry said smoothly. "I wanted her to know." It was a solid answer. It was also the truth.

"Two locations," Zavalla muttered. "The mayor is going to want to reconvene the task force." The captain could see another citywide panic in the making.

"It's more than that, and you know it," Sharpe said.

The growl sounded a lot like Silas. "Maybe we should just concentrate on one task at a time," Will suggested feeling the need to intervene.

"The way I look at it, we're informing the FBI as a courtesy," Barry said, without consulting his captain. "Vandalism is SAPD's jurisdiction." He stopped pacing and rested his hands on top of the folder filled with new information on the *Good Samaritan Killer*.

"You know what Agent Branch will say," Zavalla warned.

"I have to agree," Sharpe said.

"I volunteer to be the force of one, for now," Barry said, as if that made everything alright. "If you guys feel the need to put someone back on her house, *their* house, then feel free. We don't have that kind of manpower."

****

The warden lectured Silas on his behavior while Silas, in turn, demanded the prison inform them immediately when Samael Knight visited again. It took some convincing that there was no video footage available of the visit. It had long been erased.

As for Olivia, she was too preoccupied to argue. She was fighting off the last of the visions. The blaze of headlights catapulted her back to more humid air. It smelled of stagnant water and reminded her of home. The girl weaving her way along the side of the road was headed to a hotel for a party she would never attend. Olivia knew how this story ended. It was the night she was conceived. She tugged herself free, struggling to escape. Someone stronger than her was manipulating the remaining energy, and her protective shielding was waning with every minute they remained.

"You, okay?" Silas asked as they walked to the car.

"Now that I'm out of there," Olivia whispered, the fog already beginning to lift.

"Pittman?"

The images were coming from him, but Pittman was the conduit, merely the messenger just like she said, but she couldn't explain it to Silas. Not now. Not until she sorted it herself. Instead, they needed to focus on why they were here. They still had a case to solve.

Olivia shook her head absently. "Just get me to Melanie McCleary."

As much as Silas wanted answers, he wasn't sure he wanted all of them. Her head was elsewhere, meaning she was trying to find a way to explain it to him in terms he could understand. He loved her for that. She allowed him in her world, but she also understood what he could live with and what he couldn't.

In the car, Silas checked his notes and plugged in the address. "Be there in thirty." He reached for her hand, but Olivia stayed bunched next to the car door, holding her own hands.

Silas had a bad feeling this had nothing to do with Pittman.

****

Melanie McCleary's trailer wasn't much bigger than the tiny house had shared with her husband and daughter, but the yard was better. A basket of brightly filled flowers hung from the porch. They bothered Olivia. Maybe because they looked too happy.

There was a car under the port next to the trailer. When there was no answer at the door Silas headed around back. Olivia remained in the front, feeling disconnected. She couldn't untangle herself from the web Pittman spun at the prison.

She had believed Pittman all along. In the end, his story matched the theory she had constructed. Ava and Dorcas killed the other girls. What she hadn't known was Pittman was much more than a vigilante.

Silas poked his head inside the open car window. "Are you sure you're alright?"

Olivia blinked back to reality.

"There's nobody home. All I found was a pile of clothes on the back porch" he told her.

"I need sugar and caffeine." Her smile was thin, but it was enough to satisfy him.

Olivia focused on the parts of her conversation with Pittman so she could process the case that brought her here, to begin with. She needed confirmation other than the words of a murderer, and there was only one person who could do that. "I have to talk to Melanie McCleary," Olivia insisted. "She's the only one who can fill in the blanks."

Silas joined her back in the car and fiddled with the computer. When he was done, he tried calling Tunney but got no answer. Silas left him a message, with an update on their location.

"The car in the drive is registered to Deborah Kay

McCleary," Silas told her. "My guess is she and Melanie are together. You want to grab something to eat and come back for another pass?"

Olivia didn't have time to decide before Silas's phone buzzed. It was Tunney.

—*Found her.* —

****

Tunney and Silas waited outside the pile of burned rubble of the McCleary home. Tunney had still been roaming the neighborhood when he got the message from Silas.

"I just looked up and there it was," Tunney said, staring at the car parked in front of Sherrie Knowles' house.

Olivia was inside interviewing the women while Silas and Tunney stayed outside and reviewed Tunney's latest canvas.

"I think I'm growing on them."

"If we can wrap this thing up you could be their hero," Silas told him.

"Did Dr. Osborne make any headway with Pittman?"

"Don't know," Silas said.

His tone said there was more to it than that, but since he wasn't sharing, Tunney moved on to what he knew. "The neighbor's stories are consistent. It started with a light inside the house, before the fire," Tunney explained. "Any updates from the fire marshal that would explain that?"

Silas thumbed through the email on his phone. There was nothing he hadn't seen already. "The debrief is tomorrow, but according to the latest findings, the fire was concentrated on the inside wall of the northeast bedroom." He and Tunney looked back at the remains.

"Girls' room," Tunney said for him.

"Accelerant unknown."

****

Melanie and Sherrie both had a lot to say. Luckily, Olivia had sugar and caffeine flowing through her veins. With Tunney's eyes on Melanie's whereabouts, Silas stopped long enough to grab her a large soda before they hit I-75. It wasn't her favorite brand, but it would do. She needed something more potent than sparkling water.

Olivia had them start with recent events.

"I made Deb take a shower as soon as she got to my house," Melanie explained. "She smelled like smoke."

"Where are her clothes?" Olivia asked, thinking about what Silas found at the trailer.

"On my back porch. I wouldn't let her come inside wearing them."

"You think Deb had something to do with setting the house on fire?" Olivia asked.

Melanie didn't hesitate. "Yea, I think she did it."

"Did she confess?"

Melanie nodded. "Yea. At first, I thought she was high, but one whiff of her clothes, and I believed her."

"Why do you think Deb wanted to come back here?" The women had calmed, but there was still more.

Melanie and Sherrie looked at each other. Now knowing what Pittman knew, Olivia wondered how many pieces of their world they had already stitched together.

Sherrie reached over and squeezed Melanie's hand.

"To apologize. For what Dorcas did to my Ashley."

Olivia watched Melanie for a reaction, but there was none. Even with the talk of death, Olivia sensed nothing from her. *She was hollow.*

Sherrie's sister Tina appeared and physically pulled her sister away from Melanie. "You need to leave. Now." The request included Olivia as well.

Outside on the porch, Melanie stopped to light a cigarette, and Olivia decided to ask the question she had been holding until they were alone. "Larry Pittman killed your daughter. How did that make you feel?"

The woman across from her took a long pull and studied Olivia through a nicotine-fueled haze. "Terry said we could count on him. He wasn't wrong. Larry did what needed to be done. Dorcas is the one who ate my daughter alive. She sucked out her soul. My little girl was gone long before Larry put her down."

Melanie expelled more smoke as her eyes narrowed with a memory. "Ava asked if Ashley could spend the night, but she never made it to the house. I assumed they fed her to the croc." Melanie shed no tears as she said the words. Maybe, like Sherrie Knowles, she didn't have any left. "Ava told Terry that morning. He called me from work. I'm the one who suggested the girls go down to the pond."

Melanie McCleary sent her own daughter to her death. Olivia wondered what that did to a person. Maybe it ate their insides, leaving them hollow. "You packed them a lunch."

Melanie threw down her cigarette and snubbed out what was left of it with her toe. "Waiting for Deb to come get her daughter was a mistake. Dorcas killed my daughter, not Larry."

Melanie McCleary wasn't hollow—*she was barren.*

Olivia looked into her flat eyes. "How do you feel about Deb?"

"I brought her back here to do what she had to do. She's the one who's responsible, and the only one without a sacrifice. Dumb bitch thought burning down the house was enough, but it wasn't. The mirror is still there. The portal is still open."

A perimeter alert went off inside Olivia's head. During their ride back from the prison, Silas told her about what he found on Pittman's visitor logs. He was interested in Samael Knight, but she was wondering about Pittman's two most recent visits. The one from Deb and Melanie and the one from just Melanie. Why two visits in such a short amount of time? Was she still looking to Pittman to make things right?

Melanie had distracted her by completely controlling the conversation. Maybe that was her intent. "Where is she? Where is Deb?" Melanie hesitated, but Olivia's stare broke her.

Melanie swallowed hard and fidgeted for a cigarette she didn't have. "I suggested she take a walk."

More alarm bells clanged in Olivia's head. She looked next door and scanned the burned-out remains of what was left of the house. "A walk to where?"

Melanie shrugged. "To see Dorcas."

Olivia moved at the words, rushing to join Silas and Tunney.

"Deb McCleary is here."

"Where?"

"The crocodile pond."

****

301

They heard the screams before they saw her.

Deb McCleary was on her back. They couldn't see her face, just her hands as they clutched at the tall grass, but it wasn't enough. The tugs from below were too powerful. The huge croc had her by the leg, its jagged teeth embedded in her flesh just above the knee. Deb kicked at its snout with her free foot losing ground each time, all while the giant beast continued its backward descent into the murky water below.

Finally, Deb made contact, and the monster released her, but only long enough to readjust and swallow more of her leg. Jagged teeth sunk deeper as the croc paused to shake her like a ragdoll. Screams turned to gut-wrenching moans as the giant reptile resumed his steady crawl toward a watery grave.

Tunney got off the first shots, hitting the big bull in the head more than once. The croc stopped moving, but Deb's leg was still wedged in its mouth. Even in death, the monster wouldn't give up its prey. Deb's screams only intensified as the dead weight of the croc pulled her down with him.

Silas managed to keep pace with Tunney until his knee buckled at the steep embankment leading to the dark watering hole. Silas ignored the pain as his muscles and tendons screamed. Somehow, he managed to stay upright. Pausing to catch himself, Silas saw the other croc approaching from Tunney's blindside. Despite its size, it was fast. Silas started firing, emptying his gun into the second croc, saving Tunney's life, and ultimately his own. With his knee crumbling beneath him, Silas knew he would never make it out of the water.

Olivia was right behind them. Deb was still alive,

but the spurts of blood pumping out of the tattered leg meant the second bite must have punctured the femoral artery. Olivia dropped to her knees. Despite the pool of blood, she pressed against the torn flesh until her arms gave out.

The sun was almost gone by the time emergency medical vehicles arrived. By then Deb was long gone. Olivia was still wiping blood off her arms when Silas finally agreed to take a ride to the hospital. He was in pain. She could tell by the ill-concealed wince that accompanied every step he took.

While Silas was stuck inside a CT tube, Tunney whisked Olivia away to the sandwich shop next door to the hospital. The excursion allowed Tunney to feed Olivia and delay his talk with Fish and Wildlife. He and Silas were facing an investigation and mounds of paperwork because the crocs were a protected species. As far as Tunney was concerned, bureaucracy could wait. They would still be dead tomorrow. In his opinion, they had done the neighborhood a favor.

"He's going to make a lousy patient, isn't he?" Tunney asked as he and Olivia sat huddled over their food. Tunney didn't know if it was the pastrami on rye or the scene at the pond, but until now he had never seen Olivia hesitate at the sight of food.

"I'm sorry, I'm not feeling well." Olivia excused herself and headed to the bathroom. It wasn't long before she was back, her face a cloud of concern. "I need you to take me back to the hospital."

****

With Silas still in Radiology, Tunney waited outside Olivia's exam room. He would rather do that than face Silas. It didn't take long for someone to see her. A bleeding pregnant woman jumped to the head of the line every time.

In a darkened little room with a rolling TV screen next to the exam table, Olivia lay on the narrow bed and scooted down as requested. The nurse helped settle her feet in the stirrups. The doctor explained what he was going to do, and the probing began. He concentrated on whatever he was seeing on the screen in front of him.

"How much bleeding?"

"Enough to scare me. And I don't scare easy."

The doctor believed her. Her demographics said she was with the FBI.

"Bright red with cramping." Olivia concentrated on breathing as she said the words. She clutched her own hands protectively over her abdomen.

"Any undue emotional or physical stressors today? Sexual intercourse in the last twenty-four hours?" The doctor asked as his eyes scanned the black and white screen in front of him.

"All of the above."

"How far along are you, Mrs. Branch?"

Olivia concentrated on looking at the ceiling. "Ten maybe twelve weeks. I just found out I was pregnant. I stopped counting the days. We had given up."

"Fertility drugs?"

"No."

The doctor nodded, absorbing the information. He was older, assured, and most of all, calm. Olivia appreciated the bedside manner over mindless chatter.

"Twelve weeks looks about right." He glanced at the nurse. She moved from Olivia's head to join him. He pointed to the screen with his free hand. "What does that look like to you?" The nurse peered closer while the doctor pushed buttons to enhance the image. With the nurse in agreement with whatever he saw, the doctor looked at Olivia. The nurse grabbed a tissue and pressed it into her hand.

The doctor pushed more buttons, and Olivia heard the whine of a paper dispenser. She clung to the tissue and held her breath.

****

Olivia was done in time to hear Silas complain about using the crutches he had just been given. She agreed with the doctor that he should take the pain pills and worry about the crutches tomorrow. Olivia gladly accepted the nurse's offer to fill the rest of his prescription at the hospital pharmacy. Silas begrudgingly agreed to a wheelchair ride outside where Tunney was waiting. With pills in hand, Tunney grabbed Silas some food and drove them to the hotel. Once Silas was settled, Tunney went back to the office and sent the inquiries Olivia requested.

While Silas showered Olivia touched base with Sharpe in San Antonio. After he ate, she medicated him again. Not until he was in bed with a pillow under his knee did she tell him what he missed, but only the parts he needed to hear.

"They look like two lima beans." Silas hadn't let go of the picture since she gave it to him. The lopsided grin on his face was drug-induced but genuine. It was his first proud papa moment.

Olivia slid her arm across her abdomen and hugged herself, recalling the flutter of heartbeats. Seeing them in motion, knowing they were tucked safely inside of her was better than any picture.

Silas reached for her. "We're supposed to do this

together."

"We did."

"That's not what I meant." There was a lack of conviction in his voice. It was the drugs.

"I did what needed to be done. Regardless of what was going to happen. You couldn't have changed it." She thought of Melanie McCleary and Sherrie Knowles as she said it. They were women resigned to a fate far worse than hers.

"I need you to be okay. All of you."

"We are," Olivia reassured him as she reached for the light and snuggled in next to him. "Did you ever see yourself as a father?"

"I never really thought about it." His words were starting to slur. The drugs were doing their job, pulling him under. "I didn't think much about my personal life. Not until you came along. Until I decided I wanted this. I wanted us."

Chapter Thirty-Two

Olivia grabbed the phone and stepped into the other room before it could wake Silas. One of Tunney's many calls last night had been to the BAU Division Chief. Olivia appreciated his efforts, giving her time to devote herself exclusively to her husband.

"He's asleep," she said, still in nurse mode.

"Actually, I'm glad you answered. That way I know I'll get the real story. I'm just checking in. How is he?"

"He's going to need rehab. Depending on how well he does will tell how much time he buys himself before a knee replacement."

"He's going to hate that," Patrick said. Good thing Olivia was a strong-willed woman with a nurturing side. "Maybe it's time he realized he's human like the rest of us." Patrick might have been surprised at Silas' decision to settle down, but he couldn't argue with his choice of a wife. Olivia was just what Silas needed. They made excellent partners in the field, and it appeared the same could be said for the home front.

"Did Agent Sharpe brief you about San Antonio?" Olivia asked. She hadn't gotten around to telling Silas about the latest developments back home. Discussing one serial killer had been enough for the night.

"He did. How did you connect Smythe to the state hospital?" Her intuitive powers were more than a little spooky sometimes.

"I didn't. All I did was request Lieutenant Bartholomew look at some security issues my new client was having."

"Bartholomew's volunteered to liaise with the Bureau on the task force and the mayor welcomes any assistance the BAU can provide. That means you."

Olivia never doubted it. She was relieved Patrick didn't ask for more. "So, can Silas call you back?"

"Yea, but I really did call to talk to you. It's about Pittman. They found him dead in his cell this morning."

Olivia was silent, unsure how to feel. Finding her voice, shifted back into nurse mode. "Did he do it himself?"

"Why do you say that?"

"Just wondering."

"No obvious signs of suicide, but it's too early to tell. They said he had surgery last week. Suffice it to say, final results will take a while. No one is shedding any tears in the meantime. Did you learn anything from him? I heard you and he had quite the discussion."

He must be talking about the warden.

"Pittman confirmed my suspicions, but no one is going to like what I have to say. Put a rush on forensics." She knew that was the only way anyone would listen. "I'm ready to go home."

****

They worked from the hotel. After the Parks and Wildlife agents interviewed Silas, a request was submitted to have the now empty crocodile pond dragged for remains. Based on what Melanie McCleary said, Olivia believed it was where they would find the other two missing girls if there was anything left.

Two days later, they were back at Ocala Police Headquarters. The fire marshal's report remained unchanged. The cause of the fire that destroyed the house rented by Terry and Melanie McCleary remained an unknown accelerant originating in the girls' room. Eyewitness accounts confirmed the origin of the fire as well. The only item to survive was a mirror, that according to Melanie McCleary Dorcas brought with her and hung in the girls' room. Melanie also repeated her story of Deb's arrival at her house wearing smoke-filled clothes. They were the ones Silas found on the back porch of Melanie's trailer. As far as the fire marshal's office was concerned, the case was closed.

The forensics reports Tunney requested on Olivia's behalf confirmed her suspicions of Dorcas and Ava. Olivia was glad the Eden sheriff stayed behind to hear it. She knew he had his own suspicions about the girls all along. Pittman said as much. Sometimes the truth was too much to bear.

Patrick Monahan flew in from DC to join them. The events in Ocala had captured national attention and just as she warned, Olivia's findings would not be well received. Patrick's presence was an unprecedented show of support. The Bureau didn't mind showcasing her talents when it suited their needs or if her findings were corroborated by forensics. But there was another agenda at play. As the head of the BAU, Patrick was there to support the man he expected to succeed him one day. He and Silas had more than one closed-door conversation. Olivia suspected it was regarding career advancement for both of them.

"So, what am I looking at?" Hobbs was the first to ask. Tunney had supplied everyone with copies of the forensic report on the items taken from Ava and Dorcas' room. Hobbs tossed the paper aside as if not seeing it would make it go away.

Olivia provided the narrative. "The blood spatter found on clothing worn by Dorcas and Ava belonged to Ashley Knowles. DNA found on the soda can and candy wrapper in Dorcas and Ava's room belonged to Ashley. The soda and candy matched the ones purchased by her mother that same afternoon. The necklace Ashley Knowles was wearing the day she disappeared was found in Ava McCleary's bed. Need I say more?"

Hobbs seethed but remained silent.

Olivia kept going.

"Melanie McCleary will confirm Ava called her at work and asked if Ashely could spend the night. Dorcas and Ava McCleary lured Ashley Knowles down the dead-end road. I believe it was their intent to push her in the crocodile pond—much like they did the other girls. Only this time, something went wrong, and they only made it as far as the big rock. After they attacked her from behind, Ashley ran. Once she fell, she was too heavy to move. Melanie will confirm Ashley wasn't there when she got home. When she asked Ava about her, Ava said Ashley decided not to stay."

"My god," the sheriff said, raking a hand over his face.

Silas remained silent with the rest of the room. This was Olivia's show. He knew all along something was wrong with the case, but she was the only one who could put it all together. Maybe because she was the only one willing to venture into the darkness to do it.

Hobbs looked like he wanted to protest. He looked

to Dr. Sheppard. She confirmed Olivia's story with a nod of her head. "Parks and Wildlife recovered skeletal remains from the crocodile pond. Injuries to the skulls are consistent with the injuries to Ashley Knowles. I'm confident DNA will confirm they belong to Brittany Hoffman and Kelsey Rowe." Dr. Sheppard had worked late to get it done. Anything to get out of this town and put this case to rest.

Hobbs shook his head in disbelief. "You expect me to believe two children did this? To their friends?" Hobbs protested.

"The forensic evidence is solid enough to take to court, if you had someone to prosecute," Olivia answered in terms he could understand. "It explains the difference in method, and the inconsistencies between the deaths of Ava and Dorcas McCleary and Ashley Knowles," Olivia told him. "We never suspected Pittman for the other girls."

"No." Hobbs slammed his palm on the table. "You believed a murderer."

"Being a murderer doesn't make you a liar."

"The killings stopped when I put him away," Hobbs protested.

"Because Pittman killed the murders," she said quietly.

"Then tell me why these two little girls murdered their friends," Hobbs demanded.

"What I can tell you is further evidence, as detailed in the report, points to Dorcas and Ava as the perpetrators of the dead neighborhood pets. In speaking with Melanie McCleary. Ava's pet rabbit was one of them. The markers found on the graves was a tic-tac-toe board. Maybe it was just a game to them."

"So, that's your motive?" Hobbs shook his head. "It was a game?"

"People have been killed for less," Olivia told him. It was the best answer, the only answer she could give that he would understand. "The simple but sad truth is we may never know."

"And Pittman, how does he come into play?" Hobbs still wanted more.

"Terry McCleary went to him regarding concerns he had about Dorcas. I took the liberty of researching the nine or so schools Dorcas McCleary attended in her short life. There were consistent complaints of unusual behavior targeting other students, keepsakes missing, the same sort of thing that was going on here, minus the killings," Olivia continued. It might sound like she was piling on, but he had asked, and she wanted it to be over. "On the morning Pittman killed the girls, he said Terry called him. Ava confessed to him what she and Dorcas did. Melanie McCleary told me the same."

In the corner, the sheriff had buried his face in his hands.

"So, Pittman was what, some hero? Some vigilante?" Hobbs wanted to know.

The DA had no idea how close he was to the truth. Olivia decided to give it to him. It was the only way to make him stop. Because that was more frightening than anything else. "Pittman told me he saw them for what they were. Monsters."

Hobbs looked anywhere but at her. "How am I supposed to go to the press with this?"

"You're good at telling stories. I'm sure you'll think of something," Olivia told him.

"Don't worry, Pittman's conviction is secure,"

Silas interceded. "Larry Wayne Pittman confessed to killing Dorcas and Ava McCleary. The forensic evidence proved it. You still put away a murderer," Silas reminded him.

Tired of it all, Olivia slipped out of the room to catch up with the sheriff.

"I wanted you to be here because I know you suspected them," she said, hoping her words would stop him.

The lawman took a moment before turning around to face her. He was gathering his thoughts, debating with himself if he even wanted to talk to her. "How was I supposed to know? Who would even think of such a thing?"

"I'm not blaming you. I just wanted you to hear someone say that you were right. It helps to know we're not alone. Early on in my career I mentored young nurses. The best piece of advice I could give them was to trust their instincts. It could end up saving their patient's life one day. In our line of work, trusting your instincts can save your life or those around you."

"But little girls? Children murdering their friends? What is this world coming to?" The sheriff shook his head, wanting to make it go away. His eyes shifted away from her and focused on the sunshine outside. The light was his solace.

"Evil comes in all shapes, sheriff. It always has."

The old man looked older than he did an hour ago. He headed for his cruiser, never looking back.

Olivia was still watching him when Tunney appeared at her elbow. "Head's up. They threw me and Hobbs out of the room. The DOJ guy is waiting for you with Silas and your boss."

He meant Patrick. Olivia didn't correct him to say she no longer had a boss.

"Watch your back. Singer is out for blood. *Yours*."

Chapter Thirty-Three

Olivia reclaimed her place in between Silas and Patrick. From the look on their faces, the conversation had been anything but pleasant.

"Dr. Osborne, we were just discussing your continued participation with the Department of Justice," Patrick began. "Is there anything you would like to add regarding Mr. Pittman?"

"My report to the DOJ won't say anything more than what I already discussed in this room," Olivia told them.

"I heard about your visit to the prison." Singer's eyes flicked to Silas. He meant the altercation with the guards. "You were there a long time. Are you sure Mr. Pittman had nothing to add?"

"I shared the relevant facts of this case," Olivia said.

"Is that your final answer?"

"Asked and answered, Counselor," Olivia told him.

Singer leaned forward in his chair, meeting her stare. "Not good enough, Dr. Osborne. I want to know why you didn't mention Samael Knight."

"What does Mr. Knight have to do with this?" Silas wanted to know.

From her periphery, Olivia saw Patrick look her way. "Who is Samael Knight?" he wanted to know.

"Samael Knight is on an Interpol watch list," Silas

answered. "He trades in antiquities and maybe other things." Silas was intentionally vague. He wanted to know what Singer knew.

"Mr. Knight's country of origin is unclear, however, for the last several years he's spent a great deal of time in Las Vegas, Nevada. We believe the antiquities are just a cover for trafficking girls," Singer revealed. "Ironically, his associates are the same as Andre Roche and Ana Lutz. As I'm sure everyone at this table knows, the FBI's own human trafficking task force has had their eye on Vegas for a long time now. Roche and Lutz were primary to that investigation. Since they are no longer available for questioning, Agent Mason Deveroux is back in play."

Singer finally turned to Olivia. "That means he'll get that sit-down with you he never had. You'll be required to answer his questions about what really happened in Atascosa County. That also means he'll be talking to Lieutenant Bartholomew."

"You son-of-a bitch," Silas said. "Dr. Osborne and Lieutenant Bartholomew were victims in that cluster fuck, just like the girls Roche was holding. Dr. Osborne saved the lieutenant's life."

Singer smiled. "Then he should be more than willing to answer all of our questions."

Olivia leaned back in her chair as her skin began to prickle. "I have no more answers than the ones I already provided." She clasped her hands in her lap, in an effort to stop the flow of energy building in the room.

"I'm going to have to agree with Dr. Osborne on this one," Patrick interrupted, feeling lost in the shuffle.

"Let me connect the dots for you, Director

Monahan. Mr. Knight happens to be a not so silent partner in several substantial financial holdings in Las Vegas, all of which are owned by Ms. Sarah Larsin, Dr. Osborne's mother."

"*Estranged* mother," Silas corrected him.

"You're going to need more than that if you're accusing my agent of something," Patrick warned.

"Technically she's no longer an agent. She's a special employee. Dr. Osborne reminded me of that the first time I met her." Singer looked back to Olivia. "It was the same day you reminded me Pittman asked to see you before anyone found the latest missing girl. It was a valid and interesting point. So much so I decided to investigate what might have compelled Pittman to reach out to you if it wasn't a confession. That led me to his rather skimpy visitor log, which mainly consisted of his attorney. Then, two days before his first request, he had a new name pop up on his visitor log. Samael Knight. Some people might call that a coincidence, but none of us at this table believe in those things, do we?"

Olivia remained impassive, irritating Singer.

"I was impressed to learn you're the Bureau's highest paid consultant. So impressed, I looked it up and your contract is up for review. Your unwillingness to cooperate with me or Agent Deveroux could hamper that lucrative arrangement." Singer looked pleased with his delivery.

Olivia unclenched her hands. "Is that it? Is that all you've got?"

Silas tensed. He had heard the tone in her voice before. The night at the hotel, when Singer threatened her, and yesterday at the prison. There was the same charge in the air. It felt like a storm was coming. For once, Silas was the one reaching under the table to touch her, but she was beyond his reach.

"Did you happen to speak to Mr. Pittman's attorney before coming here?" Patrick asked. "Perhaps he would know more about Mr. Knight's visit than Dr. Osborne."

"I tried. According to Mr. Murphey's secretary he took an unplanned leave of absence. He must be taking his client's passing pretty hard. His office couldn't give me a return date."

Singer looked at Olivia, expecting an answer. Instead, he found her smiling. "You find this amusing, Dr. Osborne?"

"I asked if you had anything else?"

Singer's cheeks flared with anger at the politeness of her tone. He looked to Monahan, expecting the BAU chief to get something out of her. "Do I need something else?"

Patrick cleared his throat, but Olivia cut him off.

"My contract is up for review because I chose not to renew. I'm sure the FBI is preparing a counteroffer, but my decision is final. I don't care what they offer me."

The envelope had been waiting for her when she got home from walking the dogs and talking to Lily. The sender could have sent it electronically, but they were the government, old-school bureaucracy at its finest.

She sat at her dining room table and read through the familiar paragraphs. Her relationship with the Bureau was dysfunctional at best. They needed her and despised her all at the same time. Once upon a time that had been the only motivation, she needed to keep signing her name on the dotted line. Not anymore.

"My time with the Bureau is over. My ties are being severed as we speak."

Only his years as an agent prevented Silas from looking surprised.

Singer turned on Patrick. "Did you know this?"

The division chief remained as silent as Silas.

Singer was used to having the might of the US government behind him. Olivia Osborne should be afraid. The fact she wasn't, caused the red in his cheeks to travel down his neck.

"The law firm of *Kaine and Kaine* is representing my interests. They are the ones currently drafting the terms of any future participation I may have in FBI matters. If you would like to discuss this matter further, you'll need to take it up with them."

I'm not afraid of you or your government, Mr. Singer.

A confused look scurried across Singer's face. "Did you say something?"

"Why? Did you hear me?"

With the others watching, Singer forced himself to move on. "Brennon Kaine? Don't you think that's a conflict of interest considering he's representing the man who tried to kill you?"

"You didn't hear? Mr. Kaine's firm recently added a civil branch. His son Isaac is a partner. He's the one handling my affairs."

****

"So, when were you going to tell me?" Patrick asked once Singer was gone.

"After I review Isaac's recommendations. My parameters are very specific. Obviously, I'll make myself available for trial on any outstanding cases." Smythe, being the main one. "But don't hold your breath on anything more than that."

Patrick realized it all made sense now. During their last closed-door session Silas told him about their future plans as well as his own. "I'm sorry to see you go, but I understand. I also hear congratulations are in order."

Olivia looked happier than he had ever seen her. If anyone deserved it, it was her.

"Well then, while you're still on the payroll, the local fire marshal has a request. He wants your recommendation on how to dispose of the mirror in the girl's room. He seemed a little spooked it wasn't damaged. I also got the impression he thinks it may have had something to do with the fire, but he's not committing his theory to paper," Patrick explained.

"Douse it in holy water and bury it on holy ground, but don't break it. I can contact a local priest if the marshal doesn't feel comfortable doing it himself."

Patrick nodded slowly.

"I'm not kidding," she assured him.

"Never doubted you for a minute. I'll be sure and pass on the information."

"Anything else?" Olivia wanted to know.

"Why did Pittman kill the girls?" Patrick asked.

"He spoke the truth when he said they needed killing. He saw what they were."

"Monsters?" Patrick repeated the word she had used. She didn't correct him. "Was Pittman crazy?"

To anyone else, he would have sounded that way. It's why he would only talk to her. "No. I believed him. He could see things."

"Like you?" Patrick asked. It was nothing but a

stab in the dark.

"I see more. It's why I can't work for you anymore. I'm done proving myself."

****

"I hope you're not mad I didn't talk to you about not renewing my contract with the Bureau," Olivia told Silas once they were alone.

"Not at all. It saved me from asking you to do it. I also hadn't gotten around to telling you I turned down Patrick's request to return to the BAU full time."

Olivia was shocked. All he had ever wanted was to take over the BAU when Patrick's tenure was up. "Silas. Are you sure?"

"Patrick promised Melinda he would get out at the twenty-five-year mark. He still has another couple of years to go, but I told him right now, my answer is no." Silas reached out to touch what would soon be a baby bump. "Family first."

****

This had been the case he couldn't close. Now that it was over, Silas wanted to go home with a clean slate, but he couldn't get the words Olivia used out of his head. He also couldn't take the chance she would try and escape, so he saved his final question for their drive out of town. "Don't you think it's time you tell me about Pittman? Could he really see monsters?"

Her husband was learning. So, was she.

She would tell him what she could in a way he would understand.

"He was born with it. It was all in his rap sheet, but with the girls he got messy. Terry McCleary had it, too. It's why he killed himself. Apparently, it's familial. Pittman spoke words only my Gran used. And some she didn't. Pittman called himself a *Cleaner.* It was a slang term for someone less than a *Hunter.* The way he described them, I'm sure if a Hunter had killed those girls, we wouldn't have a confession. We'd have an unsolved murder."

"What does any of this mean?" Silas dared ask.

I know what you are. You see them, too.

"Our families have a similar history. There's a lot more of us out there."

"What do you mean by us?"

You are not alone.

"Pittman called the people he talked about, gifted. I'm not the only one." Olivia's hand went to her waist just like Silas did before. The lives inside of her already had their gifts.

Inside you are a Seer and a Teller.

"What Pittman had doesn't sound like a gift to me."

"And what about me?" she dared ask.

Silas was adamant. "You're not like Pittman."

"No. But he and I are part of the same collective."

Only you can bring us out of the shadows.

"And what about Samael Knight?" Silas had to focus on the real live person, someone he could do something about. "What does he have to do with all of this?"

"He's a Collector. That's the message Mr. Knight wanted me to have."

"A Collector of what?"

"Gifts."

****

Olivia knew what she had to do. Pittman was the one who gave her the idea. There was something trapped in her mirror, and it was up to her to set it free.

She waited until Silas left for work before shutting herself in the downstairs bathroom. The room was dim. The door and shutters were closed. It wasn't dark outside, but she didn't need it to be. What she sought lurked even in the light of day. And what did not could find her on their own time. This was for Lenore. It was time she found peace.

Olivia struck a match and savored the whiff of sulphur. She touched the flame to the wick and waited. The smell of sugar cookies filled the room, and she saw Gran in the flicker of light against the glass. There was a figure behind her, shades of gray and white, not clearly defined but comforting, nonetheless. Olivia never met her grandfather, but she knew it was him, hovering in the background.

Olivia waited until the wet girl with string hair appeared.

"*Scoi fabulum tuam. Portare me, et ego semper tecum. In illud, Ego autem constitutus a vobis in loco isto. Ite nunc. Pax et expecto amore tibi.*" I know your story. I will carry it with me always. With it, I set you free from this place. Go now. Peace and love await you.

Olivia blew out the candle.

The lights winked as the sound of a child's laughter tickled her ear.

Epilogue

It ended where it began, Amanda sitting on the floor, waiting for him when he got home. "We need to talk."

Barry unlocked the door, not planning on letting her in.

"I know you said it was over." Her voice was soft, testing the waters.

His was firm. There was no going back. "It is. Over."

Desperate, Amanda caught the door he tried to swing closed and followed him inside. "Things are different now. *I've* changed."

Barry turned around to face her. It was probably better they did this inside. He didn't want the neighbors to hear. Barry shook his head as he looked at her. "I meant what I said. We're done."

"I'm pregnant." The words just popped out, quicker than she planned. Not because they were a lie but because they were the truth.

His response was just as fast. And just as truthful. "It's not mine."

Barry watched the realization of what he had said play across Amanda's face. She reminded him of the suspect who knew they'd been caught in a lie. "You asked me why I didn't come back that night after the party. And I told you I did."

Real tears formed, but it wasn't sadness. It was vengeance. Her words were so quick he wasn't sure if they were a lie. "It didn't mean anything."

Barry had heard those words before. "It still doesn't matter."

Amanda's hand went to her abdomen. "This was supposed to be a new life."

Barry didn't even hear her. All he could see was Olivia.

****

"We need to talk."

Last night Amanda, now Silas. His week just kept getting better and better. Barry closed the door behind him and squeezed past the agent on the way to his desk. Silas Branch could be intimidating, but Barry was undaunted. This conversation was a long time in the making.

"I'm assuming this isn't about Will?" Barry slid into his chair, resigned to his fate. They should have had this conversation weeks ago.

Silas parked himself in the only other available seat. "No, it's about this." Silas tossed him a black and silver business card. "It came through our mail slot while we were in Florida."

Samael Knight - Collections and Acquisitions. Barry turned it over. *Call me.* The handwriting was almost too pristine to be real. A phone number in the same script followed. It didn't match the one on the front.

"Interesting spelling of Samael," Barry commented.

"It's biblical," Silas told him. "The number was a burner. No longer in service," Silas told him. "We found Jamie Lynne Smythe's prints on that card."

"I don't understand. Is Knight a real guy or is this from Smythe?"

"He's shadowy, but real. Smythe isn't the first one Knight used to contact Olivia."

Barry opened his mouth to say something, but nothing came out.

"The man's a ghost, but I'll send you what I have. I'll handle Knight, but I need him on your radar. I know Smythe's your pet project. I need to know you can handle him. If you need resources, I can get them for you."

"I got this," Barry assured him.

Silas nodded. "Good because you have something else coming your way." According to Will, Barry had aced his captain's exam. The next step would be the orals. Silas doubted the lieutenant would take it that far. Everything about this man told Silas he was a lone wolf. Being a captain was the last thing he wanted. Still, he deserved a head's up.

"Mason Deveroux wants another pass at you."

Barry let out an irritated sigh. "When?"

Silas shook his head. The investigation had hit a snag with the unexpected death of Marc Singer. He died of a brain aneurysm just days after returning from Ocala. Despite that, Deveroux wouldn't be content to stay on the back burner any longer. Not now that he had a second chance. "Could be weeks, could be months, but he's coming."

"Why? What changed?"

"The Department of Justice is on a witch hunt."

"They're after Olivia." Barry said it for him.

"She quit the Bureau, but she pissed some people off before she did it."

Barry looked as pissed as Silas felt.

"While we're discussing my wife."

Barry's jaw clenched. So, they were back to the start. "Maybe I shouldn't have gone to your house that night, but I knew you were out of town. If you came here to bust my balls, then let's get it out of the way. It seems we have bigger problems."

"I get it," Silas said quietly.

The confession came way too easily. Barry forgot whatever excuse he was going to make next and looked at Silas like he had missed something.

"Sharpe told me you were there," Silas said. "Jon's a good guy, and a better than average agent. He's also observant."

Barry ignored the jab and threw one of his own. "He seems too familiar with Olivia. I didn't like it."

"I could say the same thing about you."

"You know we didn't, right?" Barry clarified.

Silas knew if he hadn't gotten to San Antonio when he did, Bartholomew couldn't make the same claim. Knowing Olivia didn't sleep with Barry Bartholomew was one of the few things that made the lieutenant tolerable.

"Olivia told me. Neither did Agent Sharpe in case you're wondering. He watched over her at a time when I couldn't. That's all. You can stand down. I've got this."

Silas' words didn't carry their usual bite. "I knew when you showed up, I didn't stand a chance," Barry confessed. Before Silas Branch arrived, things looked promising between him and Olivia, but that was over now. Barry had decided to start embracing the truth. It made moving forward easier.

"My timing has always been impeccable." If Barry and Olivia only had a little more time together, Silas knew all their worlds would be different. He had just never admitted it out loud until now.

"As for that night at your house, it was a conversation we needed to have," Barry told him. By doing exactly what she asked, Olivia saved him— *again*.

"Livie told me about Amanda. Inside the marriage we have no secrets," Silas told him.

"Does she know you're here now?" Barry asked before he could stop himself.

Silas shifted in his chair. "She knew I was coming. But not about all of my reasons. You can tell her though. One day. When the time is right." Silas saw the confusion on the lieutenant's face. "You'll know when that is. I assure you."

Silas leaned forward in his chair. There were things he needed to say. No matter how hard. "I need you to do something for me, something I know you can."

Barry watched as the Silas Branch he knew slipped away.

"Olivia is having visions. Past and present." Silas kept the one of Mark Austin to himself. The possibility of an alternate version of the future was his lifeline, his only hope.

"Livie believes it's because of the babies. Apparently, they already have abilities of their own. They're sharing their thoughts."

"Babies? As in, more than one?"

The flash of a smile resurrected the old Silas, but only for a moment. "Two. Both girls."

"Congratulations." There was no joy in Barry's voice. It was Silas' smile. Something wasn't right.

"Olivia had a vision, of the future. She has no way

of knowing if it will come true, but we both know my wife." Despite his best efforts, Silas had to pause. By saying the words, he was bringing in another. The future no longer belonged to just him and Olivia. "I might not have a lot of time."

Barry pushed himself away from the desk and out of his chair. He needed a moment to conceal his own thoughts. He turned his back to Silas and stared out the window. He saw nothing of the ground below. Only glimpses of something he thought he had lost.

"It's quick. Lots of blood. As you can imagine, I can't get much out of her. She says it was just a flash."

"What do you need from me?" Barry asked, his voice husky with emotion. There were so many even he didn't know what they were. "Some kind of protection?"

"Not for me," Silas confessed.

The softness of his voice jolted Barry back to this reality. He turned and faced the man he once thought of as the enemy.

"That night in the barn, when Livie saved you, I asked her about my place in her life. She told me she loved me—followed by, she needed both of us in her life. That's when I knew what you meant to her. And that I would be sharing her with you for rest of our lives."

Barry couldn't hear anymore. "What do you want from me?" His words were desperate this time, more of a plea than a question.

"You are the only one I trust. More than that, I know you love her. That's why it has to be you. All I ask is you love my girls, too."

****

"It wasn't a haunting," Dominic told him. "Instead, I was greeted by her demon." The hiss in his ear came at the first sprinkle of holy water.

Archbishop Nicefero Saldaña Mendoza sipped his brandy in silence.

"Did *It* threaten you?"

"No."

"Was it waiting or watching?"

The memory was not one Dom wanted to recall, but it was why he came. He couldn't purge himself of it. "Both."

"This demon cannot possess her," the archbishop assured him.

Dominic recalled Olivia saying the same thing. "She said her light was too bright."

The archbishop hoped she was right, but she was also in no position to judge.

"*It* was confident, unbothered by my presence. *It* was standing guard."

The pieces were starting to come together. Olivia's last confession hinted as much. How far she had gone with the demon, the archbishop didn't ask. The act of confession earned a pardon from the Church, but absolution had many meanings.

"*It* told me she was with child."

Demons were tricksters. The archbishop hoped the statement was a bluff but knew in his heart it wasn't. This demon had no reason to bluff. "Did she confirm the news?" His mouth was dry as he asked.

"Yes." Dominic watched the old man reach for more brandy. Mendoza knew more than he was saying. He always did. "She spoke of her ancestor." The deal Sarah Osborne made beneath the gallows was over three hundred years old. More than enough time to pay her family's debt in full. This was something else. Dominic heard Barry Bartholomew's confession. He knew what Olivia had done to free him and how she had used Jamie Smythe to do it.

"Demons aren't the only ones who make deals," the archbishop reminded him.

"So do witches." Dominic watched as the hand holding the brandy shook as he raised it to his mouth. Beneath the robes, Nicefero Saldaña Mendoza was just a man. Men had fears. And regrets. "This isn't about the Smythe boy anymore, is it?" Dominic said what he already feared. There was a new deal. "This demon wants something more."

Allegiance.

****

The priest was right about so many things. The archbishop regretted not paying closer attention to a distraught old woman raising her abandoned grandchild. In his defense, he was a newly appointed priest living in a world where demons were merely a myth.

Dominic would make a fine exorcist. But it wasn't his services the Church required. What Nicefero needed was something else believed to be a myth.

Deus ex machina, the answer to an unsolvable problem. It was a term Nicefero learned in pursuit of his first passion, the theater. The bishop picked up the phone without hesitation. The lateness of the hour made no difference. The man he was calling worked under the cover of darkness. It suited his needs.

"It's time you earned your keep, demon hunter."

A word about the author...

I've been a registered nurse for more than thirty years, but my first passion has always been writing.

Growing up the youngest child of older parents I spent a lot of time entertaining myself. I discovered my love of writing through reading. I always wanted more. When I ran out of books, I started writing my own. I have lived in San Antonio, Texas for almost twenty years and have adopted it as my own. I love the diversity of this city and its endless supply of ghosts which make it the perfect setting for the Olivia Osborne series. When I'm not writing I can be found with my family and any number of cats.

LisaComptonbooks.com